Dead Cat Bounce

Dead Cat Bounce

SETH FREEDMAN

Cutting
Edge
Press

To The Fabulous Micky C

Men should be careful lest they cause women to weep, for God counts their tears.

Talmud

SUMMER 2006

The perfect mojito is a line of coke. See what I'm saying?
Rum, lime, sugar, mint – yeah, yeah, yeah, but trust me, it's
the poor man's charlie. The scared man's snow. The straight
man's chang. Not knocking mojitos, mind. I'll take one if
you're offering. Nothing wrong with them, quite like the
buzz, quite like the taste, quite like the hype and hysteria
that surrounds them. The PR machine that pumps out blend
after blend, trend after trend, all based on one fairly basic
concoction. You can milk anything forever as long as you've
got a good slogan. But it's still just a cocktail. And for all it
falls back on its Latin roots, the region's got far bigger and
better things to offer. Exhibit A. The perfect eighth. The
wrap's a good size, the material's ideal: made from a lottery
ticket, so the powder doesn't get stuck to it, or come sliding
off as soon as it's opened. That's the downside of using
shiny card – keep an eye out for that next time. Anyway,
lovely exterior, even better inside. Off-white dust, finely

ground particles, hardly needs chopping. Breathe out, lean over, breathe in. Horseradish bouquet, secondary layer of forest fruits – and a hint of strychnine, too, if I'm not mistaken, though I hope I am. Can't do much about the strychnine, comes with the territory, and anyway it's an upper in its own right, so the more the merrier. Throw it down on the mirror, looks better out in the open. Gorgeous. I mean it – heart-racingly, head-turningly, drop-dead gorgeous. My spine's tingling, my synapses are crackling. Don't tell me there's a mojito in the world could make you feel like that. Don't care how many sprigs of mint you get, how many lime segments, how much cane sugar's frosted round the rim. Bollocks to that. This is what it's all about. I'm glowing, I'm kvelling, I'm shepping nachas like a good 'un. Yeah, shepping, not shlepping. I might be a dust-head; I'm not a fucking idiot. Linguistics is a must, whether Yiddish, English or Cantonese. Got to get it right, can't come across like a shmerel. Where was I? Time for a taste test. Presentation's important, watch how I cut it. Long and thin, not short and thick – trust me, I know. No thanks, don't need a fifty – rolled up notes are so last season. Only joking, use one if you want, I prefer my long john. As in silver, as in that silver tube behind the remote control, can you reach it? Thanks. No, after you, you're a guest in this house. A line of coke is like a swordfight, you must think first before you move. Or at least check your sleeve's not dangling. Don't worry about it, plenty more where that came from. Watch a master at work. See how I slammed it back? That's years of experience, kilos of practise. Makes the eyes water, that's a good sign. Throat's iced good and proper, a full can of anti-freeze couldn't counter that. Dab a bit on the gums, great little chaser. Cigarette, Scotch, quick grind of the jaw. Got to warm the jaw up, you know, cos it'll be all systems go in a few lines' time. Gonna look like Red Rum later on, chomping at the bit and pawing the carpet. How was it for you? Good, good, have another if you're ready. I am. Apologies if I'm talking too much, I get carried away. Just tell me to shut up if I'm driving you mad. Actually I'm off out for a minute, got to grab something from the car. Take whatever you want, I won't be long. Sure, no problem. Back shortly. All ok? Had another little one, I see. 'Course it's fine – I told you to, didn't I? My turn, I think, time for a sharpener. God, I love it, look at that, what a proper little stunner I've racked up there. Makes me come out in goosebumps. This is the life, back where it all began, back in the Hampstead heim and I wouldn't have it any other way. Couldn't get back here quick enough. Should have followed my boy Saul's lead eighteen months ago instead of fucking around at university, but I'm making up for lost time now. Stuck-up goyishe gimps. I'd have hung 'em all by their old school ties given half the chance, but that's just water under the Bridge of Sighs now, isn't it? Ever been to Oxford? Lucky you, then – trust me, avoid it like the Gaza Strip. Neither one's the place for a nice Jewish boy – not that I'm nice, but you know what I mean. I belong in the City. Starting on the prop desk at Banque Nord on Tuesday, gonna trade my way to heaven, gonna ride that camel through the eye of a needle no matter what they say. Jesus, I'm still banging on, aren't I? Sorry, sorry, your turn, you speak. Don't mind me, I'll rack up. I'm a great listener, by the way, the best. More rabbit than Bugs, but I know when to shut it. Go on, seriously. Tell me all about it.

1

In one of my father's rare moments of paternalistic instruction he explained his take on the way gentiles view Jews, and despite disagreeing with pretty much everything else he ever told me, I took this particular lesson to heart.

'The world is full of racists,' he deadpanned, not a trace of irony in his voice. 'But while most prejudice is built on foundations of disgust and disdain, when it's directed against the Jews it comes from a distinctly different place. Jews are hated by people jealous of them – and that's what makes anti-Semitism unique. We're accused of doing all the things others wish they could do themselves – running the banks, controlling the media and pulling the strings of governments round the world. You'll never hear anyone making such claims about shvartses – that would be nothing short of absurd. Instead, they're portrayed as apes and baboons, as crude caricatures of cavemen and chimpanzees. They're depicted as backwards, unevolved and base creatures of the jungle, whereas we're painted as the exact opposite. As higher beings, of great intellect, cunning, and wit. They might call us evil, but they never underestimate our power. And that's a telling indicator of how inferior they feel – a sentiment with which I wholeheartedly concur.'

I think of him now, as I begin the day as I've begun every day I can remember this year – drenched in sweat, trying to work out what happened the previous night. I think of the last time I spoke to him. When he gave me the ultimatum about getting a job. Wonder if he's still the owner of north London's most well developed superiority complex. I can't confirm it from first-hand knowledge of course. I haven't seen him for months, and our occasional phone calls consist of little more than him checking I'm still with Laura, and still requiring no real effort or attention on his part. In his pocket for twenty-one years and counting. I let him think what he wants, let him tell my mum everything's come up roses for me. Why make them think any different? For now, at any rate. Bite his hand and he'll stop feeding me in a flash, and I'm a long way from ready to fend for myself. Hence my acceptance that I've got to go out to work. He spat blood when I walked out of Oxford, was close to turning off the trust fund tap for good, then settled for setting me up at Banque Nord and seeing how I fared. He's made himself crystal clear: fuck this one up, and I'm out on my own. Same goes for my relationship with Laura, as far as he's concerned. Marriage plus 2.4 kids equals a mortgage-free six-bed in Linden Lea; stray from the derech and I might as well put myself down for a council house. It's not what I want that matters, it's all about what he demands. Be the son your mother can show off. Be the husband your beck wife can sponge off. Be the dad your spoilt kids can leech off and write off just like you did to yours and theirs'll do to them too. I'll play along for now, but whatever I end up doing, I'm not gonna be another Suburb clone. Not gonna be a doctor, not gonna be a lawyer. Not gonna be a chartered accountant, a chartered surveyor, a chartered fucking anything. I wanna do the chartering. Planes, trains, keys of cocaine. No point settling for less.

That said, my opinions do dovetail with my dad's in one important area. I don't like goyim any more than he does, and that's both an ideology and a lifestyle choice in itself. I'm not to blame, m'lud, I'm just a product of my environment. The Millwall mantra 'no one likes us – we don't care' sums up perfectly the atmosphere I grew up in, though my elders and betters eschewed violence in favour of simply using cash to stick up two fingers at their detractors. The golf club nestled between my street, Winnington Road, and the almost-as-plush Ingram Avenue was a case in point. Don't allow Jewish members to play your course? Fuck you, then – we'll just buy up every ten-bedroom property in sight of the clubhouse. We're used to being besieged, from Jerusalem to the Warsaw Ghetto and beyond, so let's see how you like it now the tables are turned. At least, that was how my fevered mind told me it worked in our neighbourhood: every brick laid in a Jewish house, every tree planted in a Jewish garden, every mezuzah fixed to a Jewish doorframe – all served as nail after nail in the coffin of oppression and opprobrium that had dogged our clan since time immemorial.

Not that we did any of the manual labour ourselves, mind you. As the saying goes, DIY means something very different in a Jewish household – namely, Drag In a Yok.

Yoks are to Jews what yin is to yang. Or maybe that implies too interdependent a relationship than is really the case. I'm not sure. Oil and water's a better analogy, actually, and we're just as reluctant to mix with our goyishe counterparts as they are with us. I never made friends outside the Jewish bubble when I was growing up, and even now I still make sure to keep business and pleasure separate from each other. Tonight will see a rare blurring of the boundaries – I'm being introduced to my new trading colleagues, though fuck knows how I'm gonna get myself in a fit state for that. I'm barely awake, bathed in sweat, trying to haul my body out of bed, my mind's trying to dive back under the covers.

My Blackberry vibrates on the bedside table, I reach for it and knock it onto the floor. I give up trying, it'll only be Laura. I can tell the time by her texts, she thinks I need to know every thought that pops into her head, like I give a fuck about her latest lecture, her last set of results, her next mind-numbing module. The first rule of LSE club should be: don't talk about LSE club. Wish she'd worked that out by now.

Nope, no good. No idea how last night ended, no point dwelling on it, though. Tonight's a big night. Tonight I have to hit the bar running. However in the meantime there's nothing to do but wait. The only thing I've got to look forward to is the coked-up fear and stress and tension that a night out in Old Street will bring. Or rather, to look forward to it all in Yiddish. I wanna plutz, wanna be on shpilkes, wanna deigeh. No one will say deigeh nisht, because they're all Tonys. As in Tony McCoys, goys. Or Tillbury Docks, yoks. Except for the Essex-girl secretaries who'll be dotted round the dance floor for our viewing pleasure – the female of the species gets the best name of all: Kenwood (mixer = shikse). We've got more words for gentiles than Eskimos do for snow, but rhyming slang works best. It softens the blow, I reckon. The names are once or twice removed from the underlying insult, which is lucky because shikse is a difficult word to justify. Its literal translation is 'abomination', and while some of the Gants Hill girls aren't exactly God's best work to date, calling them abominations is still laying it on a bit thick. Not that I care all that much. I stay true to my roots.

The landline rings. Saul's number flashes on the screen. I make a weak stab at the green button, spark a cigarette with trembling fingers as I summon the strength to speak.

'Yeah? Saul?'

He laughs at my husky voice.

'What the fuck, man? You do that voice for all your punters?'

I can hear the sound of his dealing room in the background, the great and the good of Dover Securities greasing the wheels of the City bandwagon. He's been a stockbroker there for the best part of two years. After months of him asking me what the fuck I was doing wasting time going to lectures, I'm going to be joining him in the real world.

'Slightly large night . . .'

He laughs condescendingly.

'Yeah, yeah, but don't let me down tonight, and more importantly don't let yourself down. This is your debut, and you don't want your teammates thinking you can't last the full ninety. They'll judge you far more on your performance on a night out than they will on your first day's trading'

I can well believe it, and even though I feel fucked now,

I've got every faith I'll rise to the challenge. I'll be in my element, Saul by my side ready to induct me into the Square Mile-sized drinking club that's doubled as his family ever since he became a broker. I'll be the shy first-timer setting foot on the City stage, though the inhibitions should be lost after the first couple of lines.

'I'll sort myself out. What time and where?'

'It's at a bar somewhere between Moorgate and Old Street, I'll text you the address in a bit. It'll be a late start, for you at any rate. The Dover's lot will be out from about eight, but your team won't get there till tennish. They'll be trading the Dow Jones after London closes tonight cos the Fed's interest rate decision is due.'

That last sentence should mean more to me than it does. Either way, it will by next week. The only prices I care about right now are JoJo's, and he doesn't let market fluctuations affect his rates: fifty on the g, ten per cent off for decent bulk orders, ten per cent on for home delivery. Better get on the phone to him next, my cupboard's blatantly bare.

'Cool, I'll be on it by then, no problem. It'll be good to catch up with you.'

'Nice. Yeah, it's been too long. By the way, sorry to sound like a shnorrer, but you couldn't front me about a grand tonight, could you? Sorry to ask, I just had to lay out a fortune on some stupid lunchtime poker game against our European desk, and I left all my cash cards with Mya at home.'

A pain in the arse, but fuck it – cash has gone back and forth between us so many times over the years that neither of us knows who's the ultimate debtor. I've got my hunches though.

'Sure, Sauly, I'll lend you the money – I'd expect nothing less from you than that kind of chutzpah. I'd be delighted to buy my way into your affections – now who's the one turning tricks?'

He's only half-listening. I can hear him banging away at his Bloomberg terminal as he turns his attention back to the market.

'Ta – I'll get it back to you before Yom Kippur, nice one. Oh yeah, expect an unsavourily high goy-to-Jew ratio in our group tonight. Nothing you can do about it, it comes with the trader territory. If you wanted to stick with your own, you should have been a broker – trading's for Tonys, don't say I didn't warn you. Anyway, you'll just have to grin and bear it.'

Speak for yourself. I stand up and nothing too bad happens. A good start. I walk into the living room.

Sunlight's streaming through the window. The coffee table's covered with the usual detritus. Empty wraps, empty glasses, empty packs of Marlboro Lights and Dunhill Blues. Overflowing ashtrays, over-roached Rizla packs, overlooked crumbs of hash. That's why I hate stoners, they're so fucking casual about their habit. So blasé about their stash. Not us, not the true aficionados. Look at those CD cases, licked clean of every last granule of coke, the coat of dried saliva testament to the waste-not, want-not attitude of the dust-head division.

Saul wasn't always so lax on the anti-miscegenation front. Sixteen years ago – and fifty-five years after the enactment of the Nuremberg Laws – two five-year-olds stood trial in a north-west London infant school, on charges of religious discrimination against their fellow students. I was one of them. Saul was the other. As we stood meekly in the dock in our school-issue shorts and shirts, we abandoned our all-for-one approach and instantly blamed each other for the crime, in the tradition of guilty schoolboys the world over. We stood accused of having formed a Jews-only gang during lunch break and, to be honest, they'd got us bang to rights.

Brooklands had a vastly disproportionate number of Jewish students for a London school, thanks to its location in the heart of the Suburb. Somehow, Saul and I had got it into our heads that we should form our latest crew on the basis of racial profiling, rather than by virtue of who supported Arsenal or who was best at swimming. Pudgy arms pointed at each other like bayonets forming a guard of honour for truth to march beneath, we were found jointly guilty by a headmistress too incensed by the affair to spend time forensically examining our claims. I still think we could have got our convictions quashed on appeal (we weren't given recourse to a lawyer, nor allowed to call witnesses in our defence), but if anyone was on trial that day, it was the Suburb's Jewish community as a whole: we were just the fall guys for the system, our crimes merely symptoms of a far wider malaise.

I learned the lesson that we might call ourselves the Chosen People, but that the title was not meant to be literally interpreted in the asphalt playgrounds of Brooklands Infants. But the school fence was as far as my rehabilitation went. On the outside, back in the real world, I was encouraged by all and sundry to keep it in the family – at all times, at all costs. Just like their St John's Wood counterparts, the Suburb gantzer machers had marked out their territory, and were prepared to defend it fiercely from unwanted outsiders. We still do, though the occasional well-proportioned tourist is allowed through on a whim, Bhutan-style, and under strict instructions not to outstay their visa – which usually expires the morning after the night before, when the dust settles and reality kicks in. Jewish girls for marriage, shikses for practise. That doesn't apply to me tonight – I'll be otherwise engaged getting to know the traders at my new firm – but there's no doubt Saul will be living out the adage in style. Zei gezunt.

Anyway, there's no time to worry about that now. I've got serious recovering to do before tonight, and desperate measures are required. I fire up the laptop and do what I do best.

Easiest lay of my life. Just sitting there waiting for me to approach, all demure, with those come-hither eyes I can't resist. Fresh, clean, and a killer figure – I'm hooked from the off. 1.29-30's the spread, and for all the hype it's still only a two-horse race. Yeah, I said two-horse – I don't count draws, not before the match starts at least, so it's either one team or the other. United or Wigan, and given the game's at Wigan, there's no fucking way they should be a six-to-one shot on home turf. Lay United, 1.30, stake fifteen hundred to win five grand. Mouse hovers, hand pauses, last-minute appeals get heard in the crown court of my mind. Judge is having none of it, conviction upheld, hit the button, trapdoor opens. It's on. Ten minutes to kick-off. My fingers know what's coming – they're not happy. Left thumb first, grind the corner of the nail between my teeth, eyes locked on the plasma on the far wall, commentators might as well be speaking Portuguese. Not listening to them, not even really seeing the picture, just munching on nail and skin, ripping off chunks and drawing blood as I enter the zone. Still 1.29-30, dunno why I'm even looking. I know the form, know how it'll pan out. If it's goalless on ten minutes, the United backers' nerves'll fray, and they'll come out to 1.32-33, then shorten again as a second wave of buyers pile in. Not rocket science, though it's definitely a science and not an art. Herd mentality runs the show, wildebeest stampeding to and fro across the screen as the game swings one way and another. Point is, on a 1.30 lay, even if United score where can the odds go from here? 1.18? 1.14 at a push? Not exactly nightmare territory. Just double up, lay another five grand and strap in for the ride. I'm getting ahead of myself though, it's still nil-nil, and I'm only on the second finger of my left hand. Quick slug of Tuborg, few drags on the Marly Light. Might be raining outside, might be a plague of frogs, couldn't care less, couldn't even tell you which room I'm in. United pressing, Wigan stressing. All square though, eight minutes in. Finger three, no nail left after yesterday's feast, go straight for the skin round the knuckle. Tuborg chaser, lean back on the couch, pretend I'm relaxed, pretend it's all just a game. That facade lasts a second, hunch back over the screen, mouse cocked like a Magnum, eyes boring into the LCD. 1.29-31, someone's laid the whole of the .30. The backer reloads again, 1.29-30, all is calm, all is bright. Wigan free kick, half a chance for them, two thirds of a chance for me. Cunt blazes miles over, I vow to kill his kids. Nothing personal, just don't come between me and my money. Someone walks into the room, says something, says it again, possibly a third time, too. By the time I look up, they've wandered off or dived out the window, either way we're better off apart. United on top, if the screen's to be believed: 1.27-8, another half million's been placed since kick-off. Twelve minutes gone, I treat myself to a double slug of beer. Still 1.27-8, but the rally's just round the corner, and it's late as it is. Just like buses, along come two at once, the first ticks it up to 1.29-30, the next surge runs to 1.33-4. Could take a ton and a half's profit here if I wanted out, but why would I want out? What else am I gonna do, get a grip? Get a sense of purpose? Not today, thanks, not tomorrow either cos there's the cup replay to deal with. Never used to bet on cup games, they're a totally different kettle of fish. It'd be like asking a Cubism expert to value a da Vinci. Not any more though, now I take 'em all as they come, no questions asked, no eyebrows raised. A game's a game, a bet's a bet, an ego's an ego and mine's a treble. I don't do it for the money, darling, I do it for the pride. 'Course I do, just think of the naches they'll all get when they see my year-end figures. Clue: there is no 'they'. Another clue: even if there was I'd lie through my teeth whether I was up or down. If I make ten large, I call it twenty when asked. If I ever lose, it's an instant state secret, not to be declassified till I'm dead. Gamblers never tell the truth, come hell or high water, and they're on first name terms with both. Fifteen minutes, United penalty, market's suspended, big fuck-off red stamp across the screen, a million punters round the globe mimic my slack-jawed pose. They could be backers, layers or in-betweeners, but we all share one thing in common: we're all watching Ronaldo's boot like hawks. Our whole worlds revolve round his right foot right now, right up to when he jogs right up, right-left, right-left, strikes it right, keeper's guessed right, ball flies right, no chance, right? Bulging neck, bulging net, screaming fans, cocky grin, finger wagged, whistle blown, ball retrieved, centre taken, fuck my fucking bet. Screen's exploded, another mill's gone on, 1.18-19, double up, win ten if I'm right, do my nuts if I'm wrong. Hands shaking, bleeding, aching. Brain's copying hands, soul's copying brain. Just how I like it, just what the doctor ordered. Wigan better fucking score, we're all Wigan now, got a Wigan tattoo on my shoulder, Wigan shirt on my back, Wigan heart on my sleeve. My love for Wigan makes Paris's for Helena look like a teenage crush. My love for Wigan climbs mountains, bathes in springs, dances in the dappled light of forest glades. I breathe Wigan, I cry Wigan, I taste Wigan, I sigh Wigan. Wiganwiganwigan sing the birds in the trees. If I should forget thee, O Wigan, may my right hand wither. Twenty minutes up, 1.18-19, game slows down, pulse doesn't take the hint. Twenty-one, two, three, four, five – once I caught a fish alive – six, seven, eight, nine, ten – then I upped my stake again. No reason to, no reason not to. Just killing time, just killing brain cells, just killing my chances of getting out the bet in one piece. Half an hour gone, I'm exposed to the tune of four and a half. That's indecent exposure, that needs a copper's helmet shoved over it as I'm bundled into a Black Maria. Not scared though, not gonna crack. I believe. I believe I believe, at least. Trigger finger's itching, but even I'm not that stupid. Five grand's the limit on this game, and I've already put ninety per cent down in under forty minutes. Hang back, hold fire, hang Ronaldo, hold breath. WIGAN GOAL!!! Just kidding, just practising, just dreaming. WIGAN GOAL!!! Seriously, this time – big fat suspended sign over the market and everything .

. . so why's van der Sar taking a free kick? Offside? Off-fucking-side? Off your rocker more like, mate – you cunt, you tart, you greasy little northern monkey (I'm in working-class fan mode now, excuse me for a minute). Yeah, you, where'd you get that fucking idea from? Your paymasters in a Korean syndicate? Give me strength, that was never offside, not in a month of Sundays, though what do I know, it's not like I've actually seen a ball get kicked since the eighteenth minute. All I do is watch the market flicker out its own match report, like Braille for gamblers, like morse code for mugs. The fifty-inch television's only there for show, it's on and it's playing but it could be made of cardboard and I'd barely notice. It's half time there, I'm half cut here, the glass is half empty, my eyes are half shut. Lying about the eyes of course, they're wider than ever, pupils dilated like a pill-head's. This is better than sex, better than coke, better than sex on coke. I'm losing money but I'm not losing heart. It's only one-nil United, it's a game of two halves, it's always darkest before the dawn, and every dog has its day. Overdosing on clichés, overdosing on Tuborg. Nicotine level's a bit low, better sort that out while they eat their oranges. Smoking kills, but not as much as my left hand. The first half took a heavy toll, looks like a finger puppet version of *The Texas Chainsaw Massacre*. Hazards of the job, no use crying over spilt blood. Teams back out, cigarette back out, can't back out of the bet though, I'm in like Flynn, on it like Sonic. Forty-six, forty-seven, 1.15-16, stupid price now. Wigan throw, Wigan corner, Wigan slice, Wigan miss. All Wigan this half, starting to put the pressure on now. And now, and now, and how. 1.18-19, that's more like it, I knew it wasn't just me. Trade out of one tranche, bet's back down to three grand again, no damage, no fuss. Nailed-on Wigan score now, just to spite me. Fifty-three, four, five. 1.17-18. I stifle a yawn, United stream forward, I stifle a scream. Heeeere's Johnny. But the keeper saves, Wigan counter, and fucking would you fucking believe it fucking bundle in a fucking equaliser bang as the clock hits sixty on the nose, on the money, on my fucking life. I've been possessed by John Motson with Tourette's, the big bad beautiful crimson suspended sign lights up the screen, lights up my life, this time it counts, and that means I've coined it, but more importantly, more sensationally, most magnificently, I was bloody right with my lay, and look – I've got the cash in the bank to prove it. Almost. Now I've got work to do. United have come out to 2.20-25, huge spread, cos no one knows which way to bet, swinging like a metronome here, 2.10-12, 2.20-22, even printing at 2.30 but you'd need to be faster than a leopard to catch that one. Fling in a back at 2.00 cos I can work that one out in my head, put five grand on United at evens, leaves me five up on a Wigan win or draw, just over two and a half up on United. Can't lose, won't lose. Could even out the profits better though, but can't be bothered, won't be bothered. Feel a bit post-coital now, post-natal even, definitely post-shredded-fucking-nerves. That's not a good thing, by the way. I like shredded nerves, they're like shredded wheat. Keep the hunger locked up way past lunch, way past tea, way past whenever, so long as the bet's still live. And this one ain't. This one's dying. Granted there's still the small matter of whether I make two and a half or five grand profit, but that's splitting hairs. The drama's gone out of it, the thrill of the chase is over, the balloon's been burst and the air's seeped out. One more cliché, if you don't mind: it's better to travel than arrive. Always. Sixty-five, seventy, eighty five, done. Didn't hear the final whistle, wasn't even in the room. Fuck knows who won. Fuck cares either. Back to life, back to reality. Gutted. Would give it all back to start again. Listless, restless, mindless, helpless. If I forget thee, O Betfair.

If Betfair's the white horse, bullet chess is my methadone. Play a few games against whoever's online, nice little buzz when I win, nice little buzz when I lose. Just nice little buzz after nice little buzz, game after game after game. No money involved means no chance of a real kick, but the need to win means I still treat each and every battle with deadly seriousness. Two ways to play bullet chess: either keep your head down, move ultra fast and ultra safe and hope your opponent ties himself up in knots as the egg timer empties, or go in all guns blazing and scare him into submission inside the hundred and twenty seconds. Either way, it's a cheap and cheerful thrill. I'm engrossed for a while, then boredom strikes like a cobra. I switch off the computer, I leave the house. Baby blue Fila tracksuit trousers, white Air Max 90s, white Lacoste hoodie – my off-to-the-gym look even though I'm only off-to-the-offies.

I walk slowly down the High Street; I haven't got a choice. The see-and-be-seen crowd are out in force, clogging up Hampstead's arteries and forcing the rest of us to play human Tetris to get from A to B. Can't blame them – I was the same back when I was a beck. It's hard to describe a beck without falling back on all the clichés about spoiled little rich kids that so sully the reputation of me and my ilk. But I'm not complaining. I used to wear the beck tag like a badge of honour, along with all of the connotations it conjured up.

Fuck it – we were Semitic Sloanes, Jewish princes and princesses living up to the hype, so why pretend otherwise? We're not that different now, of course, but our extra-curricular activities mark us out as something more sinister than simply becks without a cause. I send Laura a quick text, write the bare minimum, tell her I love her and I'll speak to her later when I'm out. Not sure either statement's true, but I'm not under oath. Walk into Victoria Wine, there's that girl on the till. She's the main reason I set out on this expedition, she's the grail I was after. Think she's called Christine, Christina or Chrissy – whatever it is, she screams shikse from every pore, and her hyper-goyish name only adds to the allure. I flash her a smile, stride over to the whisky section. Lift two bottles of 21-year-old Glenfiddich from the shelf, walk to the counter.

'Celebrating tonight, are yer?'

The regional accent's fucking ugly, but exotic all the same.

'Kind of. Starting a new job in the City next week, gotta make the most of my freedom while I can.'

Carefully chosen words, carefully mangled sentences. When in Rome, or when in the West Midlands to be precise.

'Yeah, I know all about that. I haven't had a day off for two weeks, I can hardly remember what freedom tastes like.'

Don't look to me for sympathy, love. Not my fault you got dealt a hand full of twos and threes.

'Least you're in the right place to drown your sorrows though, aren't you?'

She laughs in a grating arpeggio, I sign the receipt, we say our goodbyes. More groundwork laid; I'm in for the long haul on this one. Back outside, the name of the game's still standing in tight circles shooting the breeze, while keeping beady eyes peeled on who else is coming and going on the wide strips of pavement either side of the street. Both the girls and the boys are scrutinising those going by with the speed of supermarket scanners reading barcodes. In one sweeping head-to-toe movement, clothes are checked for labels as well as wear and tear; weight loss or gain is noted; hairstyles and footwear are jotted down in mental scrapbooks to be recalled at will days or weeks later. The scene looks like a defanged version of teenage gangs hanging out on street corners the length and breadth of the country: bottles of cheap wine and vodka replaced by mobile phones, Marlboro Lights and tubes of lip gloss in the hands of those present. Excruciatingly little is actually happening other than a scores-strong cast sizing one another up and exchanging bland pleasantries on the Hampstead stage. I yawn, I walk. I'm tired but I'm lucid. I watch the boy becks size up the girl becks, I watch the girl becks turn the tables. No place for me here, it's no country for old men.

2

I'm the answer to a riddle. I have eyes but cannot see, legs but cannot stand, lungs but cannot breathe. Hours one to five were fine, hours six to eight not so much. Not so hot. Not my finest moment. Mind over matter, but not when the matter's eight Black Russians and x pints of Stella. x is greater than five and less than ten. The cube root of x is equal to the hypotenuse. x minus one is the diameter of y. y is a fucking good question. How is as well; where is easier to work out. The Met Bar, baby – got five of their matchboxes in my bed to prove it. Got a lot of things in my bed that don't quite belong. Two bags of cashews, half a jar of olives. One Gucci loafer, the other's on my desk. This doesn't look good, this doesn't bode well. Fear chases the pain, pain picks up the pace. Nausea joins the party, regret arrives fashionably late. Fear and pain stop in their tracks, turn around and greet nausea and regret like long-lost friends. Kiss on each cheek, bear hugs, slaps on the back. They put on music, form a line, dance the conga. I switch on the light, terrible idea, switch it back off. Try to sleep, waste of time. If at first you don't succeed, smoke. Sounds like a plan, can't see the pack though. There's one on the shelf, but that's miles away. Never gonna get there on my own. Got to be realistic, got to not set my sights too high. The immovable drunk meets the unstoppable hangover. Muhammad and the mountain. Not sure which one's me. My phone rings. My phone screams like a spoilt child. I throw off the covers, an act of unparalleled courage. I rise, I fall. I rise again, Lazarus-style. I can do this. I think I can, I think I can, I know I can, I know I can. I'm Thomas the Tank, I'm Bertie the Bus. The walls are laughing, the ceiling's in hysterics. The floor's got its mouth shut, cos the floor's furious. The floor tells me time and again to get a grip, but I never listen. Why should I? You're not my real mum, I shout, storming out the door and into the kitchen. Kettle on, open fridge, grab water, turn lid. Raise the bottle to my lips, sip, tip, gulp. Look like the girl in the Evian advert, if she had fewer chromosomes and significantly less class. And if she was a he. Watch the pot, it doesn't boil. Stand my ground, I don't back down for kitchen appliances. Kettle finally falls into line, heap a teaspoon with coffee, toss it in the mug, half-fill it with water. No milk, no sugar, no need. Clutch the cup like a trophy, stagger back to my room. Ignore the floor, hold my head high. Grab the pack of Marlboro Lights, duck back under the duvet. On a roll, onto a winner, slide open the window, it's a stunner outside. No clouds, all blue, sun's centre stage. Strange, cos I'd have sworn it was morning. Grab my phone, check the time, quarter to one. No great loss, no great drama. Today's a rest day, the worst's over. I lie back and bask in my mind's Indian summer. Coffee hors d'oeuvres, Evian palate cleanser, cigarette main. No dessert, thanks, I'm watching my weight. Smile gets wiped off my face in a flash, I'm blindsided by pain again. The only way is down, and I'm falling fast. I'm so sorry, heart, I'm so sorry, kidneys, I'm so sorry, stomach. I've let you all down, I've been foolish and selfish and stupid and weak. I've brought it all on myself, I've dragged you all down with me. I don't know what to say, I don't know how to make it up to you. I'm a mess. Leave me, I need to be alone. The floor's turned its back, even the walls and ceiling have been shocked into silence. Time to make a deal with the devil. One hour's sleep, if I go straight for a week. Clean up my act, finger my rosaries and come good on my pledge. Anything you say, any condition, any price. We shake on it, I fade to black. I wake, I laugh. I had my fingers crossed, didn't I? I'm still not better, but I fucking well will be by tonight. I'm wood, I'm teak, I'm volcanic rock. Know who's a cunt? John Maynard Keynes. 'My only regret in life is that I did not drink more champagne.' What kind of message is that for the children? Moderates never prosper, he should have hit the bottle harder. Should have come round my house, come to my parties, come down my bar. I've got a case of Dom Perignon '73 Cuvee with his name all over it. Shame he's dead. Lucky I'm not. *L'chaim, l'simcha, l'sasson.* I think I can, I know I can. Bring on Annie and Clarabel.

Can't believe the days pass so fast though, it's already six and the sun's fading fast. Friday today. Tonight's Friday night. Shabbat dinner. Family, friends, wine, challah, five-course feast. I wish. Wrong me, wrong them, wrong address. Wrong time, wrong place. Even before my parents left England for Zurich's more tax-free climes three years ago I was as good as an orphan. A loaded orphan, granted – no workhouse for me. But money aside I was on my own in the big wide world. Bundle of fifties tied to the end of a stick, I was Dick Whittington's understudy, marching off into the sunset to see if the streets really were paved with gold. Didn't have to go far, of course, didn't even need to leave the south wing of the house. Definitely didn't need to go all the way to Oxford for a pointless, yok-infested year and a half before jumping ship. Definitely didn't need to bore myself to tears mixing with the foppish boys and frigid girls I was forced to spend my days and nights with on campus. Drier than a matza factory and ten times more parev, but you live and learn and purge the memories, then pick up where you left off back on hallowed Hampstead ground.

By the time Laura arrives I'm almost back to full strength. I'm still walking round the house on foal's legs, but I mask it well. I have to. Laura's patience wore thin a long time ago, and I'm under no illusions about what will happen if I don't fall into line. We've been together since we were seventeen, and in all that time I've never really lived up to her expectations. I've been close, I've been in the high eighties, sometimes even broke into the nineties, but have always fallen short of the perfect score. I'd be lucky to make it into double figures today. Before I went out last night she gave me the 'standing at a crossroads' spiel again – it's her favourite after-dinner speech – and even though I ignored her and got wasted anyway, I knew she meant it more sincerely than ever before. Like I give a fuck. She's just lucky that she's a key part of my dad's vision for my future. Not to mention lucky that her demands match my own decision to suspend my narcotic rights till further notice: no one should turn up to their first day of school off their face, and last night's meet and greet has to be the last time my bosses see me in that state for a good while to come. I proved I could mix it with the best of them, but now I've got to be in dutiful underling mode until they rubberstamp my full acceptance into their City clique.

'All right?'

'No.'

'Sorry about last night. I had a lot on my mind'

'You had a lot up your nose, you mean, and even more down your throat.'

She's not shouting, which is a bad sign. She's not looking into my eyes either, another portent of doom.

'No, seriously Law, I'm getting really stressed out at the moment, I'm losing it. I needed to get out of my head just to get some relief from it all.'

'Don't be so stupid – the drugs and the drink are why you're losing it, not the other way round. You know that as well, you're just hoping I'm thick enough to fall for your spin.'

'Not at all, Laura, I swear.'

'What happened last night anyway? It's not like you made any sense on the phone when you called.'

Highlights of the carnage flash through my mind in no particular order. Punches thrown by us and at us; screaming barmaids slapping away groping hands; jeering traders slapping comrades' backs; coke moustaches smeared with pride under noses; fifty pound notes thrust with lust under G-strings; wing mirrors ripped off and hurled across streets; bottles dashed to the floor and ground to dust under heels. Set adrift on memory bliss. I keep my mouth tightly shut.

'I've got enough on my mind what with essays and

coursework to have to worry about you as well and get woken at three in the morning when you're wasted. You're just so selfish, it's not always all about you – uni's bloody hard at the moment.'

'Course it is. Deciding which highlighter to use to stencil your name on the desk would give Sartre a migraine. I get up from my couch and sit down on hers. She shifts position so that we're not touching. I close the gap, try to put an arm round her waist. She recoils again; I knew she would. Part of the game, part of the plan. If she thinks she's giving me a kicking with body language, it softens her up a bit on the verbal front. I pull a little-boy-hurt face at her rejection, she continues to scowl.

'Law, I'm sorry. It's not on, and it's not gonna happen again – I know you're having a hard time, and I want to be there for you like you deserve.'

'I've heard it all before, and I don't know why you don't believe me when I say I'm not gonna put up with this much longer.'

Because you're still here, because you still come back for more. The music stops when I say, not you – you're just the devil's dancing partner. I'm taking a break only for as long as it takes to learn the trading ropes, then it's straight back to hell in a handcart, darling.

'I do believe you, and I'm not even arguing, am I? I know I fucked up yesterday, I know I've fucked up a lot recently, but at the same time we both know this is the end of an era. Last days of the empire and all that, yeah?'

'So you say, but you starting work in the City doesn't exactly leave me brimming with confidence. From what I could decipher of your drunken babbling down the phone last night, most of the boys out with you were traders, and they were just as wasted as you.'

She's in real mountain and molehill territory now, but I let it slide. I don't defend anyone's honour or appeal for clemency. What's the point? I was preparing to scramble aboard the wagon anyway, regardless of Laura's intervention, and even if I fall off prematurely, what's she gonna do about it? No one's going anywhere, we're tied together tighter than Keenan and McCarthy.

'I know, but come on, Law, I always know what I'm doing, don't I? I mean, it's not as if I ever pass the point of no return. I've always managed to keep my life on track, even before you knew me. I never got kicked out of school, never got caught, never robbed anyone or got an indelible mark against my name. Look at me from an outsider's perspective – skipped a year at school, straight As at A-level, place at Oxford, job offers in the City, and already more cash in the bank than most people earn in a decade.'

'But the money's from your mum and dad, and the brains too. You've never had to work for anything, never really had to knuckle down and commit – just look at how you treated your opportunity at Oxford. I might not have been a saint either, but at least I've been changing that ever since I started uni. I'm already two years down my path, and you haven't even started mapping your route out.'

Twenty months at LSE and she thinks she's a fucking pillar of academia. Wrong reaction. Stay calm and collected. If I let her slip away, the whole edifice will come crumbling down – I'm under no illusions that the ever-flowing tap of parental cash risks getting turned off the second it looks like I'm going off the rails. I'll lose a lot more than just her if I fuck things up now.

'All right, Law, all right. I was out of order last night, I won't be out of order tonight. Don't turn this into something bigger than it really is, ok?'

But it isn't ok, she's got a lot more left to say. And why say it with flowers when you've got flame-throwers instead? I feel the fire melt my face, but it's only cosmetic. Tell myself the layer of steel under my skin can take the heat, so I stay in the kitchen.

'I don't want to see you tonight – I'm going out with my parents, and you're definitely not invited. I just wanted to pick up my watch, and to give you this.'

She reaches into her bag and pulls out a jewellery box. She opens it, I stare nonplussed. There are seven wraps in there, tied together with JoJo's signature scarlet thread. Weird fucker thinks it's a highbrow biblical reference, we all think he's got too much time on his hands, and not nearly enough seychel. I'm not sure if I'm meant to take the box, not sure if it's a test.

'It's for you, you can have them all.'

'Ok, great . . . but why would you want me to do more?'

'Cos this is it, this is honestly your lot. I told JoJo it's over, and told him you're starting work on Tuesday. I asked him not to serve you anymore, and he said that's fine. If you really want to know, he told me I was your guardian angel, that someone needed to do something before you completely lost the plot.'

I want to explode, I want to slap the halo off her self-righteous head. I don't. I nod glumly instead, then nod sagely for good measure. All part of the act, all part of the facade. An eighth of coke's an eighth of coke – if she wants to think it's my last supper then let her. JoJo's hardly the UK's sole importer, and I've hardly been a loyal customer anyway. I'll be back on it soon enough: I'm stopping of my own volition, and I'll reopen the floodgates on the same terms as well as soon as I'm good and ready.

'Yeah, you're completely right. I don't deserve you, Laura, and I'm not talking about the gift. I mean for everything you do for me, for all that you care for me. In fact I don't even want these, I'll knock it on the head here and now if it makes you happier.'

'Don't try and kid me. I know you want it, and I know you're already thinking of other ways to score as soon as this runs out. But I need you to think long and hard over the next couple of days about what you really want to do once this batch has been and gone. Because I can't take it anymore, it's gone on so much longer than I ever thought it would. Please see sense, please don't let the drugs break us up.'

'They never will, Law, I promise.'

And I mean it, for a split second. She looks so pained, so vulnerable, so fucking perfect at this exact moment. She's bringing an offering to my temple, making a sacrificial plea at my altar. She's wrapped round my little finger, she's clamped tight under my thumb. I've still got her exactly where I want her.

'I have to go, and I'd rather not see you till you've got this all out your system. I'm invited with Sarah to her sister's in Paris for the weekend, so maybe I should fly out tomorrow and not see you till after your first day. We've got dinner at Anna and Sam's Tuesday night, don't you dare try and get out of it. You'll be through all this by then, won't you?'

Yeah, I think I can manage that. And another half ounce or so while I'm at it. When the cat's away, moderation takes a back-row seat. We kiss, more for the cameras than anything else. She goes, I stay, and so does the jewellery box.

Laura's the classic poacher-turned-gamekeeper, and it suits her perfectly. Even in her hedonistic heyday she wasn't really on it like we were. You always got the feeling she was doing it as part of her endless search for meaning, her relentless pursuit of answers to her overflowing cup of questions. I never understood why she didn't fall utterly in love with substances like I did. I fell head over heels from day one. Truly, madly, deeply. I never walked alone once I learned how to hit the joint, down the shot, snort the line and pop the pill. I'd reached my destination, Laura was just passing through; hence how our paths have diverged ever since. Her loss, not mine. I'm doing fine. Always have done, always will. She's the one who worries, who carries the weight of the world on her shoulders. She shouldn't, but she always has done, always will. A classic case of Northside neurosis.

I should explain. While Suburb locals view their terrain as a private members' club, strictly off-limits to outsiders, even within their ranks a distinct caste system prevails. The Suburb was cleaved in two decades ago, when town planners routed the A1 dual carriageway through its centre like Moses splitting the Red Sea. As a result, those dwelling in streets to the north of the main road found themselves both physically and emotionally cast out of the camp – while they still had Hampstead Garden Suburb stamped on their passports, they were stripped of the full set of rights enjoyed by their peers on the south side of the border. To the outsider, all Suburb folk looked alike, but to those in the know, living the wrong side of the tracks was an indelible mark of Cain that no amount of window-dressing could disguise.

And so it is with Laura, she's been like that ever since she was a kid. Ok, her house was still worth a seven-figure sum, and both Mummy and Daddy drove around in six-figure cars whose soft-tops and alloys gave them a Southside feel even when parked in their northern drives. But there was rich, and then there was filthy rich, and Laura became another victim of the 'look up not down' virus which afflicted so many in the area. Instead of recognising her vastly superior economic status compared to those living beyond the Suburb's boundaries – in Finchley, Archway, Golders Green and beyond – she assailed herself with remorse that her parents didn't have a mansion on the edge of the Heath Extension or a palatial house behind Spaniards Inn. Even at fifteen, she was both precocious and preoccupied enough to constantly care that she lagged behind the rest of our clique, as though she lacked vital vitamins and minerals that would stunt her growth while we blossomed into fully-formed, fighting-fit adult versions of our teenage selves. Not my problem though. My bread's buttered both sides, and she's been bloody well fed from sitting at my table for the last few years.

Once Laura leaves I've got nothing to do for the rest of the day, and now that she's issued her very-last-final-I-swear-this-is-it ultimatum I've gone off the idea of a night out. Not because I'm believing any of her hype, far from it. More because it plays right into my hands for her to hear I stayed in when she does her inevitable Sherlock Holmes routine tomorrow. I know she will, she always does. Always snoops around, always checks up on me via her network of informants. So if I keep my head down at the flat, she'll find out and think the worm's turned even quicker than she'd hoped. Meanwhile I can still hit it just as hard on home territory as I could anywhere else. That way everyone's a winner. What she doesn't know won't kill her, and won't kill me either if I'm careful. Four days till work begins and the high life ends – four nights, more importantly – and nothing and no one's going to stop me squeezing every last drop out of the time I have left.

'Mip.' No response. 'Mip mip,' I type. Still nothing. I'm meant to sound like Roadrunner, but Gykus10's unlikely to get that particular cultural reference. Even if he does, what do I expect him to do? The little flag next to his username tells me he's from Slovenia, mine says I'm from Israel. I'm not, obviously, but every little helps when it comes to winding up the opposition. There are so many Muslims on this site that more often than not the blue-starred flag is red rag to the Islamic bulls, and the frothing at the keyboard begins in earnest. 'I kill Jew', 'I rape Israelien girl', 'I smash Zion' – the screen becomes another front for their jihadist fantasies, either that or they're using it as an online confessional. I'm not bothered by what motivates them, I just wanna wind them up. I'm so drunk, way past the stage where it's either big or clever. Way past the stage where I can focus on bullet chess, so I'm back on the fifteen-minute-match circuit, but I'm still getting battered, and I still can't quit. I've been hooked since I was a junior county player, when it dawned on me that chess was the perfect way to impose my superiority on my peers, and to reinforce over and over my sense of self-belief. Games of luck were out – relying on the roll of a dice or the order of cards dealt from a pack just muddied the waters. I desperately needed a medium shorn of any extraneous factors, and chess provided it. Me versus them. My brain against my opponent's. The power of my mind clashing with theirs. Winning became paramount; taking part counted for nothing if it wasn't me doing the mating by the end of the match. Seeing a face crumple a foot away from mine as they realised there was no escape from the inexorable march of my pawns, watching recognition of defeat dawn over a startled pair of eyes like the first rays of morning sun lighting up a garden lawn, seeing fury erupt when an opponent thought he had it all sewn up before being hit with a deft two-knight flurry to knock him out – those were the moments I lived for then, and still do a decade later. Their pain is my instant and insatiable gain, but the shoe's on the other foot tonight. I've lost three games in a row, and Gykus10 looks like he's gonna scalp me as well. Two pawns down, only thirty moves in. 'Mip,' I type, feet tapping the carpet, cigarette hanging from my pursed lips, ash parachuting down onto the desk. No response. My move. Bishop takes knight, pawn takes bishop, straight swap. I'd do that all day, mate. Hate bishops, love knights. It's in my genes. Bishops are too fucking obvious, they're like trains stuck to their diagonal rails: if they're born black, they stay black till the grave, if white, stay white. No room for manoeuvre, no mixed marriages. Boring, basic, bland. Easy to stop a bishop, like it's easy to derail a train – shove a pawn over the tracks and what's he gonna do? Knights on the other hand are like dandelion spores. Can't catch 'em, don't know where they're going next, can't compute their random leaps and bounds into your forecast for how the game will pan out. Officially, a knight and a bishop are both worth three points, but not to me, so I'll take the trade every time. Clock ticks, whisky glistens, eyes hurt, brain slows. Brain's been slowing for hours now, for weeks really if I'm honest, but I'm not honest. I'm a liar. I lie to my opponent, I lie to myself, I lie to the sun, moon and stars. I lie for business, I lie for pleasure. I lie because I can, I lie because I can't. Clock's still ticking, try to focus, try to think. Can't do everything at once, stub out the fag, drain the glass. Left arm's tingling, not lightly either. Gonna have a heart attack. Gonna have a seizure. Gonna have another whisky, calm the nerves, fight fire with fire. His move, my move, his move, my move, pull a pawn back, but by doing so lose control of the central four squares. Fucking clown. I love those squares, they're the Mayfair of the board. Own them, own the world. And now I don't. Walls closing in. 'Mip.' 'Mipmip.' Phone rings, it's her, fuck off, go home. 'I'll call you back in ten,' I slur. She scoffs, slurring too. We all slur these days. Me, her, them, us, bet Gykus10 doesn't though. Slovenians don't have time to slur. Too busy butchering. Nazis. Fascists. Good chess players, to be fair. Better than me at least. Fuck it, suicide mission. Kamikaze time. Swap a rook for a bishop, the crowd are stunned. They stare open-mouthed, not sure if I'm an idiot savant or just plain idiot. Turns out the latter. Village idiot. City idiot. Continental idiot. Mip, mip, mip. Fall on my sword, hoist the flag. 0–1. Gykus10 leaves in search of more prey. I leave in search of more whisky. Fat chance, all gone. Rum next, mix and match. Drink, smoke, play, mip. Clock ticks on screen, clock ticks off screen. Game's up online, game's up offline. As long as you've got your knights though, right? Wrong. Knights disappear, night disappears, day starts, I stop. Raise glass, glass drops. Shatters. Cuts my foot. Blood on the floorboards, blood on my hand as I try to stem the flow. Sleep's creeping up, sleep's got a stick, sleep coshes me round the side of the head. Pass out on the floor. Wake up in the lounge. Can't join the dots, won't join the dots. Don't know the time, don't know the day. Pretty fucking hungry, pretty fucking cold. Rum, rooks, rage, hate. Mip mip mip.

At least I stayed off the powder. Rome wasn't built in a day.

But even I have to admit things are looking bleak, even though the morning sun's telling a different story outside. Without Laura here it's like someone's cut my brake cables and left me doing ninety in a thirty zone. I'm in a serious mess, in a deep fucking hole. I don't wanna give it all up, don't wanna knock it on the head, even though I have to for the opening act of my trading career.

I take it easy for the rest of the day, and don't make any false moves till five. Which is when I open a new bottle of Mount Gay Eclipse and pour out a double. I throw in a cube of ice and let it start to melt before taking a sip of the rum. So, so good. It's like a barium meal: I can trace its progress throughout my body, feeling the nerves in my neck and shoulders flash out their message of thanks, as the surrounding muscles exhale deeply and slump into a contented, catatonic state of repose. I smile weakly, stretch out on the couch and reach for the bottle to load up the next round. I stop short in a panic, bottle dangling like the pendulum on a just-stopped grandfather clock. Panic subsides, replaced by resignation. The instinct was right, tonight's got to end here.

I wake up. I'm on the couch again, I'm terrified. What the fuck did I do? But it's only six, the bottle's still just one double short of full, and the rest of the drink's still locked in the cabinet. One hour down, rest of my life to go.

Saul calls, I don't answer. Not in the mood for whatever he's offering. He thinks we should be thick as thieves again now that I'm a fledgling trader, I've got other ideas. Laura sends another text, a reminder that she's due back in three days and counting, and I'm due at the office even sooner than that . Ignore her too, even though I know shouldn't. Jamie sends me an email, wants me to play in goal for them tonight as a last-minute stand-in. Might as well, got nothing better to do. Plus it's the perfect excuse for a quick performance-enhancing pick-me-up.

Their striker's head's down over the ball, his arms pumping furiously as he hurtles towards me. Richard's nowhere – I can see him desperately trying to make up ground to get a tackle in, but there's no way he's gonna get there. I try desperately to focus, even though the floodlights have fucked my vision, even though I can't stop grinding my jaw, even though pain grips my skull and it's all I can do not to topple to the ground screaming in agony. He's past the halfway line. I crouch down and hope my panther pose will put him off his stride. It doesn't, he doesn't even notice me, just keeps the ball at his feet and shapes to shoot. My nose is gonna burst any second, whether gushing out blood or mucus only time will tell. My throat's frozen from bottom to top, my gums iced to oblivion as well. My gloves feel loose, so do my trainers, and the cord on my ski trousers is cutting into my stomach cos I've tied it tighter than a hangman's noose. Fuck knows the score, fuck knows who we're playing, even. All I can remember is to never take my eye off the ball, and to be ready to pounce the second he unleashes the shot. He pulls back the hammer, cocks it, and – bang – unleashes a low strike across goal that's heading just inside the far post. I'm on it like a flash, sucking in air as I push down on the balls of my feet and hurl myself to my right. I've got across well, I think, and I fling my arm as far out from my body as it'll go, determined to cover every last inch that I can. Ball hits glove, and I'm a fucking hero, aren't I? For less than a second, it turns out, cos it's rebounded straight back to the striker, and Richard's still not got back to cover. Sweat's streaking my face, more sweat than normal, and normal's bad enough. I scramble to my feet, those fucking black dots of grit crunching between my chomping teeth and sticking to my tongue. My nose is flashing out a code red, telling me it can't hold on a second longer, but I haven't got time to breathe, let alone snort back into my head the liquid that's coating my nostrils. I'm hopelessly exposed to my left, and the striker knows it. He's gonna wrap his right foot round the ball and slot it home, I'd put my house on it. I've got two choices, three if passing out's included. I can dive in hope, or lunge in certainty. No prizes for guessing what I'm gonna do. Don't care where I hit him, don't care what happens next, all that matters is slamming into him like a truck. Gotta be the right leg, cos that's where my power lies. Samson had his hair, I've got my killer size-ten blades. I don't look before I leap, I don't need to. My foot's locked onto his shin, I can hear the scream before he's even opened his mouth. The connection's perfect, the ball rolls harmlessly away as boot meets bone and he goes down for the ten count. Danger over, job done, except there's no time to unwind, cos the fun's only just beginning. The night explodes into howls of rage, flurries of fists, growled threats of revenge. The ref's meek blowing on his cheap whistle is barely audible over the mayhem. In for a penny, I think, my face contorted in concentration as I fend off blows and go for soft spots on my opponents' bodies. The door of the pitch is open and subs and supporters are streaming into the cage. Ours and theirs, though theirs look far more threatening and far more likely to prevail. I'm holding my own, at least that's what I tell myself as I duck another wildly swinging fist, but then comes a haymaker from behind and I'm never getting up from that. I feel no pain, the coke's taken care of that. I can taste salt, but I don't know why. I doubt I'm bleeding, I don't doubt I'm concussed. Mouths are opening but someone's turned down the sound on the remote. I can't hear a fucking thing. Are my ears ringing? Yeah, but aren't they always? I open my eyes again and the scene's definitely different. Where the fuck's this? I'm looking up at the sky, and it feels like I'm lying on concrete now, not Astroturf. Water's splashing on my face. I squint up and see a hand wrapped round an open bottle of Evian. Whose hand? Not mine, clearly, but that's about all I can work out, cos I can't move my head an inch and I still can't hear. I'd love a cigarette, I'd love another slug on that cheap half bottle of Bell's. I'd love a rewind button so I could watch, taste, feel and admire that tackle again and again. I try to smile to myself in spite of the effort it entails, effort that's fuck all to do with the punch that floored me and everything to do with my pre-match meal of two grams and God knows how much whisky that has severed almost every tie between my mind and body. My brain says smile, my mouth doesn't hear a thing. This night's still young, I'm not ready to leave. I want more action, more football, more fighting. More coke, more drink, more water thrown on my face. More floodlights, more shots to save, more talk, more singing. I know I won't get any of it, but I fucking want it all the same. Richard's running over now – dumb cunt should have moved that fast during the match, then I wouldn't be lying here now – Jamie's next to him. They lift me up, saying something or other but I can't hear, and I can't lip-read, so bollocks to that. I'm in the back of Jamie's car, I'm nearly home. I am home, I'm on my bed. I'm the polar opposite of tired, and I'm gonna outlast the moon tonight, like I outlast it every night. I've got staying power, I've got unlimited supplies, and I've got literally nothing to lose. Literally. Metaphorically. Whatever. Just another day in Gan Eden, darling.

It's been seven hours and fifteen days. A lie. It's been seven hours and fifteen minutes. Started counting when I woke up. Feel sick to my stomach, feel sad to my soul. Feel wet, dry, cloudy. Scattered showers in my mind, hot and humid in my heart. Worst part is the void. There's nothing left. There's no tomorrow, there's not even a today. You know how on the TV page, some square-eyed spastic maps out a 'route to midnight' for the benefit of the brain-dead masses? Seven o'clock, Cooking with AIDS, eight o'clock, Ross Kemp sucks off a penguin, nine o'clock, Autism in the Attic, ten, eleven, twelve, off. That's how it was for me, class A drugs replacing class A mugs in the schedule. It was all mapped out, all taken care of: whisky, rum, coke, speed, snort, gulp, smoke, bleed. No cares, no thought, satisfaction guaranteed. Not anymore. Now I just get texts from Laura I ignore, calls from Saul I bar, headaches from hell I wouldn't wish on my worst enemy. Rub my temples, roll my eyes. Lie on the couch, feel sorry for myself. Feel sorry for my dealer, feel sorry for his dealer. Feel sorry for the dealer's dealer's dealer, all the way back to those dirt-poor Bolivian farmers – what did they do to deserve this? I'm robbing them of their livelihoods, taking food off their kids' plates. Hope they forgive me, hope I forgive me. Hope there's a God, hope He feels like dropping by to keep me company. Gonna need truckloads of cigarettes, juggernaut-loads of pizza, cargo plane-loads of Pringles, an ocean of wine. Can't drink spirits, they'll just remind me of better times. I used to soar, I used to arc, I used to wheel. Now I crawl. Now I shake. Now I kneel. Wish I didn't think in rhyme, not so funny now I'm straight. Think I'm in shock, think I'm in trauma. Definitely in hell, and not the same hell as before. That hell was heaven compared to this. That hell was temporary, that hell had a shelf-life, that hell was a fraction of the whole. That hell knew its place. This hell thinks the whole world revolves around it. Which it probably does. Doorbell rings, I'm not moving. Ceiling stares back at me, stands its ground. Oh, is that the time? Let's have another glass of water, how lovely. And a biscuit too? You really spoil me, sweetheart. Spit out the biscuit, kick over the glass. Temper tantrum time. Punch the door, kick the chair, live out the cliché. That's half the problem, that it's all so fucking clichéd. The walls aren't closing in, the silence isn't deafening, the nerves aren't frayed – but try telling that to my gullible mind. A mind that can't think for itself, that has to mimic every film it sees and song it hears. Yeah, yeah, this is *Requiem*, whatever. And last night was *New Jack*, and the day before was *Casino*, and the one before that *Kids*. I can't do a fucking thing without it getting all excited and telling me where it's seen the scene before. I exhale, I stare, I wait. I sit by the river long enough, but my enemy's body doesn't float by. Shame. Could have done with the distraction, could have done with the glee. Duty calls, send Laura a text. My nose is hurting, wonder if the nose knows. If it knows what's coming, if it knows it's out of a job, if it knows it's gonna have to break it to the wife, gonna have to sign on, gonna have to look for work in a call centre. Not my problem, I've got enough on my plate, what with the biscuits of bitterness, the wafers of self-loathing, and the Black Forest gateau of crippling fatigue. Clever wordplay, I should write a book. I should write a film. I should write a musical. *Joseph and the Amazing Technicolor Comedown*. Except it's not a comedown, is it? Don't call this a comedown. Don't believe the hype. This is like the moment after Mary gave birth, this is CE, this is AD. Get used to it, get a life, get a fucking haircut. Doorbell rings again, letterbox rattles. Yeah, yeah. If you've got something to say, send a fucking pigeon. Kettle on, kettle boils, coffee does its best, but its best ain't good enough. Call that a kick? Nestlé can go fuck themselves. You'd get more buzz out of a dead wasp. Walk round the lounge, figures of eight, mini grand prix. Pit stop on the couch. It's been seven hours and fifty minutes. Nothing compares 2 U.

'We just got back from Israel, actually'

　　Why actually? In fact, why any of the words in that

sentence? No one was talking to Becca or her faceless, nameless boyfriend. He's not from round here, that much is clear from his try-hard, high street shirt and tie and the envious gaze he keeps casting over Anna and Sam's lounge as we wait for dinner to be ready. He should be grateful to be bankrolled by Becca's clan – if it weren't for them he'd be trapped in Enfield, Essex, Edmonton or wherever the average Jew in yok's clothing ends up. Laura takes Becca's bait.

'Really? Whereabouts were you?'

Even money they were in Herzliya. Two to one they were in Eilat. Four to one on they couldn't name a single other city in the whole country. Fucking morons, but par for the course round here. Not that I give a damn about Israel and its politics, but my lack of interest doesn't translate into ignorance like it does for these hollowed-out shells. I know my Baraks from my Begins, but I've hardly got blue and white blood coursing through my veins. At least I've got a pulse though – the others look like extras from Dinner Party of the Living Dead.

'At the Accadia. We got a great deal through my uncle – he's friends with the Federman family who own it, you know?'

Herzliya it is, then. The Accadia Hotel – the jewel in the crown of a town dripping with cash, crystals and kudos, but precious little else. Been there, done that, over and over, year after year, the cycle only broken around the time I was catapulted from the comfort of my Brooklands classmates into the year above, without so much as a second thought on the part of my parents. In fact, I doubt there was even a first thought; by this point, Dad was utterly engrossed in his metamorphosis into a mega-rich magpie, buying anything and everything on Cork Street with a six-figure price tag and piling it all up in the vaults of Deutsche Bank. Mum, meanwhile, was singlehandedly supporting David Lloyd's retirement by spending up to fifteen hours a day at the club, performing various acts of time-killing banality with the rest of her parasitic peers. They signed off on the most life-changing experience yet to happen to their youngest son as though hurriedly scrawling a signature on a courier's rain-soaked notebook, then jetted off to LA without me, leaving the maid's hand to rock my cradle for want of any viable alternative.

'The suicide bombs over there are really horrible, aren't they?'

I swivel my head round sharply enough to send pain shooting through my neck. Could have been Miri, could have been Ilana, could have been Katya – all wear the same gormless expressions as they stare blankly, waiting to see who'll step up to the plate to deal with that thorny moral dilemma. Anna and Sam have got their minds on their salads and their salads on their minds, so that rules them out; Laura's caught sight of her reflection in a wine glass so she's otherwise engaged; Becca and her plus one seem to be tipsily groping each other – either that or he's trying to lift another fifty from her purse without her noticing. Jon (without the h) and John (always with) are whispering sweet nothings in each other's ears in a corner, cooing about tax-free REITs and interest rates and ABS peaks and CDS troughs and dirty cash they want you, dirty cash they need you, woah. Saul and Mya aren't here cos they've got too much seychel to stumble into a trap like this. Which only leaves me, and that's never going to happen. I turned Trappist monk the minute I walked through their double oak door; Laura managed to drag this horse to water, but I'm fucked if I'm gonna speak.

'Yes, they are, aren't they? I was just saying that to my sister the other day.'

No idea who that was, the nasal whine hardly narrows it down. I'm playing blind as well as dumb now. See no evil, speak no evil, even if I can't help hearing it. Or eating it – an oven beeps, the zombie faithful lurch as one to their feet.

Give me all your rocket, all your figs and basil too. Three courses of oohing and aahing and awe-filled speculation. How *did* Becca get the sauce so right? Is the rice *really* a fraction too gelatinous, or is Sam just being hard on himself? Where *can* one get good asparagus out of season round here? My eyes are balsamic glazed, my brain's lightly sautéed, my nerves are slow-roasted then strained twice before serving. Laura's in her element, I'm in her pocket. I'm still on thin ice with her, wish I could just let it crack but I can see my dad's face snarling up at me below the surface. Not a pond I want to plunge into yet. Pass the salt please, darling, and a couple of razor blades too while you're at it.

3

Trading is a fucking dream. I've entered the promised land. The honeymoon period's still going strong three months after I exchanged vows with my Bloomberg terminal. I was smitten from the off. We'd locked eyes across a crowded dealing room on my first day at work, but our paths weren't to cross for another six weeks. I was forced to watch jealously from afar as other men used and abused her – even two-timing her with her plain and dowdy Reuters rival. There was something so exotic about Bloomberg's twin screens on one gleaming chrome frame, something so achingly untouchable about her indecipherable system, that I had eyes for no one else. Anyone with a stuffed wallet and a pinstriped suit could get it on with Reuters, but to get up close and personal with Bloomberg you had to be something special. Alas, I was deemed nowhere near special enough during my induction at the firm, so all I could do was pine. When we were finally introduced, my heart skipped a beat, my legs began to tremble. My breath became shorter and I let out an involuntary gasp at her beauty and the come-hither look on her screens. I ran over and hugged her.

I was in heaven. We started off slowly, neither of us wanting to rush things. We did the usual getting-to-know-each-other activities common to all new relationships, taking things slowly and cautiously, occasional shy attempts at intimacy – and so it continued for a week or so. But then it bloomed into life, just as London was getting into winter hibernation mode. We were off and running through the gardens of stocks and shares – her marvelling at my trading skills, me awed at the depth of her market knowledge. She showed me graphs and charts I'd only ever dreamed about, I masterfully took control of her keyboard, and we danced the dance of lovers.

We carried on in this blissful state for weeks. There were rough patches, of course, like when she caught me using Reuters news screens behind her back, but we patched things up and moved on. We're still going strong, stronger than ever in fact. Till death do us part.

Having my own Bloomberg's done wonders for my ego as well as my trading libido. My terminal costs the firm three grand a month, marking me out as a rising star the bosses consider well worth investing in, and telling the other traders that despite my youth I'm already training with the first-team squad. I spend all day in a trance, the LCD screen bubbling over with prices, data, graphs and charting tools for every index, every currency, every commodity on the planet. It's a phenomenal piece of equipment, if you know how to use it – and I handle mine like a pro. Fingers flying lightly over the keyboard, calling up charts and order books at will. The pathways through the system are second nature, and will be for life. You never forget, like you never forget how to ride a bike (or chop up a rock of charlie, depending on your preference).

I'm happy, Paul's happy to my left, Nick's happy to my right. Across the desk, Steve's happy, Mark's happy, so are Pugh, Pugh, Barney McGrew, Cuthbert and Dibble. Grubb's not here, but I've no doubt he's happy too. He's always happy. Amount of ephedrine pills he munches, he bloody ought to be. The whole trading floor's happy on a day like today – US jobless figures are due out in an hour, and where there's uncertainty there's volatility in the market, and where there's volatility there's work to be done, cash to be made, deals to be hammered out. We're cats who'll get the cream or die trying.

'Short DAX now.'

Nick doesn't speak in full sentences, doesn't believe in them. Prefers to spit out orders like he's only got seconds left to live. He doesn't ask, he commands. Like God instructing Abraham to sacrifice Isaac, except with far more urgency and far dodgier syntax. 'Kill son knife' the St Nick version of the Bible would read. Whereas the Gospel according to Mark would be a painfully drawn out, plum-in-the-mouth affair.

'I've been contemplating just such a move all morning, but for the life of me I can't justify selling European indices at such depressed levels.'

Mark speaks, but Nick's not listening. No one listens to Mark past the first two or three words. There's just no time to. Time is money, and money talks much louder than Mark, regardless of the validity of his statements.

'DAX short here.'

Nick's worm's not for turning.

'March and Sep futures tanking, wait for a bounce.'

Paul's contribution to the debate. A pointless one, in my opinion. Waiting for a bounce is a mug's game. Let the trend be your friend. They're falling through the floor for a reason, which is that everyone's got word the payrolls won't live up to the forecasts, and that's reason enough to sell, sell, and sell again. I sell. I'm with Nick on this one.

'I've sold a tenner, and I'll work another fifty in the next twenty minutes.'

Did Nick hear me? Did anyone? Does it matter? Not in the slightest. We could be deaf and dumb and it wouldn't make a difference to our trading. As long as we're not blind. As long as our eyes can scan the screens and our brains can crunch the numbers. As long as our hunting instincts don't desert us, and we're ready to pounce at the first scent of blood. We can gang up on our prey or do it lone-wolf style, either way's fine as long as we win. That's the dichotomy about prop trading: we look like one big family, but we bear sole responsibility for our own books. United we conquer, divided we conquer – as long as we keep conquering, how we go about it is irrelevant to the powers that be.

We sit in long, straight rows in the trading room, like slaves in the hold of a Roman galley. Our chains might be gilded, but they shackle us all the same. Hundreds of options flash their rise and fall across the screens, as the Bloomberg newsbar spews out headlines like a Gatling gun. Our eyes are trained to follow every flicker. Banks of phone lines are available at the push of a button, two handsets per man –

one for the right hand, one for the left – thoughtfully built of toughened plastic to withstand the phone-to-wall smashing that takes place whenever a deal falls through. This is our world – and the flashing numbers scrolling past on the liquid crystal screens can make or break us, turning us from heroes to villains and back again in the blink of an eye.

The firm pays me twenty per cent of all profits I make. My book began life with one and a half million pounds, I'm already up to nearly one point seven. I'm taking it fucking seriously, putting all my energy into every trade, into every idea, every notion, every feeling. This is Big Boys' Betfair, nothing more, nothing less. The concept's the same: the set-up, the screens, the intuition, the hunches, the risk, the danger. And, most of all, the excitement. Every sum I've staked on every game of football, every set of tennis, every round of golf and every horserace to date has been laying the foundations, brick by brick, bet by bet. And this is the house that my habit built. I was born to trade, born to bid, to offer, to short, to long.

Trading scratches all my itches at once, I've got solid-gold pound signs where my eyeballs once stood. But I don't care about the cash for simply being cash, I care about it as chips at the poker table, as runs on the scoreboard. I trade to prove a point, to prove myself, to prove I'm right and the next man's wrong. For every penny I make, someone loses the same amount. It's a zero-sum game. It's a pissing contest. It's a dog-eat-dog world.

I stare at the laminated card that hangs from the base of my Bloomberg screens. It's a quote from the eighties, from the height of the yuppie boom. They're the words of the legendary futures dealer David Kyte, but they could belong to any trader from any era from any dealing room on earth. 'I trade anything that moves. If I lose ten thousand pounds, there's plenty more where that came from; if I make ten thousand, it's not going to make such a great advance on my equity. I don't think of it as money anymore, it's just points. If I'm up, it gives me more to play with . . .'

Spot fucking on. It's playtime all the time. When the European markets shut, there's still action in the States; when the US closing bell rings, Asia's going strong. The market never sleeps. I wouldn't either if I could avoid it, but I've got to stay disciplined, got to stay the right side of all-out compulsion. According to Laura, I've never been on such good form. But that's because it's all black and white to a girl like her. All binary. Drugs equal zero, no drugs equals one. But I know I'm slipping, I know I'm going under again. My dreams are full of flickering banks of screens, my every waking thought centres round my book's P & L. Fibonacci graphs are burned on my retinas, Doji star formations bore their way through my skull, candlestick charts slither like snakes through my mind.

But I don't do coke (I can still taste it every time I inhale, every time I lick my lips).

But I don't drink (my throat's hopes are built up with every glass of water I sip, then cruelly dashed as the awful truth is revealed).

But I don't gamble (but I do gamble. But it's not called gambling. But it is gambling. But I'm meant to call it trading, I'm meant to differentiate. I'm meant to, but I don't, because there is no difference, because they're one and the same, because a rose by any other name would smell as sweet).

I try not to think about it too much, I concentrate on my book instead. Everyone's got a book in them, this is mine. This is my life's work, this is the fruit of my labours. It's getting near the one point eight mark now. It's growing, it's maturing. I remember it when it was only this high.

They offer me drink and drugs and good times and bad times, though they don't mention the bad times, don't mention the morning after, the afternoon after, and the night after that. The hangovers, the comedowns, the shakes, the heart murmurs, the stomach cramps, the chest pains, the muscle spasms. The crawling skin, the failing sight, the shivering cold. The horrors, the terrors, the fear. Not their fault: they're salesmen, they're only doing their job. They want to be my friends, they want me to go on a 'desk night out' with the rest of the traders on my team, just like Saul keeps trying to get me back out on the town with him. They want to induct me, they want to initiate me, they want to include me. They're playing with fire. They wouldn't if they knew.

I go home to Laura instead. She seems to live at mine permanently now, that's the new regime. We watch TV, we order in, we enjoy each other's company. We go to town, we dine out, we see friends. I'm cheating on her, on all of them in fact. I never walk alone, my Blackberry's always by my side. I steal glances at its cherubic face at every opportunity – during dinner, in the theatre, at an exhibition, on a walk to the park. Even in bed. Especially in bed, because that's when I need to know most. Before I shut my eyes, I need to check one last time, snatch one last glimpse, grab one for the road. Where did the market shut, where will it open tomorrow? Where are the buyers and where are the sellers and where are the signals and signs and clues? Laura thinks it's cute, thinks I'm married to my job, thinks I'm committed to my cause. I think it's fucking petrifying. I think this is worse than anything that came before.

She wants to spend every minute by my side. She's got nothing to do till term starts again – no work, no study, no responsibilities other than moulding me into the boyfriend she's always wanted. For all my front, I came round to her way of thinking the minute I knocked it all on the head. Well, maybe not that fast, but three months in and I'm a zealous convert. Everything's started to fall into place, everything's started to make sense. I look at her and I understand why we're together, why I've put her above the powder, the pills, the whisky. The mote has fallen from my eye, the blinkers are off.

We walk down St John's Wood High Street, we stop, we eat. Harry Morgan's the venue, the choice of a spoilt generation. Mums and kids and overwrought au pairs. Au pair is St John's Wood slang for slave, the colloquialism fooling no one, least of all the prisoners themselves. I know the score, I've watched these hapless creatures up close and personal my whole life. With my parents barely ever at home, I lived as a latter-day Romulus, with this Celia or that Gabriela playing the role of doting wolf to perfection.

Now I watch these fretting Filipinos with a mixture of pity and curiosity. What do they make of such ostentatious consumption? How do they feel waiting hand and foot on children decked out in clothes and saddled with playthings that cost more than they'd spend feeding their families in a month? Does the experience make them feel mortally inferior, do they believe deep down that they could ever merit such riches themselves? Do they think that we deserve to stand so many rungs above them on the social ladder, or are they convinced that we've got this far by keeping them and theirs forever downtrodden? A cat may look at a king, but what does it truly see when taking in the regal scene?

My mind's racing, I've got no idea why. It's like a dog who's been cooped up for weeks then taken for a long walk in the woods, where it hares through the undergrowth, excitedly sniffing every leaf, twig and stone, pure relief the fuel powering its overexcited engine. I'm not impressed though, I don't want these thoughts clogging up my mental arteries. I focus on the menu, focus on Laura, focus on the bland and banal.

'What are you having?'

I care, I do care. Laura's happiness is of paramount importance, I want to feed her, water her, cater to her every whim and desire. Even though most of her meals end up being vomited into the nearest toilet bowl she can lay her paper-thin hands on.

'A salt beef sandwich, I think. Or maybe the chicken soup. Or both. Do you think it's too early for a proper meal?'

Do I? Don't I? Come on, think. This is what it's all about now. Thinking, but not about au pair chain gangs, just about salt beef. Play it Laura's way, play it the St John's Wood way, play it safe.

'Have them both, and have a glass of red too – it's a beautiful day, we've got all the time in the world.'

Good answer, though I see the apprehension flash across her face when I mention the wine. Better clarify the point, put her mind at ease.

'Don't worry, I'm not having any – but you should. I think I can cope with being around a bit of Cabernet.'

Shouldn't even have to say that, makes me sound like a proper addict. Which I'm not. Never have been, never will be. My views on vices aren't popular, but I stand by them all the same: there's no such thing as addiction, it's all in the mind. And what's in the mind is all in the mind too, if you see what I mean. Don't believe the hype about physical dependence – once you stop using, the body wises up pretty fast. It might not like it, but it gets used to it without too much fuss. And as for the brain, you have to take it in hand and show it who's boss. No ifs, no buts. Just say no. You have to be brutal, it's the only way. Exhibit A: me right now. Clean as a whistle. Functioning, focusing, firing on all cylinders.

'Ok, if you're sure you don't mind me drinking. Look, there's Max's mum and her trainer – talk about the blind leading the blind.'

I swivel my head, follow Laura's finger. Across the street, past the silver F1 McLaren (Arab) and the pea-green Bentley Continental (Jewish) and the incongruous grey Mondeo (Goyish), a middle-aged woman spilling out of her Lycra packaging strides behind a man not much younger or thinner than his protégé. Both have seen better days, both could do with a hot shower followed by a lecture on self-respect. This is no place for showing off what they haven't got – the High Street's a ruthless judge. Laura's enjoying her jury service; she'd offer to sit in the courtroom every day till she dies if she had the chance. She has the chance, of course, this world is her oyster, this way of life is her lot. Our lot. She wants it, I want her, so I want it too.

'She's sleeping with him, anyone can see that. He's been her trainer for twenty years, there's no way they're not fucking – though they must get through a lot of paper bags.'

Laura laughs. I'm good at this. I can play the bitch.

The food arrives, we start to eat. The wine follows, plus my espresso and soda. We drink, we talk, I pay and we leave. I take her hand as we walk towards Prince Albert Road.

'Laura, I love you.'

'I love you, too.'

'And I'm sorry for taking so long to listen to you.'

She's convinced. I'm convinced. The birds and the bees watching us aren't so sure, but they're just spectators, they don't know what's going on in my head, in her head. We stroll on the canal side of the street, cross Avenue Road, head for Primrose Hill. We keep going past the aviary, then swing left into the park. We're still holding hands, we're still playing nice. My phone rings – Saul's work number appears. I make a show of pretending to answer while clearing the call on the sly. Good chance to prove to Laura that it's all about her.

'Hi Sauly. Sorry mate, can't talk right now . . . I'm out with Laura and we're in the middle of something . . . Yeah, sure, I'll call you back later . . . No, not been following that stock lately, not really looking to do any PA trading at the minute anyway . . . Cool, speak soon.'

I hang up and turn round to milk her grateful applause. She's smiling broadly now, but doubt still propels her to probe around in my head.

'Can I ask you something?'

''Course you can, anything.'

She seems nervous, afraid of the dark in my mind. We sit on a bench.

'Are you sure this is what you want? Not you and me, I mean, but this whole set-up, this whole way of life. You know I'm happy, you can see it every day. I'm loving LSE, I'm totally into my course and everything that comes with it, but maybe you're just much harder to please than me.'

'I don't follow.'

'Well, you've said some pretty vicious things in the past, you've acted like the last place on earth you want to be is in the north-west London bubble, and it's hard to believe you've just swallowed all that down and changed your mind so fast.'

I sigh theatrically, I pause for effect. I let the clouds do the talking for a second or two.

'Laura, I've done a lot of thinking over the last few months, and I know you might be sceptical but I'm honestly a changed man. When it comes to the crunch, this is where I want to be, you're who I want to be with, and I'd be an idiot to want anything else.'

'Ok, you say you've changed, but that doesn't explain why. What happened to all the rage and all the scorn? And what is it you actually want to be now that you've given it all this thought?'

She's pressing buttons which I haven't got round to wiring up yet.

'I know it sounds a bit late in the day, but I think it's just a matter of maturity. I think everything up to me starting the job's been just some kind of drawn-out teenage rebellion, nothing more.'

I'm facing her, my eyes are sincere. Her eyes are searching, they look like they're finding the answers they wanted. Here, have a few more.

'I was thinking about us, about why we've been pulling in different directions recently. A couple of years ago, you were just as into the hard living as me, and that was cool for both of us. There was nothing standing in our way, no pressure, no need to knock it on the head. But at the point where you realised it was time to move on, I couldn't make myself do the same. And now I can. It's over, and I accept that.'

'Ok, but do you really think we were at the same level as each other then? I know I got high with everyone else, but you were always far more out of control than everyone else.'

Bang to rights. Try another approach, as much to convince me as her.

'Agreed, and I've been bloody slow off the mark getting my act together and changing. But not now. I've been trading for weeks, and it's the perfect environment for me. For all that betting was part of my problem, I'm still a damned good gambler, and now I'm getting to put my skills to use in a respectable industry.'

'Aren't you worried you'll get bored of it just like with everything else?'

'Yeah, I am. But I'll cross that bridge when I come to it. All I can do is give it a go. And anyway, I don't walk away from everything, do I? Look at us – I love you, I need you, and I've fought to keep you, haven't I?'

I lean in to hug her, I kiss her moisturised cheek. My Prada sweater kisses her Fendi coat. A perfect moment. We walk to the top of the hill, passing more mums, more trainers, more cowed Filipinos. We reach the summit, I pull out a cigarette and plant it in my mouth. I'm still allowed to smoke, by mutual consent. Between me and my lungs, that is – Laura's ineligible to vote on this particular issue. My autocracy's last stand.

We turn our attention to the view. We stare at London, London doesn't flinch. I can see my dealer's house from here. Probably not worth saying out loud. Probably not worth saying to myself either. JoJo's dead to me, that's how it's got to stay. Shame his number's imprinted on the inside of my eyelids, shame I could walk to his house blindfold. I've been making pilgrimages there for years. Through rain, sleet and snow. Crawling over broken glass, leaping through rings of fire. Following yonder star. Stop thinking about him, stop thinking about it. That was then, this is now. The future. Fuck the past. Forgive, forget, move on. You have nothing to lose but your chains.

4

We stop at Laura's on the way back to mine. Beck-grade three-bed in Belsize, pined for by Laura, pushed for by Mummy, paid for by Dad. Life's tough at the top. I sit in the car while Laura jogs up to the house. She opens the front door, slips inside, then emerges five seconds later looking thirty years older, three stone heavier, and bearing down on me with a grin-cum-grimace plastered over her heavily made-up face. My future flashes before my eyes. It's not bright but it's definitely glowing sunbed orange as she beckons me out of the car with a perfectly manicured finger.

'What a de-light it is to see you again, dear, it's been far too long.'

She's lying through her teeth, two can play at that game.

'You too, Mrs Rosen. You look marvellous, as ever.'

She bats her eyelashes involuntarily, I stifle a shudder in return.

'How are your parents? Michael and I would love to see them when they're next here.'

No they wouldn't, nor would my parents want to see them either, but they'll definitely all meet up regardless. Duty calls louder than any other sentiment in the Suburb, and even though the Rosens are Northsiders, their stock's rising and they're de facto A-list machers these days.

'They're fine, I think. Dad's still at it as hard as ever. I'm sure they'll be in touch soon when they're planning their next visit.'

Her smile widens, more fangs come into view.

'And you're a working boy now, aren't you? I hope you're earning enough to keep my little shayna maidel in the style she's accustomed to.'

I shrug in faux-helplessness, palms raised just enough for my left sleeve to slip down and reveal the Patek Philippe beneath.

'I'm doing my best – learning the ropes, you know? Laura's well looked after as ever, don't worry about that.'

But she does, she's in her plutzing prime, and she's taught Laura everything she knows. She leans in to brush a non-existent speck of dirt from my impeccably presented shoulder.

'Oy, you should really take more care of your clothes, image is too important to ignore – what would your mother say?'

It'd depend how many Valium she'd necked before being asked, but either way she wouldn't be too fussed. Not because she's not equally as superficial as Mrs Rosen, more because there comes a point when you're so ungershtopt that you can stop caring quite as much as you once would have –about your own nearest and dearest, at least. The richest people eat with their fingers, but the Rosens have got a long way to go till they find that out for themselves. I pretend to sweep myself down more.

'Thanks, that'll be the cleaner – she's new, and she washes about as well as she irons, which isn't saying much.'

We laugh knowingly, we act like we're bonding, and the act's all that matters. I'm dying for a cigarette but the risk-reward ratio's all wrong. A moment on the lips is nowhere near worth the lifetime of her barbed comments and petty criticisms.

'Anyway, lovely to chat, but I must dash back in and get my purse – I only dropped round to check on the flat, I do worry about how Laura looks after the place.'

She's already backpedalling up the path, string of pearls swinging from her neck. I wave her goodbye, watch her wobble her way through the front door. I spit on the pavement and jump in the car. Nasty piece of work, her and the rest of her cackling coven. Bad taste in my mouth, though I hope that'll go once Laura brings Daisy out. Daisy's mine, but she lives with Laura. I used to see her on weekends, then every fortnight, and lately not at all. I've been dreaming of this moment for months, and finally it's here. Reward for my sacrifice. My hands are sweating onto the steering wheel, I'm a bundle of nerves. The front door opens, I catch sight of her. She hasn't seen me yet, she's seen the car but she doesn't recognise it. She should, but it's been ages and she's only three, so I can't really blame her. I press a button, the roof slides down. Now she's seen me, now she's running, now she's jumping, now she's diving into the front seat. Now she's panting, now she's yelping, now she's licking my face. Now she's remembering, now she's recalling, now she's making up for lost time. Laura laughs, so do I. Daisy barks.

The engine growls. We drive off, reunited, playing semi-happy families for the first time in a long, long while. We all live in a yellow BMW.

Daisy looks tough, but she's acting like she's not. Laura's cosseted her, siphoned off her ferocity and replaced it with sugar and spice and all things nice. Not ideal. Not for a Doberman. She's put on weight too, got soft around the middle. She seems lazy as well. She jumped straight on the couch when we got inside and hasn't left it since. Not gonna let her get away with that kind of slackness. If playtime's over for me, then it's definitely over for Daisy. Or Dock-tailed Daisy, to use her full title. It wasn't me who cut it off, by the way, though if her original owner hadn't got there first I might well have been tempted. Aesthetics over ethics. The stump only adds to her allure. Jet-black coat, piercing stare, broad shoulders and a thick skull. Just got to sort out the extra pounds and she'll be perfect again. The pride of Hampstead Heath.

Daisy stays, Laura goes, Daisy plays, I doze. Wake up in a daze, can't remember where I am, who I'm with or what I'm on. Disappointed by reality, thought maybe clambering on the wagon had been just a bad dream. Turn on the TV to check who's playing later. Turn it straight back off – can't take the risk. I've got no safety valve, I don't believe in moderation. I can't do anything by halves, by thirds, by quarters. If I watch the game, I'll have to bet. If I have a bet, I'll have to drink. If I have a drink, I'll have to rack up. And if I rack up a line, it's goodnight Vienna, good morning Vietnam, and goodbye to any hope of keeping Laura. I've used up all my lifelines, she'll never get over it if I sin again. To err is human – that's my usual excuse – but expecting her divine forgiveness for the thousandth time is asking a hell of a lot.

If I have to suffer, so does Daisy. Got another hour to kill till Laura's back from the gym, so Daisy and I head out into the night. Darkness reigns – outside the door and inside my head. There's a void that needs filling, a hole that needs plugging. We stride along the street. I scowl, Daisy smiles. We pick up the pace, we march down Haverstock Hill, we reach Kentish Town. We keep going, up Islip Street, back to where it all began. My alma mater, my old stamping ground, my first taste of freedom and my first encounter with life outside the gold-plated ghetto of Hampstead Garden Suburb.

My paternal grandfather put his foot down when my parents were going through the motions to send me to a private school along with the rest of their sheep-like peers. 'The last thing he needs is to be kept in a gilded cage at school as well as at home,' my savvy granddad barked at them over Friday night dinner. He'd been brought up in the rough-and-ready climes of the East End, his parents straight off the boat from Odessa without a penny to their names. Despite his having fought tooth and nail to make sure his own children didn't have to suffer the same hardships as him, he recognised the innate dangers in our cushy surroundings.

'There's plenty of time for him to become just another north-west London brat, but he needs to see that there are others who don't have it anywhere near as easy as he does – if you don't prise open his eyes, they'll stay shut forever.'

I'd long since departed the table by that point, and only heard the argument thanks to having positioned myself on the upstairs landing to spy on the new maid who'd arrived that week. I was definitely on my granddad's side in this one, though for different reasons: I had no intention of taking anything other than pleasure from being exposed to the NOCD crowd (Not Our Class, Dear: usually delivered with an ironic tone by the speaker, but the irony was all for show – or else why say it in the first place?). Either way, I was hardly daunted by the prospect of expanding my horizons as Granddad was demanding; after all, he was only talking about JFS, the Jewish school in Camden, which suited my homogenous streak far better than having to intermingle with treif types in some mixed-race local comprehensive.

Even before my first day at my new school, it was clear that those running the JFS show weren't that concerned about their actors' safety as soon as they set foot on the inner London stage. 'Here – is arrive for you today,' mumbled Paulina-from-Latvia, Lithuania, or wherever. She thrust a cellophane-covered royal blue blazer at me, with a bright yellow logo sewn over the left breast pocket in what can only be described as retro thirties Berlin chic. What the fuck? Were we that in thrall to the National Socialist designers of yesteryear that we now marked out our young with yellow stars of our own accord? Lucky it wasn't a boarding school, I thought, or no doubt we'd have been issued blue and white striped pyjamas as well.

Yellow star on my chest, trepidation in my heart, I set off for school without fanfare – of course, my mother 'would love to be able to take you, but Michelle's stylist is only in town one morning this month, and you know Mummy loves Moschino'. Dad was doing whatever shipbrokers do best, so I got Paulina to order me a cab to Hampstead station, and followed the other blue-blazered faithful onto the next south-bound train. No cattle cars for us, which kind of spoiled the image, but the Holocaust humour was in full swing again once we alighted at Camden Town: 'JFS students to the right,' barked a London Transport employee who'd been asked to help direct the incoming new recruits on their first day in the concrete jungle. The selection had begun – and we trudged silently up Camden Road like lambs to the slaughter.

I was assailed with a strange sensation within seconds of taking in the view ahead. For all I'd had snatched glimpses of extra-Suburban life through the tinted windows of Dad's Bentley or from the back of black cabs ferrying me to and from the gated drives of friends' homes, I'd never been this up close and personal with the gritty, grimy side of London – and I was entranced. The hairs on the back of my neck stood on end as I gazed open-mouthed at the sheer hardship all around: this was night to the Suburb's day, and I was both repelled and seduced by what I saw.

For all the Suburb's faults, aesthetically it is a joy to behold, thanks to the vice-like grip exerted over the neighbourhood by the omnipresent Suburb Trust (never say their name louder than a whisper: they run the area like the Cosa Nostra, demanding money with menaces, dictating everything from whether an extension can be built at a house's rear to handing out permits for washing lines in residents' gardens). The lengths to which the Trust went to wield their power meant the Suburb looked exactly the same almost a century after the day it was built. Every house was constructed from the same brown bricks, every roof was tiled in matching fashion, and the lush hedgerows and abundant trees gave the area a verdant hue unparalleled across the capital. By contrast, Camden was a grey, empty void: framed beneath similarly drab low-hanging clouds, the buildings ached with age and discomfort, decrepit structures on their last legs, propping one another up like late-night drinkers not knowing when to give up and go home. The cars looked like escapees from a scrap dealers' guillotine. Granted last-minute reprieves, the years they'd spent on Death Row had irrevocably crushed their spirits, if not quite finished off their battered bodies. Graffiti adorned walls and bus shelters like fading tattoos on a middle-aged brickie's arms, and rubbish lay strewn along pavements and inside front gardens as though integral items of street furniture.

But best of all were the faces of the people passing by. Even the young looked world-weary; whereas in my neck of the woods an innate sense of entitlement permeated everyone – from child to teen to all ages of swaggering adult – here hope had been abandoned by all who'd entered, and nothing I saw gave me reason to think they'd been wrong to take such drastic action. Had I known how comparatively well-off Camden actually was, when set against real inner-city deprivation and hardship, it would have made no difference to my intoxicated mind. Just like the first-time smoker gets high from hash despite knowing skunk would get him even more wasted, so too was my rush so instant and intense that nothing could have taken the edge off it: I floated along on a private trip that seemed set to last forever.

All these years later, the effects still haven't worn off. I sit on a wall, stare at the sights, drink it all in again. The hardship, the hard luck, the hard knocks. Daisy's growing impatient with my reverie, but she'll have to wait. The school was knocked down a few years after I left, the United

Synagogue owners cashing in on the property boom and relocating out of town. Flash townhouses stand where JFS once stood, but they seem out of place against the backdrop of crumbling council flats and tumbledown terraces. We walk on, slower than before, more for Daisy than for me. I'm still raring to go, physically at least. I could keep going all the way to JoJo's. I pause, I shake my head, I banish the thought like a leper. Back through Chalk Farm, back to beckdom. The cracks are starting to appear though – Laura's gripping one hammer, her mum another, and there are plenty more queuing up for their turn to smash my sanity to smithereens.

Laura's making coffee. The kettle's whistling a cheerful tune, two cups stand side by side on the counter. Daisy looks from me to Laura and back again, can't believe her luck at the way things have panned out. Laura's looking pretty pleased with herself as well, sunny day, everything's a-ok. It's a bit sickly-sweet for my liking, but I know how to grin and I know how to bear it, or at least how to give a passable impression. Laura's washing up, still smiling, still humming, still driving me fucking mad. She stops, reaches into the fridge. I glower at her back. She tosses me a Granny Smith, puts one on the side for herself, turns back to the dishes. I walk into the lounge, pull my cigarettes from my back pocket, lie down on the couch.

There's blood on the apple before every bite. I know my lip's cut, but I don't know why it won't stop bleeding. It's been bleeding all afternoon, onto my cigarette, my thumb, my pen, my teeth. And now onto my apple. There's something biblical about the splash of red on the white-green flesh, something related to original sin. That's the second time in as many minutes the apple's got me going all religious. When I went to take the first bite, I held it tight in my right hand, a Marly Light dangling loose in my left. Unlit, unloved, unwanted, but undeniably there all the same. I looked at them both, then looked at me looking. I was Moses, they were the coal and gold. Big moment. Defining moment. Make your bed, lie in it, line your lungs with tar or your stomach with vitamins. Choose life. Yeah, right. Actually I did, but only to shut up the voices. I'll wolf down the apple then give my undivided attention to the cigarette. I bite, I bleed, I grimace. I bite, bleed, grimace, scowl, the apple gets smaller, the blood gets fainter, the core gets nearer, the seeds get blacker. So does my mood. I'm not on good form, I'm on mid-table-and-sliding form, I'm on keep-this-up-much-longer-you'll-be-in-the-drop-zone form. End of season's coming up, I wouldn't bet against relegation. I wouldn't bet on it either though, cos I'm not betting anymore, am I? Not betting, not bingeing, just fretting, just whingeing. Whining, moaning, pining, droning. I'm a barrel of laughs, a whole brewery in fact. All Laura's fault, she's the fucking serpent in this sedra. I absolve myself of blame – I was only joking about wanting to go clean. This was Eden, this was paradise. I was happy, I knew it, I clapped my hands. Then she came along, made me eat from the tree, and suddenly all was revealed, all became clear. I grabbed a fig leaf to hide my shame. Not good enough, said the snake. New leaves aren't for hiding behind, they're for turning over. Twat. Her, not me, I hasten to add. I didn't need her intervention, didn't need her sermons. It was meant to be the other way round anyway. I call the shots, I run the show. I'm the sorcerer, she's the apprentice. Not anymore. Now it's me asking her for permission to breathe. Me asking her how high to jump. My Pinocchio to her Geppetto. Something's gone horribly wrong, horribly fast, horribly here, horribly now. I can hear her in the kitchen, scrubbing and scouring and singing and dancing. Mocking me. Menacing me. Murdering me. I don't want her type round here. What a girl like her's doing in a place like this only God knows, and He's not talking to me these days. Not like He used to. Not like when I could chat to Him for hours, pour my heart out, pour my whisky out, pour my powder out, and nothing and no one could come between us. Now I've got Little Miss Motivator breathing fire and brimstone in a leotard, and God's decided three's a crowd. Think. Think. Bloody think. What would Jesus do? Babble on about the meek. Useless. What would John Wayne Gacy do? That's more like it, and I don't mean the clown costume. Though that'd make a nice little flourish. But there's no time for that. I've got to get her out, got to knock her off her high horse, off her pedestal, off that perch she sits on all day cawing like a fucking crow. Before she was a crow she was a dove, a rolled-up twenty her olive branch. Lot of water's passed under the bridge since then. That was the past. Got to live in the present, but the future's leaving me seriously dazed and confused. How did she switch so much, so fast? Give the Jesuits the boy till he's seven and they'll give you back the man. Give me Laura for a few years, and suddenly it's me who's gone from man to boy. Medical science is baffled, my dealer's even more nonplussed. I can't live with her, but I can't live without her either – my dad'll explain why not. Well, she's not getting off that lightly. I've got to get back to how it was before, how it was when we first started, how it was before she made me eat the apple. How it was before the blood came pouring from my lips.

Maybe the blood's coming from my tongue, I've been biting it all week. I'm exhausted from keeping a lid on my bubbling cauldron of rage, I'm spent from silencing all the screams. It's consuming my mind, it's eating up my body from the inside. I'm going to collapse in on myself like a dying star.

The vultures are circling overhead, they're expecting a feast. They can sense our relationship's on its last legs, they're already planning how to carve up the carcass. But I'm not giving up without a fight. I'll fight anything, anyone, anytime, anyplace. I'll fight the demons, fight the monkey on my back, fight the urges and cravings and lust and desire. And Laura won't know a thing. I'll keep her well out of it, keep wearing my mask and swallowing my pride. Keep up the facade until fiction becomes fact and I truly mean what I've been saying over and over and again and again.

5

DECEMBER 2006

We wait for Neil in the boardroom, steam from our coffees misting up the glass of the cabinets on every wall. Nick's Patrick Cox-clad heels are resting on the thick oak table, a sure sign he made at least fifty grand trading in the States overnight. I glance at the papers spread out in our midst, scan the headlines for danger, for clues, for luck. I only care about what the market cares about. Floods matter for their effect on crop futures, war in the Middle East for its impact on the oil price. Lives lost, hopes shattered and dreams dashed are all very sad, all very unfortunate, but there's no death-toll index to trade, so there's no point sitting shiva. No time either. Neil kicks his way through the double doors and sits in his throne. Paul clears his tar-lined throat, he's holding the conch.

'Trouble in paradise, boys – we're running a big position in Synamed futures, and it looks like they're not gonna get FDA approval for their latest miracle cancer cure.'

Steve's face tightens, his Hermes tie looks like a noose round his neck.

'What's the pre-market seem like?'

Paul flashes an evil grin, enjoying Steve's agony.

'Like your wife on her period – blood on the carpet time. They've already printed at nineteen seventy two, down a full pound on close. And if you manage to get above nineteen fifty by the time morning meeting's through, it'll be a Christmas miracle.'

Steve bolts for the door, Neil glances up from Page Three, then back down again. Nine-bob Neil's not fooling any of us, Nine-bob Neil doth protest too much. Especially cos today's offering barely merits a second glance – too chubby round the waist, not nearly enough up top, nose like a pig and eyes to match. Ruined my taxi ride in, rocked my faith in the *Sun*'s selection process.

'Paul, you should be running after him, not sitting here gloating. Steve might be a fucking idiot, but he's your fucking idiot. I told you to take him under your wing, didn't I? Just get him out of those Synamed and give him the cattle-prod treatment.'

Neil's drawl tells its own sorry story. He looks how I used to feel in the bad old days. Bloodshot eyes, throbbing veins, forehead covered in sweat. Parched, pursed lips, but he talks a good talk. From his mouth, that is. From his nose, not so much. The road map of burst capillaries and hollowed-out pores says it all. He's at the bottom of the barrel, at the bottom of the bottle, at the bottom of the bottomless pit. Yet he still reigns supreme over each and every one of us. He's still lord of all he surveys. He's still the jewel in Banque Nord's crown.

That's the beauty of this job. As long as you get straight As when you trade, you can be a grade A cunt, do all the class A drugs you can eat, live it large and hard and like there's no tomorrow. So long as tomorrow you're back at your desk, back on form, and back in the black. We all want to be Neil. He's our hero, our idol, our David but with far bigger balls. Michelangelo's marble dealer would have had a field day.

The briefing breaks up, the troops assemble in the trenches. One last prayer, fix bayonets, charge.

I'm in heaven. The seraphs sing and the angels pluck their harps. Gabriel hands me down my silver trumpet, but I pass it back. I've got no time to play. I'm losing, I'm winning, I'm losing again. I'm throwing good money after bad, I'm breaching my limits, I've gone through my stop loss. I'm ok again, I'm treading water, I'm gulping down air while I've got the chance. The pound's getting smashed on the currency exchanges, the knock-on effect on the FTSE is brutal. I'm fine though, I'm riding the wave. I'm staying afloat, I can see where it's going. My book's flat, my nerves are calm, my powder's dry.

Saul's sent yet another solicitation to meet, masquerading as a trading tip. I barely give the email a second glance – I'm still steering clear of his type of night out, and I definitely don't need any advice on the market front. Nothing personal, boychik, but I'm my own best friend when I'm glued to my dealing screens. The only message I need to send is a quick sugar-coated declaration of love to Laura, then it's back to the futures and options and graphs.

Trading bridges the gap perfectly between my innate lethargic streak and my unquenchable will to win. For all the high-octane excitement of a day in the dealing room, there's no real effort required other than a basic grasp of the markets, an instinctive feel for the lay of the land, and a steel-coated set of nerves. Just like chess, it's me against them – no dice, no luck, no variables beyond my control. Or so I tell myself.

'Seen you were doing your nuts in March puts earlier – you sorted yourself out?'

A full sentence from Nick, he must be bored. Nick likes to act the concerned parent when he's got nothing better to do. Nick sticks his oar in without a second thought. Nick thinks he's Neil's heir apparent – he's probably right, hence I have to play it safe.

'Yeah, got a bit carried away thinking the pound had dropped too far but I came to my senses. No real damage.'

Platitudes over attitude, no point pulling the wolf's tail.

'Good, but be careful about going back in before the FTSE's settled down. It'll be up and down like a whore's drawers till there's clarity from the FX market. I'd stand well back if I were you.'

Sir, yes, sir.

'Thanks, Nick, gonna do just that. Appreciate the advice.'

Yeah, right. I need his advice like a lokh in kopf (hole in the head, sounds better in Yiddish though). I don't like kibitzers over my shoulder – not at my desk, not at my chessboard, not here, not there, not anyfuckingwhere. The heat's rising, my blood's boiling, Nick's really got to me even though he probably didn't mean to anything like this much. I'm not in the best of moods anyway, cos I hate uncertainty, I hate not knowing how to make my next move. Nick's Laura and my dad rolled into one, garnished with a layer of barrow-boy arrogance to boot. We are not amused. We are not contrite. We will not be silenced, we will not sit on our hands. I load up my order book, I fire off a few rounds. Fuck it – it's my book, my rules. I'm short of the FTSE, the FTSE plays ball. It sinks like a stone, falling far enough for me to take a quick couple of points profit. I reload, I go again. And again, and again, and again. All afternoon – winning some, losing some, winning some, losing more and more.

Nick's not watching, Nick's doing his own bidding, his own offering, his own sighing and stressing. Lost in his own world. We all are. Each one of us held captive in our own private heaven or hell. Mine's definitely the latter, I'm getting caned here. I've not stopped at the lights, I've sped straight through, turned left, got lost, found myself in Oyabrochland. Population: one. Me. Bobby McGee fucked off ages ago.

I stagger out of the office twenty minutes before the close, three hours after I should have thrown in the towel. Down a hundred and five grand, down a peg or two or ten. Battered, bloodied, bruised. Hate that Nick was right, hate that I was wrong, hate my book, my trades, my Bloomberg, myself. If Neil hadn't stepped in when he did I'd still be there now, eyes locked on the screens, doubling up, quadrupling up, and onwards and downwards to try to recoup my losses. Works at the roulette table, doesn't it? Yeah, yeah, bottomless pockets, whatever. I would have won in the end. I always do. Should have told Neil to back off, should have told Paul to fuck off, should have told Nick to suck me off. Shouldn't have let them shut down my system, shouldn't have let them send me home and give me a week's ban from trading. Shouldn't have nodded and shrugged and believed their hype. I don't need time off, I don't need a break. Neil's the worst. Fucker acted like a barman slinging a drunk out the pub. I spin on my heel, I'm going back up there. I spin back round, don't make it worse than it is. Not the end of the world, not the end of the line. The book's still up, still over one point six. Worse things happen at sea. Worse things happen at a backstreet bookies. At least I've still got my kneecaps. At least I'm not walking in the valley of the shadow of debt. I sit on a bench, I smoke like a chimney. Four in a row, then one more for luck. Luck's not listening, luck's a lady sat on some other cunt's lap.

Laura's ringing me. I silence the call and let it go to voicemail. She's not the answer to my prayers, she's just a fucking albatross. Not interested. Not now. Not while my head's in my hands and my heart's in my mouth and my dad's eyes glare at me from halfway round the world. Not while I'm dying for a drink and a line and a sweaty six-hour session with my beloved Betfair. I flag down a cab, I slump in the back. Home, James. No point digging this hole any deeper. No point shutting Laura out. No point letting the demons back in.

6

Busy doing nothing. Still barred from the trading floor, still in suspended animation. Had a walk with Daisy, a talk with Laura. They're both sated, they've both exited stage left. I'm starving though, chalishing for something, anything to fill in the blanks in my mind. Can't sit still, can't take it easy. Can't gather my thoughts, can't calm down. My IV's been yanked out, my oxygen supply cut off. I'm itching like a kid with chicken pox. At least I've got Arsenal tonight, at least I've got Saul. This'll be the first game I've gone to since I started trading. I haven't had the cheishik to turn up while I've been on the wagon, there are too many temptations both inside and outside the ground. Maybe that's a good thing tonight. Haven't told Saul what's up, it's none of his business. He'll only lecture me on trading, even though he knows fuck all about my side of the market.

He looks down on traders like me, I look down on brokers like him. Everyone looks down in the City, we wouldn't have it any other way. Saul's power lies in his silver tongue, mine lies in my lead-lined stomach. I can take the pressure of riding a non-stop rollercoaster every day in the market; Saul prefers to sit back and let his clients' bank accounts take the strain. He spins them a yarn, sells them a dream, siphons off his cut from each trade and never risks anything more precious than his reputation as a stock-pusher. He wines, dines, sixty-nines – whatever it takes to win the business and send his commission figures soaring. He struts about free-range in Ford Open, I'm holed up in solitary in a maximum security jail. I wouldn't swap places for the world. Only difference is I'm coming up to four months clean, whereas he's still hammering it as hard as ever. Lucky bastard.

I gun the M3 down Frognal and swing a hard left into his drive. Saul winks at me from his perch on the low garden wall. I wink back. We could be auditioning for the part of Sid James's stunt double. Carry On Up the Arsenal. He's got his away shirt on, Gant jacket open to let the club crest breathe. Mya taps on the bedroom window, waves at Saul with one hand, clutches a full glass of red with the other. No prizes for guessing what she's doing tonight. It's a game of two halves for us, it's a game of two bottles for her. K'nayna hora, she can put it away. Looks great, drinks even better, perfect little package for Saul to come home to every night. Laura could learn a lot from Mya. Actually, I could learn a lot from Saul. Like how to call the shots, wear the trousers, crack the whip. Not that Mya needs much encouragement, but still. I'm stuck living life on the hard shoulder while they weave from lane to lane doing one-twenty, never indicating, never giving a fuck about anything or anyone other than themselves and their base urges.

'Well, well, well – nice of you to find time for me at last. And there I was thinking I needed to be saying Kaddish for you. I've been checking the death notices for weeks.'

Kaddish for me? Yeah right – odds on I'll be the one saying the mourner's prayer for him, the way he's hitting it these days. He's definitely been on the powder already. He's jabbering away like Daffy Duck, his nose is twitching like Thumper. I make do with my Marly Light, I make do with seething quietly and letting the gears do the talking.

'I swear, if we don't beat Inter I'm setting fire to my season ticket. Complete waste of money so far this year, complete waste of time as well.'

I nod for the record, he's not expecting a verbal response. He's in soliloquy mode, I'm just the skull in his hand.

'Adebayor's taking the piss, Rosicky's a waste of space, Ljungberg's more worried about his six-pack than the fact he can't score from further back than the six-yard line. Wenger indulges them, the board indulge Wenger, we indulge the board, and it all just spirals ever downwards. We should have packed up and gone home the minute Adams made it four in May '98.'

I smile at the memory, I scowl at the here and now. At my here and now, rather than Arsenal's. May '98 was a defining moment for me as well as them, a high I've never managed to surpass despite years of trying. North Upper, front row, dead centre, skinny thirteen-year-old legs dangling over the side of the stand. Eyes crimson from the L-skin we'd smoked en route to the ground, ears pounding from the roar of the Highbury faithful, skin glowing from the rays of the early summer sun. Yoks to the left of me, goyim to the right, here I was, stuck in the middle with Saul. Five minutes to go, and the on-stage drama was building up to its magical crescendo. All we needed was to beat Everton to win the league, and at three-nil up we were home and dry. But cometh the hour, cometh the raging alcoholic – Adams latches onto a Bould through-ball, one touch, sets his sights, left foot, bang, right underneath us, right on the money, everything right with the world right there, right then. The stadium erupted, the eagle landed, this was how the West was won. The North Bank bounced like a Spacehopper, the concrete turned to rubber as ten thousand lords of the dance jumped to their feet. I really cared, I really felt it, I really belonged to that heaving mass of red and white. I loved the players, the fans, the time, the place. I had no money on the outcome, no ulterior motive, no iron in the fire other than a deep, pure lust for my football team.

That was then, this is now. Older, wiser, colder, snider. It's not that I don't want to go to the match – I do, but for all the wrong reasons. I want to go because of what it says about me, my possessions, my status. I want to go because thousands can't. I want to go because I can. Because over and above my being a fan, I'm a debenture holder, a shareholder, a season ticket holder. I stopped caring about the team's fate long ago, but I keep up the act like a veteran thespian. I've spent my whole life as a chameleon, I know how to blend in, how to do as the Romans do. I ham it up when I'm at the game or watching in a pub; after all, partisan and primal emotions are bubbling beneath all our surfaces, looking for any chance to burst out like lava from Mount Merapi. But really I'm only an armchair supporter – whose armchair just happens to be the best seat in the ground.

I only want to be at the match for the same reasons I

spend £500 on lunch at the Ivy, a grand on Dom at the Sanderson or five bags on a Vuitton three-piece. I'm no food connoisseur, no wine buff, no sartorial expert – but I'm a master of the 'Cos I can' philosophy. It's all about having been there, done that, got the T-shirt. Problem is, these days the cotton chafes my skin and the neck's too tight. This emperor needs some new clothes made up, and without drugs, drink or gambling there's a distinct lack of material to work with.

We park in the usual spot, I palm two tenners to the fat man on the gate.

'All right, boys, 'ow's it going? Up for it, are ya?'

Fucking twenty-stone Tillbury. I flash him a forced smile, Saul latches onto the fresh meat and spits out coke-tipped bullets like a Browning 50-cal.

'Yes mate, you reckon we'll do the business? One-nil down from the first leg is fuck all, innit?'

His affected accent puts mine to shame. He doesn't fool Michelin Man, but he could talk in patois and the guy'd still have to bow and scrape like a shoeshine boy.

'Yeah, son, we'll be fine. Three-nil, Henry hat trick, no fuss. Here, you wanna give me your keys? Just in case I have to move your car to let the others out.'

Didn't realise he was talking to me at the end, I'd tuned out of his Cockney frequency after the first dropped h. Saul nudges me, then grabs the keys out of my hand. I barely notice. My eyes are glazing over, I'm retreating into my shell. The day's trades line up in the back of my mind and wait for the starter's pistol. They hurtle down the track, full pelt towards the finish line. The top three ascend the podium, little blonde girls wreath their necks with laurels. The MIB-30 short's the winner, raises its arms in triumph as the medals are handed out. Worst trade of my City life to date, a proper yisgadal moment. Got to snap out of it, got to put it behind me. We walk to the ground. Saul buys a beer, I buy a Coke. All I can taste is shame.

'Wait for me a sec, will you? I'm just ducking into the gents – actually, do you want a bit yourself?'

Fuck yeah/fuck no. Delete as applicable. Flip a coin, pick a card. My willpower snaps, my head bows, my last barricades are breached. I follow him in. I follow his lead. I follow him up, up, and away. Back where I belong, back where I started, back to square one. Out the door, grab a beer, beeline for the bookies. Scan the prices, brain rushing like it's gonna miss a train, eyes darting, ears pricking, gums numbing, heart racing. Guilt can go fuck itself, this town ain't big enough for the two of us. Same goes for doubt, same goes for remorse. Back Arsenal to win, back Arsenal half time/full time, back Arsenal -1 on the Asian handicap. Back to backing, back to betting, back to fucking black.

'Got something I reckon we should talk about on the way home, something you trader boys won't have picked up on your radar. I'd tell you here, but it's a bit too hot for forty thousand Tonys to hear, if you know what I mean.'

Saul's off, I'm running. Down on the pitch, the teams are shaking hands. The tension mounts, the nerves start fraying.

'Sweet, hope it's an NLR. I don't get out of bed for anything less.'

An NLR is a north London ramp. A north London ramp is a 'for us, by us' initiative which uses the Jewish grapevine to get a share price moving, via a series of well-placed rumours that spread like wildfire from Baker Street to

Bushey. Saul loves a good NLR, he was born to ramp. He speaks of them in hushed tones, with the deference of David Attenborough talking the viewer through a pride of lions' hunting tactics. He can tell an NLR is brewing by the sequence in which the buy orders come in. First the Soho House crew, then those dining in St John's Wood High Street, then Hampstead, then Golders Green . . . By the time the Dyrham Park Golf Club set come calling, he knows the ramp is complete. At that point, a stock could have surged eight or nine per cent, as fabricated news of an increase in profits or a massive tax rebate entices new buyers. Once the price is up, those who were in from the beginning sell their stock and bank their winnings. Whispers and gossip like this are the very foundations on which the City's built, and everyone has their source: the Etonians, the Essex boys, the blacks, the dogs, the Irish. But no one does it better than the Jews.

'Kind of, kind of. Except this one might not be a ramp – looks like there's fire as well as smoke this time.'

I want to know now, I want to be let in. I've got a tab with Saul's firm, he throws me the odd bone or two every now and again. I let him wash whatever illicit trades he wants through my account, then give him back half the winnings in cash. Easy money, but nothing too serious. He can't make the trades too large or too frequent otherwise he'll attract attention from the firm's compliance department and the FSA. Not that anyone's ever got much more than a slap on the wrist for low-level insider dealing, but there's no point putting his head too far above the parapet.

My Blackberry starts beeping, it craves my attention. Won't get any though, I'm broiges with it ever since last week's bloodbath on the Bloomberg. It won't shut up, I flip open the cover. Laura's texted me, wants to know if we're having fun, wants to know the score. I have to check the scoreboard, can't even remember if there's been a goal yet. Thirty two minutes, nil-nil. Not telling her, not replying to her message. Put her to the back of my mind, relegate her to the second division. Live in the moment, grind my jaw and lick my gums. Dab a bit of powder from Saul's wrap, look forward to the half-time top-up in the toilets. My bets are still live, but they're no substitute for the real thing, the Betfair thing. The slips don't burn a hole in my pocket, don't even keep it warm. They've been placed, they can't be changed, can't be traded. Born to die, from cradle to grave in a lifelong coma.

Game's over, game's up. Our strikers are fucking weak, can't carve out a single chance. Three blind mice, see how they don't run. Inter do though. Three class goals, three strikes and we're out. But it can't kill my buzz, can't rain on my parade. The crowd's livid, there's hate in the air. Saul's furious too, so I fake it like an orgasm just to fit in. He wants to drown his sorrows, I'm already in for a penny so I dive in for a pound as well. I drive round the corner to Highbury Park Road, we push our way into a packed Galino's. Couple of bottles of red, slam back the rest of the coke. I'm three sheets, Saul's four and rising. I drink, I drive, I listen to Saul. When you're hot, you're hot, when you're not, you're not. Saul's hot. Saul's boiling. Saul's turning to steam.

'You know Brownings?'

I shake my head. I could have rattled or rolled it, Saul wouldn't have noticed.

'Proper low-end shmutter business, used to be kosher,

got bought out by treif management in the early nineties when the recession was biting. Still capped around ninety million, heavy volume on a good day's trading, and right now it's majorly in the spotlight for all the wrong reasons.'

He pauses for breath, for effect, for the time it takes him to lick the empty wrap in a futile attempt to get one last hit.

'Head for mine, I've got another eighth there. I'll text Mya and tell her we're coming. Anyway, so Brownings have had two profit warnings in six months, and their next statement's due out on Monday. Nothing has three warnings in a row – either they go bust or get bid for by a vulture crew. Always the way, and this'll be no different. The arse has fallen out of the price for months, it's gone from two pound fifty to eighty pence in almost a straight line.'

Flecks of spit appear at the corners of his mouth, his eyes dance like a bear on hot coals. I'm still waiting for the money shot, I'm bored of the build-up.

'Nu, so what's so special about them then?'

'Listen, listen. Everyone knows the business is fucked, everyone's expecting the worst. But the stock's being propped up by talk of another MBO – the management can get it for next to nothing, and their property portfolio alone's worth about sixty-five pence of the share price. But – and this is the killer part – we know they're not gonna bid for 'em, and we've seen the wording of the statement. They're going into meltdown, they've breached their bank covenants *and* they've found a hole in their accounts. *Oy vayz mir*, over and out.'

Flecks become froth becomes foam. He's bubbling over, he's bursting his banks.

'How do you know for sure? Cos this is one that could seriously backfire if it goes pear.'

'Mya's brother's one of the liquidators being lined up for the salvage job – he came straight to me, cos he's as shady as any other Sephardi working over here. A hole in their accounts will see them carted off to the knackers' yard – as soon as the statement comes out, the stock'll be suspended, and they'll announce they're bust before the suspension ever gets lifted.'

Fair play to him, this is a thing of beauty. This is a Rubens masterpiece, a Grayson Perry tour de force. Best of all, if it's already a target of the bear raiders, going short on the stock won't raise a single eyebrow either inside or outside Saul's firm.

'So what are you saying, that it's literally got no floor?'

'Fucking right – no floor, no support, no nothing. You could sell twenty grand's worth at any price and it'll only cost a few hundred quid to close the minute they go bust.'

'Ok, but why stop at twenty, then? I'd do fifty, a hundred, even two hundred if there's that kind of volume.'

That's the coke talking, the wine shouting, the ego screaming its head off. But I mean it, cos from the minute the light bulb flashed on above my head, I've been hatching a plan. A plan that could see me laughing all the way to Bank station and home from the City for the very last time.

'You can't do that much, you've never dealt that sort of size with us before, and that's the kind of thing someone might spot.'

Saul's such a little girl, such a broker-turned-gamekeeper. Who the fuck cares what size I've dealt up to now? A dead cert's a dead cert, this is a remortgage job, not a time for restrictions and restraint. I glance over at him, he's crushing his cigarette pack into a ball with both hands, blowing smoke out of his nostrils like a dragon.

'Yeah, but you're saying it's a stock with volume, that it's been in the news for weeks. What difference whether I make a five- or six-figure trade?'

He kisses his teeth like a sulking Rasta. I mount the pavement outside his house, we climb out of the car. A fox panics, darts from the garden and straight across the road. Saul slings the pack of Dunhills after it, then jogs up the gravel drive to the front door. I should text Laura, I should go home in fact. I'm not going to do either, I'll make it up to her later if this trade comes off.

We sit in the dining room, Mya's out for the count. It's three in the morning, Saul's still chomping at the bit. I'm matching him line for line, word for word, shot for golden shot. I'm still trying to grind him down over the Brownings trade, he's still sticking to his guns. We play chess, I smash him, we play Gran Turismo, he smashes me. We smash our livers, smash our septums, smash the navel-gazing world record. All I care about is me, all Saul cares about is him, so close no matter how far, forever trusting who we are, and nothing else matters. I slam the door on the BMW, slam the engine into second, slam the brakes on at my house. I slam my eyes shut and pray for sleep, pray for Laura not to wake up and smell the recidivism on my breath.

Wide-eyed and bathed in sweat, I hear the bird before it sings. I know it's coming: the sky has that black-becomes-grey look, clouds roll swiftly past the window and that fucking first bird's never late. Once it sings, the domino effect is put into motion. Within ten seconds the entire avian populace of north London is up and at it, their dulcet tones chastising me with their two-note rebuke.

I don't even know if I've been asleep. The sweat that covers my back and legs and stains my pillow is no indication, it's as much a part of my nocturnal coke routine as the satin sheets I lie on. The CD case fallen down the side of the bed, the rolled up twenty, the dregs of whisky at the bottom of the glass – all standard too. I remember the mocking tones of the World Service just before the six o'clock news. I can tell from my phone that I emailed our US equity trading desk at five. I definitely dreamt – yeah, but you don't need to have slept to have dreamt. It's six twenty-five, so does it really matter if I did or didn't get a maximum half hour's kip before getting up now?

Yes. It's fucking critical. It's of paramount importance. My whole day, my whole existence rests precariously on the answer. If, and I hope to God it's true, I did sleep – even only for quarter of an hour – then I can bite the bullet, force myself through the next twelve hours until I score again. If not . . . well, physically it makes absolutely no difference, but mentally it's hammer time. Mind over matter and all that.

I decide that I have slept. First hurdle clear, nineteen to go. Half six isn't the hour for self-reproach and regret, instead I use the time to splash my face with cold water, all the while avoiding eye contact with myself in the mirror. I shave, I dress. Boss pinstripe suit, pink Hermes tie, the ever-faithful Gucci loafers. But it's like tying a ribbon round a pig, no one's gonna get fooled.

Laura's still asleep on her side of the bed, so tiptoeing round the house seems like a good idea, but so does another line. I do neither; the line jettisoned because I've finished the bag Saul gave me as a going-home present, the tiptoeing because two grams and half a litre of Scotch doesn't really wear off that quickly. I can barely walk a straight line flat-footed; take my heels out of the equation and I'll be spending the day getting a cast set at the Royal Free A & E.

I clatter down the stairs, tumble out the door. My Burberry trench coat's buttoned up against the savage wind that slaps me round the face, over and over, unannounced every time and increasingly brutal. On the walk to the station I go through my own version of the twelve steps, but it's only one step long, because I'll never give in and admit that my life has become unmanageable. I'm not fucking addicted – not to coke, not to trading, not to anything. I get to the station, I play my trump card – I buy the *Sun*, forcing the self-assessment and doubt to the back of my mind for another day. The walk to the station's the only time I really care, really think about it at all. Really have even the slightest notion that the wheels are coming off. One flick through the *Sun* and one cab ride later, and I'm back in the game. Eyes stinging, desperately dehydrated, but chalishing to read the Bloomberg headlines and gear up for another day's trading. Fuck the pain. Fuck the worry. Fuck the warnings. This is it, free rein for ten hours – go long, short, even sideways, put down the cash, take a position, trade and trade and trade and trade. And then, for want of anything better to do, bell JoJo, get him to deliver the wrap to the office, and that's another day done. Another day closer. Another dawn chorus where I'll have a front-row seat. Another night where the clouds are my only companion.

'What the fuck are you doing here?'

Nick's a rude cunt, but he's a rude cunt with a better memory than me. I look sheepish, he looks wolfish. I want to be a wolf too, I want to howl at the moon, I want to moon at the Hang Seng as I short a basket of Asian futures in the run-up to the US opening bell. Not today though, not tomorrow either, not till mein Fuhrers Nick and Neil say I can come back.

'Dunno, Nick, I was just on auto-pilot I suppose. I feel like a right mug.'

Nick flashes a Fred West smirk. He gives me a curt nod, then elbows his way into the building. I shuffle off down the road and fall into a cab. I fall asleep in the back, I fall out at my house. I fall on my feet, because Laura's already left for class and I've got the place to myself. I switch on the laptop, log into Coutts to check my balance. I transfer every last penny to my account at Dover's. It's showtime.

I fight for my right to party, Laura cracks down on my protests like the Burmese junta. I'm put under house arrest, my constitutional rights are suspended. I beg for leniency, she softens ever so slightly. She tags my ankle and tracks my every move. I don't breach the terms of my parole, now's not the time to rock the boat. Not when my planets are starting to align, not when I can see light at the end of the tunnel.

Saul's agreed to my compromise offer, the stage is set for the Brownings announcement. He sells a quarter of a million at seventy-five, just shy of a hundred and ninety grand's worth of stock. If it comes off as planned, I'll bank one-twenty, he'll keep the balance and trade it as though it's his. No more sharing the profits, no more fifty-fifty. Fine by me, cos I'm only in it for the ultra-short term. I'm yanking the emergency cord, I'm jumping off the train with a bag full of swag. A hundred and twenty'll easily match what I'd earn in twelve months on the trading floor, a hundred and twenty gives me a year to breathe even if my dad cuts me off for a while, a year to assess, a year to find my feet. Disposable income, disposable career. No bills, no mortgage, no fuss. There's only one essential item in my life, and a ten grand rock from Hatton Garden Chaim should seal the deal on that front. I can't beat her, I'm gonna join her instead. Jack it in, walk the plank, turn myself in and collect the reward.

I've dealt with the doubt, my heart's come round to my mind's way of thinking. One final fling to toast Brownings' demise and then it's on the wagon for life. No ifs, no ands, no pots, no pans. If not now, when? Drugs are the piece of grit around which I've built the pearl of my life, but the pearl's lost its lustre and cracks are starting to appear in my shell. I haven't worked out what's going to fill the void, but I will, and I want to, and I won't back down from the challenge.

The eleventh hour's the longest of my life. Three days till payday, till old acquaintance be forgot and never brought to mind. Laura smells a rat, she can't believe I'm so casual when I'm still suspended from the dealing room. I can't believe I'm so casual when I'm about to ask her to marry me – the time to take the plunge has come, no point fighting it anymore.

'Laura, if you had a year to do anything you want, what would you do?'

That's how fucking bored I've become, cooped up in the house like a battery hen. Wish Sam I Am was here, would much rather be discussing green eggs and ham.

'Go travelling, I suppose. Probably South America, though not if you and your septum were coming too.'

Yeah, yeah, very good. I can score anywhere, darling, but stick the boot in if it makes you feel clever.

'And if you had a year to kill in London, what then?'

'I'd take a course, find a passion . . . hold on, what are you getting at? You not telling me something about what's going on at your work? Have they fired you?'

No, 'course not. I've fired *them*. I'd fire you too if I went with my gut feeling, but my survival instinct's bigger and tougher than my gut and won't let it have the last word.

'No, nothing like that, Law, not even close. I was just daydreaming about what I'd do if I didn't have to work for a year, if I could take a step back and properly work out what it is I want to be.'

'Go on.'

'Go on what?'

'Go on tell me what it is you're planning, because I know you wouldn't just say something like that if you weren't already striding along the diving board about to jump off.'

I light my nth cigarette of the day. I cough pathetically, hoping to tap into some latent motherly streak in Laura. Got to get the conditions as clement as possible for her to back my plan.

'Thing is, I've come into a bit of money – actually a hell of a lot of money – and I honestly feel it's a sign, you know? The timing's perfect, just when I've started to realise being a trader's a far too corrosive life for me.'

She's hyper-alert now, hyper-nervous and hyper-cautious. She always is when I mention money, typical fucking Northsider.

'What money? Please tell me it's kosher.'

'It's glatt, Law – what do you take me for? It's from a load of bonds from my bar mitzvah that matured last month. There's over a hundred grand sitting in Coutts, waiting to be invested or put to good use.'

She exhales again, the doubt dissipates. Then it's back in a flash as she joins up the dots.

'But surely the last thing you need is to have all that cash in your pocket and all that time on your hands – you'll just go back to your old ways, you'll be even worse than you were in the summer.'

Oh ye of little faith. I'm a changed man, I've had my Damascene moment. My love, I'm finally ready to leave it all behind, and I want you with me as I march into the sunset.*

'Look, no one knows better than me what happens when I slip up. The other night at the football was fucking awful, I was up all night and nearly had a heart attack. Seriously, Law, I can never go back to that state again. I trust myself, I really hope you can too.'

We've both heard it all before, we both know the drill. We've read the programme notes. She criticises, he apologises, she doubts, he spouts, she pouts, truth outs. The painted ponies they go up and down. I keep the music playing.

'Look, I know you don't see it the same as me, but there's a world of difference between bad habits and addiction.

---

* Terms and conditions apply. The value of my promise can go down as well as up. Your home life is at risk if you don't keep up repayments on my emotional mortgage.

Nicotine's my only addiction, nothing else. I don't wake up in the morning and crave coke, I don't wake up in the morning and fancy a glass of Scotch – all I want is a cigarette.'

'So where does the gambling fit into your compulsion spectrum?'

'That's borderline addiction, I think about it far more than I think about drink or drugs. And that's exactly the point, Law – trading is just another form of betting, and it's doing my head in. The only difference is that the machers and shakers round the Suburb call it a respectable profession, whereas they'd never let their kids spend all day backing horses at Coral's. But I know from firsthand experience that they're just two sides of the same coin, and that's why I have to walk away from it.'

She looks like she might agree with me, but it's hard to tell from this angle, hard to tell if she's frowning in disapproval or concentration. The conversation peters out, I've thrown enough damp towels on the fire to smother the flames. We go our separate ways, her to the gym, me to the balcony. I keep counting my chickens even though they won't hatch till Monday morning at the earliest. The Brownings statement could hit the screens any time between pre-market and the close, every second's going to feel like a year. Monday's going to be a long, long day, and an even longer night too if everything falls into place.

The weekend has landed, I couldn't care less. Laura could, though it's unclear why. She's hardly going to paint the town red, she's far too low key for that these days. Becks just wanna have brunch. Twice in two days. And since I'm still in the doghouse, that means I get dragged along as well. I kiss their cheeks, I slap their backs, I bite my tongue. I listen to soporific tales of stultifying banality. I make sure not to use words like soporific, stultifying or banality so as not to stand out. I smile at Sarah, I laugh along with Lucy, I empathise with Emma. I nod at Nathan, I shake hands with Harry, I bang my head against every brick wall along the High Street. The whole scene's like a magic-eye picture that everyone's cracked except me, or maybe it's the other way round. I don't know how Laura does it. Don't know why, either. She looks as bored as I feel, but no one's holding a gun to her head. At least I've got an excuse.

Monday's here, right on time. I knew it wouldn't let me down. The Sunday papers were full of mixed messages, some tipping Brownings to ride out the storm, others eulogising the stock in funereal hushed tones. Saul's called me twice already, he's as nervous as me. But I'm not nervous about the trade, I'm nervous about what happens next. Laura's conceded more ground than the Dutch in Srebrenica. She's backing my early retirement, she's agreed to turn a blind eye to one last blowout. I've got her ring in the same jewellery box she filled with charlie in the summer – thought that'd be a nice little touch to ram my point home when I pop the question. Can't decide when to do it though; part of me wants to do it at the Royal Opera House tonight, but the rest of me knows I'll be a long way from compos by the time the curtain falls.

I spend the morning plutzing about the present and kvelling about the past. I watch the market through my Blackberry lens, I look back at my life through coke-tinted glasses. I log into Bloomberg on my laptop and stare daggers at the screen. There's only one price I care about, only one stock that matters. Brownings, stock code BNG. I type BNG

LN <Equity> Q a million times, I stop, look, listen, then do it all again. 72-72.5, massive volume, massive uncertainty. Swings and roundabouts, slides and monkey bars too. It's all over bar the shouting, but the newsbar's keeping shtum. No announcement, no indication when it's going to be released. Time passes, time stops, time reverses back to the house to turn off the gas. I shut my eyes and massage my temples. I need to speak to Nick 'n' Neil. I need to tell them I'm not coming back, I need to make sure we part on good terms. Not a bridge I want to burn, especially since I'm not entirely sure this is the right move.

I rub my hands together like Fagin, I'm getting more avaricious with every minute. It's the means I truly love, not the end – though there are a hundred and twenty thousand reasons why the end's pretty loveable too. This is the beauty of the stock market, it's just there for the taking, and if we can do it this easy, those at the top of the food chain must be raking it in. When in Rome, build a fucking aqueduct. Saul's line, not mine: it's a classic. Sums it all up. Everyone else is doing it, why can't we? If your dad's a doctor, he'll give you a check-up for nothing, if your uncle's a lawyer, he'll do your conveyancing gratis. So if your best mate's a dodgy little broker with his ear to the ground, you'd expect him to sling free money at you when it's on offer. So here we are. For what we are about to receive, may the Lord make us truly thankful.

The town crier's pounding the streets. Brownings are dead! Long live the short sellers! Too fucking right. My wheelbarrow runneth over. I stand triumphant on the couch, I take bow after bow after bow. I wait for the applause to die down, wait for the roars to abate. I force out a couple of tears, it's what they expect. I step up to the mike, I steady myself. I just want to thank everyone who made this possible, the inept management of Brownings, the corrupt liquidator at McMillan's, the adept broker at Dover's – yeah, that's you, Sauly boy! – and most of all me, just for being me, just for standing by me through everything, just for always knowing the right thing to do and the right words to say. If it wasn't for me, the world would be a poorer place, a darker place, a colder place. While I accept this award with great gratitude, really it's me who deserves it, not me. Thank you all, I love you, I love me, I hope you do too.

Five grams of coke. Four box tickets, three Cristals, two dyed blondes, and my best mate Saul in tow. Not sure if we'll make it to the twelfth day, but right now we're seeing out the year in style. Royal Opera House, suited, booted, wasted. La Bohème by Puccini. Champagne by Roederer. Powder by some Peruvian peasant family. I'm walking slowly, Laura on my arm, I'm watching men watching her. You wish. Place is mobbed, I'm too hot. I keep smiling, keep walking, keep elbowing my way through the crowd. The drip down the back of my throat has stopped, not sure why. Definitely buzzing, but not as wired as usual. Drink more, clutch Laura. Saul's off to the gents, Mya's at the bar. Horses for courses. Laura's forgotten her role: seen and not heard, there's a good trophy. Swaying slightly now, need to sit down. Back to the box, lean heavily on the dividing wall. Rub a bit on my gums, bit on my tongue. Curtain's up, I'm not. Coke's not working, nor's the drink. Can't sit still, nowhere to go. Stare at the stage, nothing to see. She sings, he walks, they fight, I stare. Cymbals crash, violins screech, oboes moan, I hear. Next break, same again. Back to the bar, back to the gents. Jack and Jill went up the hill to fetch a glass of Cristal. Eyes red, tie too tight, need some air, need some nicotine. Can't focus, nothing new. Laura's talking far too much. Rub my eyes, she's still there. Hate her, hate them, hate the others too. If looks could kill I'd be in the Hague. Find a toothpick, snap it in half. Feel worse, an hour left. Fuck this, so tired. Stop watching the stage, start watching the crowd. Peer over the side at the punters below. The box is Mount Olympus, I'm Zeus. Down in the stalls sit the NOCD faithful: those two have saved all year for their tickets, these three are up from their country village for a big night out in the capital. That one's never been to anything grander than a recital at the parish church, this one's only here cos the woman she cleans for couldn't make it. Fucking proles. Having their day in the sun, something to dine out on for months. Lean back, bored again. Stroke Laura's back through her dress, pretend she's a cat. She purrs, in character. Trace my fingers round her throat, she arches her neck. Press a bit too hard, but not hard enough for her to think I mean it. She can't say anything anyway. My box, my coke, my cash, my rules. Head heavy, eyes shutting. Play with my keys. Scratch my arm, draw blood. Dab more coke, down more water. Fat cunts on stage, fat cunts off stage. Something's got to give. Bet it's me. It is. Out the door, hit the bar. All alone, not another philistine in sight. Tip the barman a twenty, grab the bottle, fuck the glass, fuck the rules. At door, light fag. Outside, quick drag, quick swig, quick glance, quick jig, quick dance, quick run, think deep, don't look, just leap. Jogging down Bow Street, drop the wine in a bin, sweat pours. I pause – no breath, no pulse, no clue what next. On a bench, in a cab, at a door, not mine. Ring bell, run away, come again another day. No keys, long lost, get up, get cab. Hotel, Baker Street, minibar, dust. Laura, Saul, Mya, me, what a happy family. Facial twitch, fucking pale, only simchas, beta blockers. Four, three, two, one, fat lady, curtain falls. Brain, heart, eyes stop. Two days pass, encore. Freedom's just another word for nothing left to drink.

There goes the bride – sobbing, screaming, storming her way out of my life for the final time, my trust fund hot on her heels.

But the hall's already booked, seems a shame to waste it. My knight's my best man, my pawns are the ushers. I stand under the chupah, I smash the glass. You may kiss the mip. Can't wait for the honeymoon.

7

She ruffles my hair, I emit a low, warning growl. She laughs, trills out her instructions.

'Put out the cigarette, brush your teeth, and come give me head like this morning.'

My eyes narrow to slits, I'm the Kim Jong Il of the castle. She doesn't get licked out on demand, it's not a pay-as-you-go contract. I control the rations, I call the shots. Good things come to those who wait, to those who deserve the red carpet treatment. That's no metaphor, not this week anyway – half her womb's bled out already, and there's still no sign of the crimson tide turning. Doesn't bother me, spurs me on if anything; you don't go down for the taste or the scent, it's all about ownership, all about spray-painting your tag on her labial bricks. Fuck saying it with flowers, the flat of my tongue and the edge of my lips speak the lingua franca of true blue lovers. I cut my teeth, or rather my teeth cut my frenulum, on Laura's grateful pussy from the word go. I heeded her early advice, let her coach me till my skills were as finely honed as a brain surgeon's. The three Ts: timing, touch, tenderness, with a garnish of controlled pain and a dash of ferocity to season. I'm so fucking good, I'm the man of the match, I'm the week-in, week-out MVP. Tina knows the score, can't get her knickers off fast enough, can't spread her legs wide enough, can't grab my head hard enough when she's soaring through the sensual stratosphere. K'nayna hora, a layban on her – but as long as we work round my schedule.

I flash her a strained smile, I stalk out of the room and pad across the lounge to the sofa. My Blackberry rests on Daisy's front paws, she nuzzles it gently with the tip of her nose. Lassie she ain't, there's no subliminal message behind her munching my handset, no fire to put out, no orphans to rescue. I hurl my lighter at her thick skull, she dives for cover in a flash of black and gold. She cowers under the coffee table like it's a Morrison shelter, memories of bombshells fired by her former owner still exploding in her mind. Time she got over it, she lives a charmed life with me, just like Laura did, just like Tina does, just like anyone else lucky enough to have the sceptre extended in their direction. Daisy looks at me mournfully, I hold her gaze and stare her down. She's in the doghouse for a reason and she can take her punishment on the chin. I spark my cigarette, keep eyeballing Daisy, wipe my phone on the couch and weigh up my options. Tina's in the blue corner, Glenmorangie's in the red, and the versatile little wrap in my pocket will go nicely with either option. Or just as appetisingly on its own.

Tina's still in bed, Daisy's still under the table. I'm still on my own, my mind's still seeping sanity like a sieve, I've still got more screws loose than the Townsend Thoresen. Tina's a welcome distraction in the ultra short term, but she can't stop the rot on her own, nor is she that way inclined from what I've seen so far. Neither of us are under any illusions about what's going on here: we've found a port in the storm together, but it's only a matter of time till we go back to being just ships that pass in the Hampstead High Street night. Setting up shop in my penthouse is a no-brainer for her, she's milking the *Pretty Woman* role for all it's worth while the going is good. The alternative is too bleak to bear, it's crushed her ever since she hitched her way to London from inner-city Stoke. Six days a week at the off-licence, a cell-like room in a Tufnell Park bedsit, no cash, no class, no fucking clue. She touts herself as an aspiring actress, she's got the aspiring down to a fine art but the acting not so much. Auditions come and go, dreams fade and die, days flash by and failure beckons a bony finger up ahead. I can't help her career, wouldn't even if I could, but I can cushion her fall for as long as it suits my agenda to do so. It does for now, so there's still room at the inn for her and her kitbag full of troubles. She's my little pony, her blonde hair scraped into a perfect braid down her back, starting high atop her head in keeping with haute Kenwood couture. I'm a sucker for a high ponytail, nothing screams tola louder or prouder, and right now I want her treif status shouted from the rooftops. I'm an equal opportunities employer, this is multiculturalism at work, at play, in business, in pleasure. A bile-filled, bitter old hag in Elephant and Castle doesn't agree, she's shouting at me via the graveyard shift phone-in on LBC. 'I don't want my grandson in a predominantly non-white class,' she spits. 'I know just what you mean,' the equally bigoted presenter concurs. Somewhere in Mississippi a church burns contentedly. Can't really have a go at the kettle for hating blacks though, not given my pot's history. For us, by us: despite my recent veering from the derech, that's still the long-term plan. Someday you will find me, wearing my tefillin, in a Stamford Hill yeshiva in the sky. Not today though, I've got my mind on my shikse and my shikse on my mind.

I catch her staring at me if I turn around quick enough. I watch her watching me watching the days tick by. She can't work it out, can't compute the inaction and inertia. She works every hour God sends, she scrimps and saves and squirrels and stores, she puts away what she can for a rainy day, knowing full well that the forecast is thunder and lightning for months and years to come. She sees me busy doing nothing, can't join the dots. Cash rules everything around her, her dreams stack up like planes over the runway, but air traffic control never give the green light to land. I've already hit the ground running, already disembarked, picked up my bags, jumped in the M3 and sped my way home. She looks at me with two parts resentment to three parts admiration, she can't help marvelling though she wishes she could. The ant looks up to the sluggard, this is the new world order.

She puts two and two together, I see her search for my horns. Jews with diamonds aren't a girl's best friend, not if she's broke, from Stoke, and her life's a bad joke. I can see the cogs whirr in her mind, hear the abacus click in the frontal lobe – it's all black and white, and it doesn't feel fair. I'm not saying sorry though, not shedding a tear, it's an accident of birth, not of design. A seven-foot shvarts doesn't weep for his five-foot friend, he just picks up a basketball, shoots a few hoops, and cashes the cheques that the world hurls his way. How odd of God to choose the Jews. Pause, rack, sip, smoke. Not odd of God, the goyim annoy 'im.

I am gone like the shadow when it declineth, I am tossed up and down like the locust. And that's on a good day.

Time is no healer, Time's a bovver boy with steel-capped DMs. Time waits till I'm not looking, then knocks me clean out with a metal pole. When I come round, Time's still there, sticking the boot in over and over, crushing rib after rib after rib. Time's merciless, but I know it's nothing personal. Time's got its own problems it needs to take out on someone, anyone. I'm just the unlucky punchbag caught in the wrong place at the wrong time.

Laura's long gone, true to her word – bad news for me, even worse for my bank manager if my parents find out what happened. Got to make sure they get my spun version of events, got to make sure they reject her testimony as wholly unreliable. Time to play the bulimia card, probably throw in a few self-harming bubbemeisers too, for good measure to really hammer her credibility. At least my Banque Nord bosses aren't kicking up a fuss – both Nick and Neil fell for my hypertension routine and offered to hold my job till I sort myself out. Could be a long wait, though I'm sure they give even less of a fuck than me.

It's one thing to wake up and not know what day it is, but try waking up and struggling to decipher the month. The spread's wider than an OFEX stock: February–April's the bid-offer. I'd be a tentative buyer of March, nothing firm though. My Blackberry laughs bitterly on its coffee table perch, Daisy's eyes are fixed firmly on the front door. Daisy hates me, I hate Daisy. Daisy's been acting up ever since Laura left, she won't cut me an inch of slack. It's all my fault, she reckons, I'm the evil tyrant who banished her beloved princess from the land. Even though that's not how it happened, even though I'd do anything to get her back (but I won't do that. I won't beg. I won't grovel. I won't admit I was wrong, there'll be no midnight selichot. I won't back down).

We deal with our loss in very different ways. Daisy goes for the classic sequence: denial, anger, bargaining, depression, acceptance. I laugh in all their faces, my five stages are far more fun, they're a far better fit for my frame: smoke, sip, coke, mip, rip my mind to ribbons. Run at my memories with a chainsaw, grind my emotions to dust under my heel. Use a sledgehammer to crack every last Laura-laced walnut rolling round in my soul. She's been written out of my history, she's a burnt-out star whose trail has long since ceased to blaze. Daisy's struck down by the power of love, I'm emboldened by the love of power. It's all about power now. Same as it ever was.

Out with the old, in with the new, and that goes for JoJo as much as for Laura. Fuck knows why he let morals trump money when it came to my custom, but he won't be sorely missed. He got far too big for his boots, far too confused about our relationship. He was my employee, he wasn't my friend. I needed him to serve, not protect – especially once Laura made for the exit. But he decided to follow Laura, decided he was doing me a favour by belatedly honouring her plea not to do business with me. His loss, Steve's gain. It makes fuck all difference to me. By and large.

Run out of small talk. Run out of big talk. Run out of frowns, sighs, coughs, whistles. Saul's in the same boat, we're like the owl and the pussycat. I catch sight of my reflection in the window of the Previa driving past. I swear I'm getting fatter, must be the only coke-head in London who puts on weight. I should apply for a refund. Waiting for Steve. Always waiting for Steve. Could be the title of my autobiography: Waiting for Steve – things to do in Kensington when you're half-dead. Been leaning on these railings for almost an hour, can't do a fucking thing about it. Possession is nine tenths of the power struggle. Want someone to throw their arms around me and tell me not to worry, he'll be here soon. Want a dealer who shows me a bit of respect, who cares about my feelings, who treats me like a prince. Want to be curled up by the fireplace out of the cold, just me and my gram, staring into each other's eyes, not saying a word, not needing to. Want a new start, want a new leaf. Want a new dawn, a new day, a new life. More than anything, I just want Saul to stop kicking the fucking lamppost. Mug, dick, wanker. Etc, etc, etc. Car turns left, we look up, it's not Steve, we look down. Car turns left, we look up, still not Steve, we look sad. Car, left, not, fuck. Car, left, not, fuck. Two, four, six, eight, who do we appreciate? Steve, Steve, Steve Steve Steve, Steve-Steve-Steve-Steve, Arsenal. At least it's not raining. I yawn, I crack my knuckles, I study my phone. Another car turns into the road, my head jerks up to look but my heart's not in it. My heart's been buried at Wounded Knee. My heart's flown south for winter. My heart's doing a twelve-stretch for aggravated assault. Can't remember if I used to spout such bollocks before coke crowbarred its way in through the back door of my life. Wonder what I'd be like if I'd stayed on the derech. Not much different, I bet, just with another brand of addictive streak. Probably be standing outside LA Fitness before it opened every day, desperate to get on the weights, desperate to bench press my way to nirvana. Or hooked on work, hooked on girls, hooked on cash, hooked on food. Whatever the substance, I'd definitely be hooked on something. It's not my fault, those older kids made me do it. Steve is still just a figment of our imaginations, Steve's just in theory and not in practise. He'll be wearing striped pyjamas when he comes, he'll be wearing striped pyjamas when he comes, he'll be wearing striped pyjamas, wearing striped pyjamas, wearing striped pyjamas when he comes. Forget how the next verse goes. Would ask Saul, but I hate him. Would ask Steve, but he's not here. It's a full half hour later. Steve's been and gone. I was at the shop, didn't get to see the Messiah reveal himself in all his glory. I'll survive. In the pub with Saul, he's slipping me my wrap, I'm pretending not to care. I'm pretending I'm far more interested in sedately sipping my Stella than wanting to kick down the door of the gents, throw the entire eighth on the ledge by the sink and inhale the pile like a fucking hoover. Saul's playing the same stupid game. Aren't we clever, aren't we grown up? Definitely not two 21-year-old fiends whose whole lives revolve around feeding the monkeys on their backs, who run halfway across London to stand in the cold for the length of a football match just to pick up, who can't see past the end of the next line or the bottom of the next bottle of cask-strength Caol Ila. Not that I'm bitter, mind. I'm genuinely not. I'm genuinely happy. I'm genuinely delighted with my lot. You think it's only the gear talking, but I know the coke's just the icing on the cake. It's all gone, playtime's over. I'm lying on the couch, I'm looking at the moon. Was gonna jump over it earlier, don't want to anymore. Saul's left, so have the others, so has my sense of well-being and joy. Wish I had another line, and another, and another. Wish I had a mute button to make the voices in my head shut up. Wish I had a penny for every wish I've made. Wish I had a line for every penny I had. Wish, wish, swish, swish. I should audition as a windscreen wiper. Wish I had a rewind button, wish I had an off button. Go to bed. Can't go to sleep, go to hell instead. Wish I was in Kensington.

I'm Saul's pet project, he's taken me under his wing. If it wasn't for him ferrying me back into the real world on a regular basis, I'd be truly both a rock and an island. Hiding in my room, safe within my womb, I touch no one and no one touches me. Tina aside, but she hardly counts. That's a dangerous way to spend the rest of the month, rest of the year, rest of my life. Saul's not exactly the ideal alkali to my acid – he's more like the nitro to my glycerine, but he's the best I've got and we both know it. Better the blind leading the blind than just leaving them sitting all alone in the corner. Saul leads me astray, leads me up the garden path, but at least he leads me. Far more in sickness than in health; it's strange how my decline's brought the two of us closer together again.

Only six weeks into my Ferris Bueller's year off, I've still not got a clue what to do with my days. My nights are fine, all taken care of, but my daylight hours are as empty as my promises. Saul's put me on a strict regime, one that I say'll kill me but he swears will make me stronger. He's got no interest in curing me of any of my vices, which immediately catapults him above Laura in the top ten. Instead, he's singled out my solitude as the weak link in my chain. I can keep doing what I do, keep getting drunk, keep getting high, keep keeping Tina as a pet, as long as I get out of my house and surround myself with like-minded accomplices. Most of all, he reckons I've got to kick my Betfair habit. Online's out, offline's in. Instead of spending every day shackled to my laptop, I've got to cash out, back out, log out once and for all. I have to walk on to the bookies with hope in my heart, and I'll never bet alone. He's spot on, but knowing I'm doing the right thing doesn't soften the blow.

The Ladbrokes on the High Street becomes my second home. I'd be happy to make it my first, but they take a dim view of substance abuse. Plus the place is heaving with all manner of Tonys, and that's not the kind of environment in which I want to raise my kids. Fuck knows where they come from, because they're certainly not the kind of Hampsteadites you see in the brochure. They're probably day-trippers up on a coach tour from Kilburn; either that or they're refugees claiming political asylum from Chalk Farm. Whatever their roots, they spot me a mile off and circle their grease-stained wagons the minute I push my way through the front door into the semi-darkness. They blink like bats at the bright light streaming in from the street, then look me up and down with unbridled disdain. You're not from round here, are you boy? Well actually I am, it's all of you who seem to have taken a wrong turn somewhere between the giro and the job centre. I give them the cold shoulder, they mutter into their bacon butties and ignore me, too. I'm in and out in a flash: quick scan of the prices, fill out the slip, pass my money under the counter, wait for my receipt, then a beeline for the exit. I'm only there to stake my money on the night's football, and that's how it stays for a couple of weeks, but soon the four-legged siren's song lures me onto the racing rocks. I'm powerless to resist, my curiosity piqued by the daily sight of the pilgrims standing reverentially at their altar and offering up their sacrifices to the golden calf on high. The TVs are mounted on the western wall, and the punters are no less deferential than the Kotel faithful, no less ethereal either. They pray all day long, pushing their betting slips into the cracks of the counter and beseeching the Almighty to intercede on their behalf one last time, then shockeling nervously as they await the celestial decision.

I mock them at first, I scoff at their hangdog stares, their wistful smiles, their unabashed desperation as the day grows long and their wallets wear thin. I'm a sceptic, a cynic, even a borderline atheist – at least, I don't bow down to the same god as them. My God only cares about football punters, we are His chosen people and the rest are out on their own. The pagan rituals of the equine disciples are an affront to Him, to me, to all that we stand for. But where familiarity at first bred contempt, now it's curiosity that's welling up inside me, and when the dam eventually bursts, I'm swept away on a tidal wave of sinful pleasure. It's such a mug's game, such a shot in the dark, that I can't help but be seduced by the wild abandon that a day at the races offers. Or rather, a day at the bookies watching a day at the races on a twenty-inch screen through a twenty-foot cloud of smoke. There's none of the skill of trading, none of the science of gambling on football, just a blind roll of the dice and a full-armed toss of caution to the wind.

That's not how the rest of them see it, of course, but they're cunts and I'm not. They put their faith and funds in barely sentient quadrupeds, hoping against hope that the beasts won't bolt off the track and the hurdles won't snap their fragile legs in two. They study form all day and umm and ahh to themselves like they're the high priests of meteorology. Red sky at night, gelding's delight, or so they say, or so they wish, or so they hope, or so they never know for sure. Backing anything over evens is more random than flipping a coin, but still they line up to be shot by the bookies at dawn, noon, and dusk. They bet to win, they bet to place, they exacta and yankee and tricast and forecast. They beg, steal and borrow, they come back for more, and Ladbrokes wouldn't have it any other way. The shareholders get high on the punters' supply, and the party never ends – for either side. The sheep enjoy the fleecing as much as the farmers, I can see it in their eyes: despite all the money that's siphoned out of their accounts, despite all the pain and misery and dashed hopes and dreams, they're in seventh heaven as each race gears up to start. Been there, done that, I know the score. I might be a football elitist, but the chance to slum it isn't one I can pass up for long. The spirit is willing, the flesh is bang up for it as well.

One old boy catches my gaze on my first day at the screens. The glint in his eye spots the glint in mine, they get acquainted and swap war stories. The man doesn't say a word, just arches an eyebrow and nods at my betting slip.

'Two-Tone Joan to place.'

The others can hear, they don't seem to care though. They're too busy ogling the runners like a stag party getting lathered up over the stripping nurses.

'How much you on for?'

The alterkakker's still trying to size me up, trying to work me out. Hope he has more luck than me.

'Seven hundred at five to four.'

He puckers his lips, narrows his eyes. A few other members of the synchronised scowling team do the same.

'That's a big bet for a little boy – you putting it on for your dad, are you?'

Nothing big about it, this is loose change. Elementary, my dear Tillbury – can't you tell from my Moschino romper suit?

'Just liked the price, thought I'd put my money where my mouth is.'

No point rubbing his nose in it, if he wants to think this is a big deal for me, I'm happy to play along.

'Well, I hope your mouth knows something the bookies don't. Two-Tone's been on the drift for the last half hour, she was odds on earlier but now they reckon the ground's too soft for her. Plus she didn't eat up when they arrived at the course.'

I nod like I know what he's on about, I nod like I care what he says.

'So what would you be on then?'

Give him the chance to spread his gospel, I can see he's a budding preacher in need of a congregation.

'Townshend Road to win, no fuss. I'm a backer at twelves, you can still get on at the price if you're quick.'

I don't want to be quick, I don't even want to be slow. Why the fuck would I back anything, anywhere, at twelves, elevens, tens or nines? Only two things are made of that price: pipedreams and paupers.

'Cheers, but I'm all in on this race, got to keep a bit back for the three-thirty.'

Thanks but no thanks, darling. The horses line up, they're under orders. My new best mate forgets me in a heartbeat, I forget him even faster. Strapped in, strapped up, locked and loaded, ours not to reason why, ours but to do and die and fucking love every last second of the ride. Two-Tone's a slow starter, no idea what Townshend Road's up to. I've only got eyes for Two-Tone Joan and her red-and-black striped jockey who straddles her like a pair of fruit pastilles. Two jumps down, three fallers so far, not Two-Tone, not important, not my problem. The glue factory'll have their hands full tonight. Two-Tone's fourth of eight runners left, Two-Tone's third, Two-Tone's fourth again. The commentator's voice quickens, so does my heart, blood gallops round my body to the beat of the horses' hooves. Another faller, another punter moans in despair to my left. Mug. Should have gone with Two-Tone, mate, should have listened to the Golden Jew. Two-Tone's third, looking for a gap between the leading pair. My pulse quickens again, my heart flutters like a coquette's eyelashes. Round the last bend, two more fences to go, Old Man River's babbling away in tongues from his corner of the room, daft codger still thinks he's in with a chance. Two-Tone's stepped it up, found the extra juice, breathing right down the leader's nose, right on the rail, right at the right time and the right place and the right fucking day of the week. Final fence, tiny stumble, another faller, another whimper behind me. Two-Tone leading, home straight, full steam, eyes front, legs pumping, whip cracking, ahead by a length but two and three are closing in, neck and neck, back into second, the room's buzzing, the heat's rising, arms flailing, urgent shouting, feet stamping, high pressure, high octane, high as fucking kites, to the post, photo finish, couldn't give a damn. Two-Tone's placed, that's all I needed from her, I've romped home, back to earth, back with a bump, light a fag, slump in a chair.

Glance around, survey the scene. Pretty heavy collateral damage, some serious anguish on a dozen or so faces. Sackcloth and ashes, gloom and doom, down, out, sent home in a box. Not my man though, he's grinning like a paedophile. He knows the form, knows not to gloat, but he knows that we know that he knew best. He'd do a lap of honour if it didn't mean getting lynched on the way, he'd wag a finger at us all if we'd promise not to snap it off. He walks over to me, poker face back on, nonchalant mask covering the glee beneath.

'Townshend Road came good, didn't he? Great little gelding, that one – keep an eye on him at Cheltenham next year.'

Go on, old man, have your moment in the sun. Dance in that limelight, bask in that brief flash of glory.

'Yeah, well done mate, should have listened to you, but I'm still a bit green round the gills, and anyway I did ok in the end. I like to keep my stake high and my risks low, you know? Short odds, deep pockets, that kind of thing.'

Easier said than done, of course, but it's all relative. A man with a ton in his pocket shouldn't bet any different to a man with a million: there's no tax, no hidden costs, just straight profit or loss. I watch as he shuffles off to collect his jackpot. The man behind the counter flashes him a weak smile, pushes a fifty pound note and change towards him.

I wait for the rest to follow, but I'm the only one who does. The lucky punter wanders back to his corner, the bookie goes back to his computer. A rare twinge of guilt crosses my mind like it's looking for something – not gonna find it though. If his world revolves around five-pound bets, zei gezunt. Twelve-to-one to him's the same as twelve-to-one to me, but I still can't believe anyone takes pocket money like that seriously. No time to dwell on it, next race starts in ten. Cash in my chips, massive wad, can't be bothered to count it, can't believe they'd rob me in here. Onward Christian soldiers: pay up, pay up, and play the game.

8

MARCH 2007

Saul's on the edge, Mya's aghast. A good word, aghast – conjures up images of horror and fear and most of all helplessness. Which is about right for her, she's fucking powerless to stop his decline and fall, she should get out now while she's still got other options. Not right now, I suppose, might as well live for the moment seeing as we're already at the airport. Saul's nerves are frayed, they hang from his shoulders like a worn-out tallit, he's looking frail and forlorn but at least he's still standing. Tina's plutzing off to our left, or whatever the goyishe equivalent is, screwing up her eyes at the Travelex prices, furious with the numbers they're quoting for the euro-sterling spot rate. She's not alone, a whole horde of others do the same, would-be f/x wizards thinking they can outfox the markets like Soros devaluing the pound. Fucking Tonys, and they call us misers. Tina succumbs to the pressure, pushes two fifties reluctantly across the counter, grabs the thin wad of euros with an even thinner-lipped grimace, pouts and potters back over to us.

'Bastards, can't believe they're so tight.'

I can, treacle, they're only doing their job. Just like him, just like her, just like you. The world of big business meets the world's smallest violin.

'Yeah, but don't worry Tee, this weekend's bought and paid for by Messrs Dettori and Fallon, so all's well on the Western Front.'

She doesn't know who I mean, but she knows what I mean all right. I've spoken of nothing else since the double came in thirty-six hours ago. Even by my standards it was a major score – fifteen grand in tax-free takings, enough to match her annual income on the one hand, take the four of us on a Barcelona blowout on the other. Tina's never had it so good, she never will again, this trip'll mark the high point of her life's candlestick chart. She's drunk on the excitement, Mya's drunk on the Merlot, I'm drunk on the power, Saul's sober as a judge. Can't snap out of it, can't raise his game. Hollowed-out eyes matching his hollowed-out septum, he's making me feel like a picture of health and that's a bad sign for both of us. It's not like I haven't got my own demons to banish, but I don't let it show, do I? My dad's last email made explicit reference to what will happen if I don't immediately uncouple myself from the 'shikse bandwagon' I've hitched myself to – can't fault his network of informers at any rate. I didn't bother replying, but he won't care about that. His words are all that count.

Hours flash by, sights and sounds and scratch and sniff. Remember eating, don't remember what, where, when. Credit card tastes of horseradish, tongue tastes of Tina. See her stripped bare, all fours, all mine, all night. Doing lines off the small of her back, crouching tiger, hidden coffee table. Get me to the casino on time, I'm getting hammered in the morning. Bet, dice, spin, touch, move, grin, walk, run, trip, force out another laugh, down another Johnny Blue, drop another half. To the victor the spoils, to the loser the cashpoint, wadded up, waddle up, double up the stake, double up in pain, the pain in Spain's cured mainly by cocaine. Day becomes night becomes here becomes now becomes blurred becomes clear becomes vicious and cruel. Saul missing in action, Mya absent without leave, Tina a fish so far out of water she could be in the Gobi desert. Bait my hook, reel her back in, she flounders on my deck just how I like it. Dice again, down again, hell is round the corner, rock bottom's just along the hall. Dice, cold, walk, turn on the tunnel vision, flick channels, blink. Dice and doom and gloom and dark, walk the plank and plunge to the depths. I lift up my eyes to the mountains, from whence shall my salvation come? Tina naked, shaking, crying, smashcut to the street, flashback to the plane. Saul's not singing anymore. Blood from my nose, taste metal, turn on a sixpence. Blood cries me a river, I try to swim upstream. Dice are my armbands, cards are my water-skis. Speak when I'm spoken to, walk Tina outside, slash, crash, burn. We'll be running round Barca with our willies hanging out.

City Airport car park, Saul in his Targa. Shivering, cold, shaking like an epileptic, Mya on shpilkes riding shotgun. I lean in through Saul's window, cup his chin in my hand.

'Come on, Saul, you're not doing yourself any favours. Let's head home, we'll go for a pint and a chat, just you and me.'

He scowls, stares out of the windscreen at nothing and no one.

'Saul? What the fuck, man – you're starting to worry me as well as the girls.'

He glances my way for a second, grips the steering wheel hard.

'Yeah, ok, let's do that – there is something I need to talk about.'

Mya's ears prick up, she's as in the dark as me. I catch her eye over Saul's thinning hair, motion for her to keep shtum.

'Nice, no problem. Go home and unpack and meet me at Freemason's at nine?'

Saul nods once, turns the keys, revs the engine. Tina slips her hand into mine, her fingers are freezing. We walk to the car, I can't be fucked to speak. She can, but my silence speaks louder than her asinine words. We buckle up, I slip behind Saul in the queue for the exit. Jungle Fever '98 comes forth to carry us home, the bass resonating in every bone of our battered bodies. I'm briefly at peace. I'm feeling semi-benevolent towards Tina, quite impressed with how she lasted the course. Still can't remember large chunks of the weekend, still not convinced there wasn't some serious damage done, be it fiscal, physical or psychological. Saul's definitely a mess, but then he was beforehand as well. I'm intrigued to find out what he wants to tell me, can't imagine what all the fuss is about. Nothing could rock his boat any more than it could mine, we're both still afloat in every sense of the word. Maybe he's hitting it a bit harder than he should, but he knows how to take that in hand. A good slap round the face and a good slam on the brakes, we all have to do it from time to time. Tina turns down the volume, looks me dead in the temple.

'Listen, maybe I shouldn't say anything, but some fucked-up things happened in Spain, and I want to know why.'

I say nothing, spark a cigarette and wait. I'll hear her out, but only to help jog my memory. There's no way on earth I'm getting lectured by my underling.

'What happened between us on the second night was really scary, you know? I mean, I've been in some weird situations before, but that was something else. I know you didn't mean it, but it's made me wonder what sparked that behaviour in the first place.'

Not a clue what she's on about, though it sounds like I should have. I rack my brain. It's impervious to racking though, not yielding an inch. I rack harder, it still won't budge. I'm not asking Tina, it'll only pour fuel on her poor little fire.

'Maybe this was your mind's way of telling you to sort yourself out, maybe you're closer to the edge than you think.'

Careful, sweetheart, you'd do well not to keep pulling this lion's tail. I still keep my counsel, I'm a champion tongue-holder.

'I know you've got cash, I know life's all a big joke to you, but seriously, don't you think it's doing you more harm than good?'

She falters, she knows she's treading on a minefield. I admire her courage, I hate her fucking chutzpah. I watch the road, I let the latent energy collect in my chest.

'Cos you don't seem right at all, you're even worse than when I met you and you were bad enough then. Don't you

want to get a job, get away from the drugs and the gambling?
I mean, hard work never killed anyone, did it?'

'Oh yeah? Ever heard of Dachau, darling?'

Course the Kenwood hasn't, but it's beside the point. I've
had enough of her sermonising, not sure what qualifications
she has to start biting the hand shovelling meal after meal
down her avaricious throat. My spring's uncoiled, I'm on
the offensive now, but I've got to control it, got to rein in
the rage. This isn't quite the time or the place for the
both-barrels treatment. I'll hold fire till the time is right, till
I'm back on home turf.

'I'll let you into a little secret here, Tee, and you can make
of it what you will.'

Turn to page 180 if you want me to turn all sackcloth
and ashes and fault my tortured childhood for my lot. Turn
to page 210 if you want me to absolve myself of responsibility
and lay the blame at some abusive teacher's/playground
tormentor's/paedophilic uncle's door. Turn to page 265 if
you want me to break down and confess to my inner turmoil,
fear and despair. Or just stay sat where you are, in my car,
in my house, in my bed, in my world, with your mouth shut
and legs open and eyes front and nose twitching contentedly
with the best powder money can buy.

'I'm sorry for what happened in the hotel room . . .'

Whatever that may be. I'm keeping it vague, I'm not
making a full statement till I speak to my lawyer.

'. . . and I'm sorry for all the times I've lost it a bit in front
of you . . .'

There's a microscopic trace of remorse somewhere on
the back seat, though I doubt even a forensics team would
find it.

'. . . and I know what you're saying about what I get up to, I'm getting a bit uneasy myself, to be honest.'

To be utterly fraudulent, obviously. Let's not get too carried away. Let's not give her more than the faintest glimmer of hope. She's already smiling cautiously, already thinking she might have found a chink in my armour. Close, but no Romeo y Julieta.

'Plus, looking at Saul, I reckon I'm not the only one on the verge of slipping off the tightrope, I think this weekend's shown both of us that.'

It might have, though it's odds on neither of us will pay the blindest bit of notice to the warning signs. We're near Hounslow now, I'm gazing out the window at the goyim grazing in the streets and gardens. Pointless bastards, so low down the food chain I have to squint to see them from my perch. Funny how one's sneaked onto my passenger seat. I laugh nastily to myself. Even funnier how I'm wasting my time giving her the same speech I used to give Laura, as though Tina comes anywhere close to Law on the sliding scale of people I give a fuck about. Not funny, actually, more pathetic than anything. Tina's as disposable as a carrier bag, I could kick her out the car here, in five, ten, or twenty miles' time, now, tomorrow, or the day after that, and I'd barely register her absence. So what am I doing still chatting to her as though she matters?

'I want to make it up to you, Tee, I want you to know how much I care about you, how sorry I am for messing with your peace of mind.'

Really? I'm having an out-of-vocal-chords experience, my trachea's playing tricks on me. The honey keeps dripping from my lips, the saccharine cloud hangs thick in the air.

'Let's go out for dinner on Thursday, just the two of us, I'll get my table at Locatelli or the Ivy and we'll make a proper night of it, ok?'

'That'd be great, I'd love that. As long as I can switch shifts with Karen, that sounds perfect.'

And we stop at the lights, and we lean in for a kiss, and we follow it up with a hug, and I stroke her thigh, and she strokes my arm, and I can read her mind like a book but I still can't make head or tail of mine. And as we keep tailing Saul down the A1 I pat the eighth in the condom pocket of my jeans and all is well with the world. Cue theme music, cue credits, cue three minute commercial break.

Saul's indicating right, he blasts the Porsche into Kingsley Way. I do the same and reach for my cigarettes. He's flooring it, whatever evil spirits might be devouring his soul clearly haven't got started on his Ayrton Senna complex. I'm happy to keep up, happy to chicane round the Suburb hot on his heels. This M3 was made for barrelling, and that's just what it'll do, up Kingsley Way, left on Meadway, right onto Norrice Lea and then the double-width straight of Winnington Road. Saul's pulled away, he's flying up towards the Heath at full throttle. I hang back a bit, I don't trust my reflexes all that much given the three-day battering they've just endured. I flick my cigarette in the ashtray, glance up and see Saul arrowing straight for a gap between a reversing truck and a lamppost, he makes it, just, then swerves to avoid an SLK coming the other way. He's stuck between a Honda and a hard place now, the hard place a skip full of demolition detritus which he definitely won't beat in a fight. He's gonna slam into the Honda, that much is clear as day, the screech of his brakes the soundtrack to the head-on collision that both parties are powerless to avoid. The Targa flips over, the Honda's sent into a tailspin, the deafening crash as the Targa lands sends birds panicking out of the trees as the upended car screams towards the golf course fence. Tina's shrieking, which sounds even worse than the metal-on-concrete concerto we just sat through, fuck knows what to do, where to start, how to help. First things first, scoop the wrap out of my jeans, empty it out the window, ball up the paper and toss it in the skip, self-preservation's a must whatever the circumstances. Smoke's pouring from both bonnets, no one's emerged from either car. Other drivers are rushing towards the wreckage, but that's a fucking bad move if one of the engines blows up. I jump out of the M3, shout at Tina to call 999, then take in the scene from a semi-safe distance. Still no sign of drivers or passengers, that's a fucking bad omen, even worse are the flames that lick at the Honda's windscreen. That car's gonna explode, this is a proper nightmare, every one of us watching is utterly powerless. Can't hear any sirens yet, can't believe this is real, can't breathe from the tension, can't think or act or move or even stand. My legs give way, I slump back against my door, the first police car screams round the bend from Ingram Avenue, just in time to see the Honda's bonnet cave in from the heat. A ball of fire engulfs the vehicle, accompanied by screams from the onlooking army of gawpers. People dive for cover, but this ain't a Hollywood blockbuster, the flames aren't that high and they've only got eyes for the Honda and its occupants. Gazes swivel to the Targa, smoke's still gushing from the front, the policemen rush to the doors, assess the situation, Mya's voice carries with the wind and she's in serious fucking pain judging by the tortured sound of her moans. Both policemen get busy trying to free her, they wrestle and tug and stand firm against gravity's bullying tactics. They save the day, or Mya's at least – she's passed like a parcel to the just-arrived ambulance. Saul's still inside, Tina's still shrieking, I'm still no more than a pillar of salt. Firemen fan the last flames, then the cutting begins and Saul's pried loose from his snare. Death sighs in frustration, thought there was the chance of a hat-trick, but two out of four's not a bad day's work.

Mya's been unconscious for over a week, there's a good short to be done in Majestic Wine shares. Saul wishes he had the luxury of a coma to hide behind, but he's wide awake, wide eyed, wide open to the brickbats hurled his way, even more exposed while he's lying in traction in the Wellington. They're baying for blood, the witch-hunt is on: police, parents, elders, betters, tinkers, tailors and anyone else with an axe to grind. His main problem's the mob of Nigerians whose two kinsmen went up in smoke in the flame-grilled Honda – hell hath no fury like a pack of angry shvartses, and Saul's firmly in their sights. The bulk of them hail from Strawberry Vale, twinned with Gomorrah and twice as depraved, and they're all blessed with the kind of council estate of mind to guarantee Saul a round-the-clock nightmare for years to come. The dust doesn't look like settling any time soon, it's hard to see what his best option is when all roads lead to Gehinom. His lawyer reckons he'll do a minimum two years for a multitude of sins, ranging from possession to DUI to death by dangerous driving. His family have all but disowned him, Mya's family have all but disembowelled him, the Suburb yacheners are circling overhead ready to pick his bones clean of every last speck of juicy gossip. The myth-making's begun in earnest, the bare facts aren't nourishing enough for the nests of chirruping starlings. According to the hype, it was a suicide attempt, an insurance job, a drug-induced game of chicken. Saul's a major coke runner, a minor gangster, owes a fortune to his dealer, robbed a fortune from his firm. Even Mya's not safe from the bubbemeiser brigade: she was sleeping with me and told Saul seconds before the crash, she wrenched the wheel from him when he told her he was sleeping with her sister, she was giving him head while he was gunning up the hill, she spat rather than swallowed so he swerved to avoid the splashback. There are some creative minds out there, albeit vituperative and vicious; I catch Laura's eye as we pass in the hospital corridor and it's clear she's jumped to conclusions along with the rest of the talking heads.

'Happy, are you?'

She spits like a cobra, I counter like a mongoose.

'Bulimic, are you?'

She fucking is, I can smell the acid on her breath from here. Old habits die hard. She flounces off, my little praying mantis in Prada. I head for the car park, this hospital's not big enough for the two of us, despite her being half her normal size. There's an angry aubergine-coloured clown staring at my car, he spins round at the sound of my remote unlocking the doors. I get the full once-over from his pinprick pupils, I'm not his flavour of the month. He prises apart his mouth and spews out his opening gambit.

'What you looking at?'

'Dunno, mate, I'm not David fucking Attenborough.'

I follow it up with a broad smile, more for my benefit

than his. I'm on a roll, two killer lines out of two in the last two minutes. My fists are clenched in my jacket pockets, but I'd be laying the chances of a fight here. I've got five inches on him, I'm bulked up beautifully as ever under my top. He's thinking twice, he's hesitated so he's lost, plus the Attenborough line's soared so far over his head it's made him snap his neck in confusion. He steps aside, I saunter into the space left by his backpedalling Reebok Classics. He's still looking nonplussed, I'm still looking smug, then the roles reverse as a blade flashes into view. Not desperate to get Damliolaed on my day off, I stay very still and await instructions. He points the knife between my eyes, the tip less than an inch from the bridge of my nose.

'Prick, you better watch your mouth now.'

Simon says, Damocles does, I'm happy to go along with that given the circumstances.

'Your partner Saul owes us a fuck load of cash, and cos he can't pay while he's in here, you're gonna have to come up with it for him.'

I'm not following at all, don't get the partner reference, don't get why I've been put in the frame as guarantor for Saul's debts. I'd argue the toss, but the switchblade seems to have tipped the scales of justice in the plaintiff's favour. I try another tack.

'Ok, well, I've probably got close to a grand in my wallet, that'll more than cover whatever tick money he owes you, so why don't you take that and we'll call it a day?'

He flares his nostrils, which weren't exactly narrow to start with, grabs my wallet from my inside pocket and empties it on the tarmac.

'Fuck a few hundred quid, we're talking eighty bags, and that's without interest.'

That's not a pretty figure. My mind races as I try to work out how and why Saul's in so deep with this kind of crowd. My interlocutor doesn't seem the type to be trading precious metal put options, the commodities he deals with must be a bit more under the counter than that. Even so, how can Saul be down eighty thousand on coke? There's no way he's done that much, even less likelihood that he hasn't got the cash to cover whatever ticks he's running. Either way, I've got to extricate myself from this situation immediately. It's not my problem, not my debt, and I'm not getting sucked into Saul's quicksand just because he's given some shvarts thug my name and number.

'Look, mate, I don't know what this is about, but I'll get you your money, let me go and chat to Saul and sort it all out.'

He presses the knife into my right cheek, runs it down my face slicing the top layer of skin. A sharp pain trails in the blade's wake, but he's an expert butcher, barely drawing blood as he guides the weapon carefully along the outermost tier of flesh. I wince out of duty, it's what he wants to see.

'Fucking right you'll sort it, you've got three days to get it. We've got your address, you better be waiting for us at home on Thursday, you get me?'

Barely, he sounds like he's in an Um Bongo advert.

'Yeah, yeah, I follow.'

Can't believe the cunt cut my face, can't believe I can't do anything about it either. He spins round and jogs away, I scoop up the notes from the ground, jump into the car and drive in a fury to my house. I don't want to see Saul right now, I'll go back to the hospital later when I've calmed down a bit. My cheek doesn't seem too bad, I quite like the look, if I'm honest, not sure it'll enhance my job prospects but it'll definitely leave a tough little scar. I head to the safe depository on Finchley Road, take out eight wads of notes from my box and stash them under a couch in my lounge, no point not being prepared for Thursday's visit.

Back at the hospital, Saul's cutting a pathetic figure, strapped in and strapped up, and strapped for cash, too, if his whining is to be believed.

'Listen, I swear I never thought it'd come to this, I never thought you'd become involved at all.'

'So why'd you give them my name, then, you spastic? Who the fuck are they anyway?'

'I don't know, I panicked. I was all over the place after the crash, wasn't I? Two of them came to see me here and were getting heavy. I needed some breathing space so I said you were good for the money cos you were my partner in the deal.'

'What deal? Seriously man, what fucking mess have you got yourself – and me – into?'

He sighs theatrically, hamming it up to buy himself time. Tears start to form in the corners of his eyes, he's got a bad case of the yisgadals coming on.

'Ok, this is what happened – it's such a nightmare. About six weeks ago I lost a fortune on a lunatic trade I went into with a few of the Hendon lot, shorting Palco just before a bid, you know. You remember how thin the order book is on Palco stock –'

'Saul, man, I don't need the whole megillah, just tell me

why some orang-utan's waving knives at me in the middle of St John's Wood.'

'Sorry, sorry. Anyway I was down about fifty grand myself, but the others started going mad, telling me I had to cover half of their losses too because I'd brought them the trade, so the long and short is I was down close to a hundred and had fuck all way of paying it.'

'Why fuck all? Where's all your back-up cash? You can't be putting it all up your nose, a fucking hoover couldn't suck up that kind of money in a few months.'

'I don't have any – at least, none that I can touch. I had a fucking bad run trading PA ever since Brownings – the Batman deal was meant to be a get-out-of-jail move.'

'Nu, that still doesn't explain why my face looks like a chopping board. Spit it out.'

More sighs, more tears, more of the woe-is-me and mea-culpa routine.

'So that guy who cut you works for this Muslim bastard Maz in Hyde Park who I got involved with – they serve coke all round that part of town, and I was middleman on a few deals for them. After the Batman trade I needed to make some quick cash, and one of the prop traders I know told me about a couple of dealers who needed a new supplier cos their last one got sent down. I spoke to Steve, told him my problem, and he said he and I could go in together connecting his seller and my new buyers. It was all going well for a few weeks, I was taking a couple of grand's turn every time we dealt, then suddenly it all blew up because they reckon Steve ripped them off with a huge batch of grade Z powder. Now Steve's gone to ground and it's all fallen on me to deal with.'

Sounds like the yacheners were pretty spot on in their speculation about the car crash, they've clearly got impeccable sources. There's too much information to process here, I need a line. I do one, don't bother offering any to Saul, he can go fuck himself as far as I'm concerned. The only reason I'm staying the right side of the red mist is that I need to know all the facts now that I've been dragged into the firing line as well.

'So what does it all mean? What am I meant to do, given these cunts know where I live, want me to pay them eighty grand, and think carving little reminders into my face is a better way of doing business than writing it on a Post-it?'

'Look, I'll get you the money as soon as I'm out of here, of course I will, you know that. I just really need them out of the picture, so if you can sort them out the cash I'll give it back to you a.s.a.p. once I leave this bed, plus another five to say how sorry I am.'

He thinks that's a fair offer, I think it's a fucking liberty. First of all, I should never have been involved in this in the first place. I'd never have pulled a stunt like that if it was the other way round (probably). More importantly, he's just told me he doesn't have any money, that he still owes thousands to his disgruntled Batman investors, and that he's got precious little prospect of clawing anything back in the near future, so he can offer me five, fifty-five or five hundred grand and it's still just an empty promise. He's been robbing Peter to pay Paul without doing a very good job of either transaction, and now I'm the next mug to become one of his creditors – and there doesn't seem to be anything I can do about it given my three-day deadline for delivery.

'Saul, you're scum. Seriously, I have no idea what's going on in your fucked-up head, and I don't really care either. All I know is I should never have been caught up in this, and if it wasn't for you already being in hospital, I'd put you in one for what you've done to me. I'll give them the money because I've got no choice, but I'm gonna threaten you the same way they threatened me. You've got three days from when you get out of here to pay me back, I'm not joking, otherwise I'll bring your world crashing down around your ears. I've got too much on you Saul, your insider trading, your cheating on Mya, the dealing, the stealing, the works, and don't think I won't go down that route cos I swear to you I will.'

He looks like he believes me. He definitely should. I've got far less to lose than him, all I care about right now is my money and my pride. I'm spitting blood – I've got to get out of this room, back home and bury my head in the powder.

Two days later and I've still not slept, my heart's on its last legs and my legs are in oleh v'shalom terrain. I crawl around the flat in concentric circles, finally coming to rest next to the TV, Daisy looking on with a mixture of condemnation and concern. Life begins at three-forty a.m. My doorbell is ringing – I snap out of my trance and check the videophone. Three figures stand on the front step, bearing no frankincense or myrrh but flaunting gold jewellery on every available surface. The charge of the chav brigade. I buzz them in and leave the door ajar, want to get it over and done with as fast as possible. I'm beyond exhaustion, I lean heavily on the wall as I make my way back to the lounge. They barge their way in, chests puffed out as they strut around me like peacocks.

'You got our money, boy?'

The dan dada of the operation, presumably. Not sure why he calls me boy, some kind of slave-era payback going on, I suppose. I start to mumble something in response, dribble a bit as I crack apart my chapped lips.

'Speak up, boy, we ain't got time to waste.'

You might not; I do. Assuming I make it only to three score and ten rather than meah v'esrim, I've still got a good five decades to kill while I wait for the chariot to ascend. I try, try and try again to get my mouth moving, make it on the eighth or ninth attempt.

'Sorry, I'm just a bit fucked up right now, your money's here, give me a second.'

Daisy's got the three of them in her crosshairs, she better not try anything stupid. Even if she took a decent chunk out of one of their legs, I'm in no position to tag team, and chances are all three are armed with more than just their wits.

'Get on with it, boy. I know an oven dodger and his cash aren't easily parted, but you ain't got much of a choice.'

An extraordinary turn of phrase for one so dark. I'm impressed. I've always loved the oven dodger insult – when I first heard it I wished I was a Tony myself just so I could use it. I lean under the couch and retrieve the stacks of fifties, and six eyes light up in unison. An arm slips round my neck from behind – a headlock is the thanks I get for my generosity. Getting choked on coke isn't pretty, my iced-up throat is crying its heart out, my lungs can see what's coming, my mind goes even blanker than before.

I wake up to an empty house, devoid of both guests and anything fenceable – I've been bled dry, there's not a penny to my name nor a pot to piss in. Daisy's gone too, though I can't believe she'd have gone with them without a fight, probably just gone out for a jog when she saw the front door wide open. I don't have a clue where to start, don't know who to call or how to fucking call them if I did – no Blackberry, no laptop, no landline, no doubt in my mind that there's no M3 either. I've been well and truly pogrommed.

9

Nightmare on Hampstead High Street II – the Revenge of the Kenwood. Tina wants to talk as soon as she finishes work, which bodes ill for me and Mario. My man and I are still in our second honeymoon period, childhood sweethearts who went their separate ways then fell back into each other's arms years later. All the water under the bridge couldn't wash away the attraction, couldn't take the shine off the lust or dampen the ardour, and it's infinitely better making love on a fifty-inch screen, no matter how old-school my partner may be. Mario's company, Tina's a crowd, but I've put her off for a week already and she's getting increasingly irritating with her constant harassment. I walk Daisy on a short leash down the road to Victoria Wine, smoke a cigarette as I watch Tina fuss round the shop getting ready to leave.

She's looking flushed. I attempt a perfunctory kiss as she sits down next to me on the bench but she ducks my lips and flashes a moue of distaste. It's gonna be one of those nights, then. I batten down my hatches and brace myself for the onslaught.

'Can we go back to yours? I don't wanna have this talk in public.'

My mind yawns, my senses snore.

'Sure, darling. I hope it's nothing serious.'

Like cancer or AIDS – heavy stress on the AIDS – I've still got my doubts on that front. Major doubts: I'm playing with fire shtupping a shikse. My views on HIV don't tally with the WHO's, but I still maintain you ain't gonna catch anything from an untzerer girl. At least, odds are against it; we're immune to immunodeficiency, in my book. Which is why I fuck bareback – always have, always will, it's a calculated risk and so far so good – though doing the same with Tina is far harder to justify. I blame the parents.

'It is, kind of. Can't we just go?'

She's already up and straining at the leash. Daisy's not so eager, I'm even less keen. We trudge up the hill in silence, I'm not blinking first. She will, 'course she will. They all do. Quiet grates on the nerves of the nervous and scared.

'Look, I hope we can have this talk without an argument, you know?'

The pre-match build up gathers pace; early indicators are we're in for a full-blooded evening's entertainment.

'Sure, Tee, why would we get in a fight? Here, you buzz the lift, I've got to have a word with Boaz.'

She looks frightened as she walks through the hall. I pause at the doorman's desk and slip him a ten-pound note and an envelope.

'Boaz, a friend of mine's dropping off a package in about

an hour. Can you make sure he gets this? And that tenner's for you to say thanks.'

Easy money all round. That'll supplement his day's wages substantially, keep him in falafel and pita for a good while to come.

'No problem, I call you when it get here, yalla.'

He laughs knowingly. I don't return the compliment, don't care what he thinks of my life and times. He should realise he doesn't command quite as much respect in his doorman's uniform as he did in his Israeli special forces' fatigues, should know his place and be thankful for the scraps thrown his way. I lead Daisy over to the lift. Tina's still fretting and frantic. I switch on the NES while Tina gets changed out of her work clothes, put So Solid on the B&O, play them both from the start. By the time 'Haters' comes on I'm on World 1 Level 2 and Tina's back in the room wearing jeans and a jumper and a jaundiced smile. I keep playing, get Mario some wings, fuck up the turtles and keep munching the coins.

'Well I've spent keys make money for centuries, had dough then that's when I spent my Gs, people on my back always wanting freebies, get out my face watch me on TV.'

The gospel according to Asher D. He's on Track 3 Verse 6; I'm on World 1 Level 4; Tina's on Whine 2 Moan 8.

'I've got to tell you something. I don't know how to make it sound any better than it is so I'm just gonna come out and say it.'

No you aren't, you've been beating round the bush ever since we met up an hour ago. Mario jumps onto a falling log, only just scrambles to the next one in time, makes up for it by killing another turtle. Ms Dynamite steps up to the plate on 'Envy'.

'I've got a tongue like a trigger.'

Her and me both. Mario loses his wings. He looks embarrassed as he's forced back down to ground level. Tina's twisting her plait with both hands. Mario eats a mushroom.

'I'm p-rrrrrrrrr-eeeeeeeee-g-naaaaaaaaaaaaa-n-tttttttttttt.'

Time elongates and snaps back like a rubber band. My hands are locked on the controller, Mario slides down a snowy hill smashing all creatures who stand in his path. A Venus flytrap snaps at his heels, he skips past and gets wings again.

'Are you ready to get cursed? But first me and my shadow exchange words. Listen, I said shadow shall I fuck that bitch? He said no Megaman keep an eye on your shit, and I said, shadow can I kill that man? He said no Megaman don't you understand.'

Mega's words reverberate round the room. Mario's world is quiet save for the sound of his end-of-level score being added up. I grip the controller till my knuckles whiten, I clamp my mouth shut with jaws of steel. Annie get your coat hanger. Mario get your fucking fireball.

'Aren't you going to say anything?'

Teardrops gather in the corners of her eyes, beads of sweat break out on my forehead. Congratulations, it's a goy. My dad's naches will know no bounds. I speak in a monotone, mouth on autopilot as I gather my thoughts, and Mario misses another 1-up opportunity.

'How do you know it's mine?'

Bit of an Albert Square response – I can do better than that. She can't, her lips tremble like Sam Mitchell's. I sigh through my teeth, weigh up my options, such as they are.

"Course it's yours. What do you think I am, some kind of slag?'

Darling, if I rounded up and shot all the men you've had since primary school I'd be done for ethnic cleansing. I'm a Jewbious Jew, reckon the odds of me being the dad are five to one at best. Mario slides down the flagpole, still miles from the princess, still a prime hate figure in the turtle community.

'Sorry, Tee, that was out of order. I'm just a bit stunned, that's all.'

Buy a bit of time, think fast, ços I've got to make a move soon. The risk-reward ratio of sleeping with Tina is just way outside acceptable parameters, it's pure downside and fuck-all up. It's the old grenade analogy so beloved of traders, and it sums up this situation perfectly. Walk into a room holding a grenade and the best-case scenario is you walk out again with the pin still in. Worst-case scenario and you get your brains plastered over the walls like a Dulux topcoat. Exhibit A: the expanding zygote two feet away from me on the sofa. Why do bad things happen to good people? Daisy, Daisy, give me your answer, do.

'I know, I am too, but still you don't have to be so fucking rude to me. It's hard enough telling you as it is.'

Sing a song of semen, a pocket full of coke. Hit pause on the NES, whip out the wrap. Mario's frozen in mid-flight, Megaman's still boasting about his TT in the background. I'm struggling to keep a lid on my rage, my fear, my shock, my horror. I slam back a line, spark a cigarette, turn to face Tina and stare into her ice-blue eyes. I want to gouge them out, want to tear her limb from limb, want to excise the offending foetus like pitting an olive. I've done some stupid things in my time, but this stands head and shoulders above the rest. A hundred years ago their men used to rape our women to fuck up our bloodline, and just look at me now.

'Yeah, I know. It'll be ok. We'll work it out, I promise.'

Rather, I'll work it out and you'd better strap in for the ride. This can go one of two ways, three if I let my fury get the better of me, though I'd do well to keep a clear distance between my hands and any sharp objects right now. She can do the right thing and get rid of it, and I don't mind paying for both the procedure and a golden handshake to see her on her merry way. Or she can do the wrong thing and keep it, but she won't see me for dust – fuck paternity suits and the CSA, where there's a coked-up will there's always a way round these trivialities. Might as well be up front with her, honesty's the best policy just this once.

'Tee, I don't think either of us is ready for a kid, do you? I mean, it's not like we've been together long or either of us really knows where our lives are going.'

Even though I've got a fair idea. She and I are passing like angels on Jacob's ladder – we met on the middle rung but we're headed in polar opposite directions. She'll forever dance and drink and screw because there's nothing else to do, whereas I'll get it out of my system in a matter of months. Scout's honour.

'I want to keep it, I definitely want to keep it. We can do it, it'll be a beautiful thing to share together.'

Jesus wept. I run a hand through my hair and keep my eyes locked on Tina's. Time for a bit of bad cop, time to lay down the law.

'Tee, this really isn't a good idea, and I should have as much of a say as you in this. I one hundred per cent don't want you having this baby, it'll fuck up our lives and do all kinds of damage to our futures.'

She's crying properly now. I think about batting an eyelid but that's as far as it goes. I keep talking – in for a penny, in for about ten grand and change if she's lucky.

'I mean it, Tee, we've got to be rational about this, it's not a game.'

She wants to interrupt, wants to make her case, but I'm not pausing for breath.

'I know it'll be painful if you get rid of it, but believe me it'll hurt less in the long run. And I'll take care of you, I'll pay for everything. I'll do more than that as well. I'll put some money aside for you while you recover, I'll be there to cover your every need.'

Her eyes glaze over, then harden, then stare daggers at their opposite numbers.

'You're such a fucking tosser, it's always about money with you, isn't it? You think you can just buy me off, that I'm some little problem you can throw money at and I'll disappear.'

Spot on. And?

'I knew you'd react like this, I knew there was no point trying to find your human side. Fuck you, actually, I'm keeping it whether you like it or not.'

Wish we were running a plc rather than a dead-end, mixed-race pseudo-relationship. If I don't want to be part of her cross-pollination plan, I shouldn't have to be. If this was a democratic system, I'd hold fifty per cent of the voting rights, I'd have fifty per cent of the say in the matter, and nothing would get done without a minimum fifty-one per cent majority. We'd go to arbitration, we'd hold hustings and live debates and have a second round run-off, but instead we've got a situation where she calls the shots because it's her belly holding the beast. Hence my hostile takeover bid; everyone's got their price and I can't imagine a girl like her letting morals trump money for too long.

'Tee, please don't be like that. It's not about cash, it's about bringing a child into the world in the wrong circumstances. Neither of us want that, and for my part I won't let it happen, whatever the cost.'

I can't see my children in her eyes, there's no room now that the pound signs have started barging their way in. Attagirl, let's talk shop. I offer ten grand plus expenses; her opening bid's fifty all in. That's not a gesture of goodwill, that's a fucking pension plan, and we both know it. She thinks she's got me over a barrel; she's probably right. I spin back to the NES, we can reconvene anon. Mario bitch-slaps another turtle, bounces off its head onto a ledge, crawls into a pipe, emerges in a room full of coins. I get the picture.

I seethe therefore I am. Tina's still holding out for the biggest pay day of her life, Saul's been spirited off to the Priory without paying me back a penny. Money's too tight to mention, I can't back a winner for love or money, my septum's falling apart at the seams. I wander round like a bomb victim, dazed and confused and covered in dust, some of it legal, most of it not. *Je ne regrette rien*, but even so. I walk round and round the Rose Garden, Daisy trots up ahead, leaving me alone with my thoughts and my cigarettes and my ever-trusty hip flask. I'm coping, with my usual blend of stoicism, fatalism and alcoholism. Can't do much about Saul, although I'm chalishing for revenge. He'll be out soon enough, and I'll be in ton-of-bricks mode the minute he walks through the clinic gates. Tina's another story – wish I had even fewer principles than I do, the world wouldn't miss another checkout girl for too long, and I'd be doing her a favour putting her out of her misery. If I have to raise the fifty I'll do it, but for a tenth of that she could be at the bottom of Regent's Park Canal with the rest of the also-rans. It's not even about her, really. At least, it's nothing particularly personal – I'd feel the same about any other Kenwood regardless of their individual characteristics. Just like a car connoisseur recoils from a potential purchase as soon as he sees the Skoda badge, so it is when shacking up with a shikse. The specs don't matter – the brains, the beauty, the bodywork – once you know the make, it's a straight no from the off. Tina could never have been more than a gentle stroll down a cul-de-sac, a dummy hand of poker for no cash, a throwaway put option when your real money's invested in a basket of blue-chip stocks. No point telling her any of that, no point feeding her from the tree of knowledge, it'll only make things worse. A goy doesn't know they're a goy till they're told by a Jew, like an animal doesn't know its name till it's classified by a zoologist. Better she stays in the dark about my reverse National Socialist doctrine and just thinks I'm a bastard for ninety-nine other reasons.

She calls me when I'm halfway up St John's Wood High Street. It's not the time or the place, so I hit silent and go back to watching the becks breeze by. I'm drowsy from the whisky, from the walk, from the way of life that I lead right now, from the way of life that awaits me if I jack it all in and hitch myself to the beck-wagon. In vino veritas, in whisky oy vayz mir. I skulk up Fitzjohns Avenue with a heart full of lead, a lead full of Doberman, and a Doberman full of heartache for the life we once knew. She can read the runes, knows it's not gonna get any better for either of us, however many brave faces we put on it. I feel like mipping tonight.

Boaz glances at me as I pass him in the foyer. I barely muster a nod. I'm not in the right frame of mind for pleasantries or peasantry, my mood's getting blacker with every step. Fucking a gold-digger and getting fucked by my best friend has cost me a hundred and thirty grand cash, not to mention the twenty thousand spent replacing the goods looted by the ganefs. That's serious damage by anyone's standards. My temper's rising faster than the lift, I'm incandescent by the time I step out at my floor. I kick my way inside, Daisy scampers to her usual spot and buries her head in her paws. I fling open the balcony door and spit at the city, boot the railings with my right trainer, spin round and storm into the kitchen. Nothing in the fridge worth eating, plenty worth drinking though, white wine time and white line time too. I grab the bottle and a corkscrew and stomp my way back to the lounge, kick open the door and get the fright of my life. Bottle hits floor and mind hits roof. Two skinheads sit facing me, one either side of the TV like stone lions framing a doorway, their faces just as impassive and uncompromising. Daisy's whimpering from the other side of the locked kitchen door, I start shaking, stop breathing, stay rooted to the spot and try to appear as docile as possible. Definitely don't want to rattle this pair's cage, far better to roll over and play dead than have to do it for real. The ice is broken by the heavier-set of the two, sitting to the right of the plasma with all the archangelic confidence of Gabriel.

'Any idea who I am?'

I can probably do this by a process of elimination, but I don't reckon he'll give me that much time. Smart money says they've got something to do with Saul and Maz, the next in an endless line of pillagers sent to relieve me of my worldly chattels. They fit the stereotype, plus the second one's eyeing up my electronics with an avaricious leer. I shake my head, can't speak yet, apparently can't move from the neck down either.

'Stop panicking. Come here and sit down.'

Not as easy as it sounds; I'm wearing a Wile E. Coyote face as I contemplate the thin air beneath my feet. He gets up, face softening slightly, walks towards me with a loping gait.

'We're not here to hurt you, we're on your side.'

I haven't got a side, haven't got a team, haven't got a clue what's going on or what I'm meant to do to protect myself. He reaches into his jacket pocket, draws out a business card.

'Here – take this. It's got all my details, you'll be needing them pretty soon. I'm Nicky, and this is Yuval.'

Yuval nods slowly, I stare at him and then turn back to Nicky. I keep shtum, my mouth bone dry and my palms soaking wet. Nicky puts a bear-like paw on my shoulder, guides me firmly to the sofa, pushes me down onto the seat.

'Listen, son, I'm gonna get straight to the point cos I haven't got long. I've been watching you for a while, I've seen how far you've fallen and I know you've still got a long, long way to drop.'

Too fucking weird for words, too fucking weird for thoughts. Dying for a smoke or a line or a bodyguard.

'I know all about you, every last sordid detail. The coke,

the banged-up shikse, the pay-offs, the whole sorry story. And I'm here to put it all right, right now. It can all end tonight if you want it to.'

He sounds like a cheap advert urging the underclass to consolidate all their debts into one easy monthly repayment, he's got the mock sincerity down to a T. Think I'll wait for the small print, think I'll have my lawyer go over it with a fine-tooth comb.

'Yuval and I are recruiters, basically, we work for Israeli intelligence, and we're here to make you an offer you'd be a fool to refuse.'

I let out an involuntary laugh, Nicky cuffs me round the head with a fat forehand, then immediately feigns contrition so as not to scare me back to silence. My ear stings, but I keep smiling at the absurdity of the situation. The slap's brought me back to life, my stage fright's fading fast.

'Sorry, but what the fuck do I have to do with Israeli intelligence? And what the fuck are you doing watching me?'

I look over at Yuval, but he's clearly only here for show. Nicky leans back on his chair, rests his elbows on the leather arms, brings his palms together pointing upwards like a bonehead Buddha.

'Our job is to scout out potential candidates from the community, Jewish kids who for one reason or another stand out as suitable for the kind of work the organisation does. That rules out most of the clones you've grown up with, cos we're looking for a very specific type of character to take on. I'll be blunt with you, we're far from convinced that you'll make it in practise, but you've definitely ticked enough theoretical boxes to make it worth our while dropping in for a house call.'

I pull out a cigarette and light it. I'm highly suspicious but far less frightened than before. I don't doubt for a moment they are who they say they are, but that's not necessarily a good thing given where the conversation seems to be heading.

'Ok, but since you know everything about me, warts and all, what's my appeal? And what makes you think I want to sign myself over to some Israeli spy set-up?'

'Again, I'll tell you very plainly what we think of you, and if it hurts your poor little ego I apologise profusely in advance, though I strongly doubt it will. Stretching back to your infant school dalliance in ethnic supremacism, it's clear you've got a massive chip on your shoulder about mixing with the goyim, you embrace the 'nation that dwells alone' line with a hyper-bigoted zeal. You might be a mess right now, but you've still got plenty of the attributes that can be forged into the exact shape we want. The chess prowess, the sky-high IQ, the ease with which you learn new skills are all well and good, but not enough on their own. It's the gambling, the solitary lifestyle, the manipulative streak, and the base callousness you show to those weaker than you that mark you out as both a cunt and a candidate. I don't like you, but I don't have to like you to bring you in. And it cuts both ways.'

I light a second cigarette with the first, blood pumping through my veins as I take it all in. I've still got a smile fixed on my face, but it's only for decorative purposes; inside I'm struggling to keep up with the bigger picture. The details make sense, but the overall ludicrousness is way outside even my usual parameters.

'Psychologically speaking you'd need to sort yourself out in a big way before we'd let you anywhere near our work, but that's what the first stage of the process is all about.'

Nicky looks to his right, Yuval leans forward and clears his throat, starts speaking in a thick, grating Israeli accent.

'If you do as we're telling you, you'll go straight into the army in a month's time as the first part of the training . . .'

This is getting more laughable with every sentence. Objection, your honour. I motion for at least a two-year recess.

'What the fuck? Do either of you know how insane this sounds from my point of view? I walk into my lounge and find you two sitting here, next thing I know I'm getting smacked round the head and given the king's shilling, and it's not even for my own country's army.'

Yuval attempts to reply, Nicky waves him quiet.

'Firstly, it is your country as much as it's mine or Yuval's. We're not trying to sell you the Zionist dream, but the whole point of the place is to provide a refuge for Jews, and God knows you need one right now. Secondly: yeah, I'm sure it does sounds pretty mad to hear all this, and do you know how I know? Because I was in your exact position about twenty years ago. When I was nineteen, I got in a row with one of my dad's mates at our snooker club in Gants Hill, and – being the lairy fucker that I was, and still am – I dealt with him in the best way I saw fit. Namely, waiting outside and beating seven shades out of him with a crowbar.'

He pauses for dramatic effect, though he hardly need bother.

'So, in order to get me away from trouble and the Old Bill, my dad packed me off to the one place where little

Jewish boys can always go to escape their troubles. The land of milk, honey and dark-skinned Sephardi girls just waiting to spread 'em for a white boy from the West. I spent four years out there, had the time of my life, and when my dad said it was safe for me to come home, I practically begged him to let me stay. I came back in the end, but wish to God I hadn't. And think about it – you're screwed if you stay here. The net's closing in on you from all sides. Saul's hardly your best buddy, number one cos he's already given your name to the police saying you got him into the dealing, and number two cos the whole eighty grand number was a set-up – how you didn't see that coming is beyond me, by the way.'

I jump forward with a start, eight million pennies dropping with an ear-splitting crash.

'What? What are you talking about?'

Nicky sneers back at me, enjoying the moment.

'What I'm talking about is there was never an eighty grand debt for him to pay off. He just needed a quick way out of his other troubles and paid a couple of wannabe-thugs he got hold of to shake you down. Didn't you even stop to think there might be something a bit sus about the whole thing?'

I'm blind with rage, but I know it makes sense. Saul's a fucking eel at the best of times, and when his back's against the wall I mean about as much to him as a mug market maker at Merrills he wants to stitch up. I punch the wall theatrically. No one's impressed. My thoughts immediately turn to Tina, but Nicky's beaten me to it.

'That tola bird, on the other hand, really is pregnant – don't worry about that. Actually, do worry, but not that she's having you on. Point is, on your own. You've got no way of getting your money back from Saul, and for all you know the shiks will keep squeezing you for cash the longer she threatens to have the baby. What can you do about it if she decides to fuck off up north bearing your offspring in her womb and your cash in her hand?'

Another barely sufficient cigarette, another barely suppressed scream of fury.

'Trust me, you need us more than we need you. We can make both problems vanish, and more on top – we'll get you out of this rut, let you put it all behind you, give you a fresh start and a new challenge and a one-eighty shift in direction.'

They're like fucking Jehovah's Witnesses, preying on the weak and vulnerable to further their own messianic agenda, though at least the Witnesses knock before entering.

'There's too much hanging over your head, and you know it. You'll never work in the City again, you'll get stitched up for running class As, not to mention having a mamzer running round Stoke sporting your chromosomes in a few months' time. You'll have all your family and friends on your case wanting to know what went wrong – I know how it works in the north-west ghetto. You can start again in Israel, and everyone'll think you're just following in the footsteps of the Zionist pioneers. They'll be bursting with naches and not bat an eyelid at you going.'

I slump back into the couch. I'm still screwing about Saul, can't believe how naive I was. Tina's another story, but one that needs fixing just as fast – if these two are really offering what they say they are, I've got precious little choice but to play along.

'Listen, son, I'm telling you, your best bet – your only bet

– is getting on a plane in a fortnight and making a fresh start in Israel. Scores of Jewish boys round the world volunteer for the IDF every year without even needing to get an Israeli passport, and that's all we're asking you to do at first. If you make it through that stage, that's when it'll get interesting for all of us. I'm putting my neck on the line for you, you'll count as my personal project, my discovery, my star signing. But that means total compliance, because I'm not someone you wanna cross once I've done you a favour. I'm offering to do you the biggest favour of your life, and I can see you've already worked out it's the answer to your prayers'

He's got me where he wants me, but I'm still not signing on the dotted line. High-pressure sales tactics are a fucking wind-up, I want to be alone with my thoughts and my NES. What would Mario do?

'Ok, I hear you, I hear you loud and clear. But I need to think, and I can't do that right now for all kinds of reasons . . .'

Nicky holds up a hand. Yuval stares blankly somewhere over my forehead.

'You've got two days, then we'll meet up again. I'll call and tell you where, but don't think this offer lasts longer than forty-eight hours. The more time passes, the less likely it is we can step in on your behalf. Babies grow bigger, cases grow stronger, patience grows thinner, understand?'

Chai, chai, v'kayam. You can see yourselves out.

10

I'm nailed to the cross, all I can do is count down the minutes. It's both a stranger coming to town and a man going on a journey, all wrapped up in one seriously strange package. I'm warming to Nicky's ideas, juices are flowing and synapses are crackling. Too many unanswered questions, but then there always are; I just don't normally step outside my head and look at my life from a wider perspective. For all the madness of their visit, it's hardly breaking news that Mossad are on the prowl in all four corners of the globe. I'm not the first foreigner they've tapped up, nor the first fuck-up they've had on their books. I'd do a bit of background research but they're not the most open of organisations – the internet's just full of hearsay and speculation rather than cold hard facts about their modus operandi. Doesn't matter really, it's not as though I've got any better offers. No point getting on either Tina's or Saul's case for the time being – if Nicky means what he says, they'll be dealt with shortly and sharply without me lifting a finger. Good. Fuck them. Fuck the rest of them as well, in fact, fuck every last face who makes up the facade of the gilt-edged world I live in. If they're gonna judge me for the way I've behaved, then I've got the right to turn the tables. The army should run through this neck of the woods killing everything that moves, it's the only way. Like getting rid of rabies for good, same process with the disease that poisons us all from cradle to grave. It's all a fucking scam. We grow up on a diet of money, yachts, mansions, the works, and we're taught to worship it all like deities. Fuck the creators – the scientists, the thinkers, the artists – all that's sacred are the money men, the scions of the property world, the retail kings, and it's all a fucking con. They're all crooks, but you'd never call them that, would you? No way, mate. They swan into shul, throwing cash at their favourite charities – patrons of the arts, Jewish Care mega-donors, you know the drill. Meanwhile, how did they get rich and stay rich? Dodging tax, becoming exiles in Monaco, shafting the Exchequer, robbing the poor to stay filthy rich – and we clap along and beg for encores. Mafia without the guns, Cali cartels without the product. Nino Browns serving turkeys to the neighbourhood, but with kipas on heads and mezuzahs on the Bishops Avenue gateposts. So fuck it. If the end justifies the means, I'm gonna do it my way as well – and I'll see them all in the front row of Norrice Lea shul on Yom Kippur. I'll be the one with the Xs on my gun and the blood on my hands. Al Chets all round.

I wait at the table flashing a scowl at the world. The world doesn't seem too fussed. Nicky chose the time, let me choose the place. Locatelli at half eight, just him and me, no Yogi

Bear Yuval gawping at the gnocchi to distract us. I could make my way blindfolded from here to the gents: a couple of chicanes past fellow diners, through two doors – one glass, one wooden – and then to the far end of the row of cubicles, where I'll decamp between courses for a dose of off-menu palate-cleanser. I play with my Blackberry half-heartedly, I'm in bored teenager mode – at least that's the image I hope to convey when he gets here. I'm way past second thoughts, I'm on tenth and rising, I'm far from convinced about all this. Following Nicky's yellow brick road to the West Bank and beyond sounds good on paper, but in glorious Technicolor it's a very different story. I don't wanna die for his country, my country – any cunt, in fact – I'd much rather dig in my heels in Hampstead and make it on my own. Nicky's rasping voice bores its way into my eardrum.

'We all know you're a budding Kasparov, but can you play nim?'

I nod sullenly as he takes his place opposite me. He whips out a matchbox and empties its contents on the tablecloth, sets up four rows of matches: one of seven, one of five, one of three, one of one.

'Go on then, you start'

I take four off the top row. He clears out the row of three. I take two more from the top, he takes four from the second line. I can't win. I flash him a sarcastic smile.

'Rack them up again.'

He starts this time, wins again. And again. And again. Doesn't speak other than to tell me to line them back up, barely looks as he flicks matches off the table and into his hand. I redouble my efforts, still lose, retriple them, makes fuck all difference. We keep going. I'm ten-nil down, fifteen-nil. When he hits twenty I give up.

'Ok, great, any other little pub tricks you wanna show me? Can you make a pretty swan out of a beer mat?'

He raises his left eyebrow, cocks his head to the right and stares at me.

'Sore loser, are we? It's only a game, son.'

He's winding me up. I'm not in the mood for this.

'Yeah? So why are we spending the night playing it, then? I've got places to go, even if you don't.'

He remains placid, watches me with beady eyes.

'I'm trying to teach you something, boychik, and trying to learn something about you at the same time.'

'Do you have to talk in riddles? What's the tachlis, O wise one? What lesson was I meant to learn from that five-minute session?'

'First off, there's no skill to nim. It's not chess, it's just a straight memory game. Remember all the combinations for winning and work backwards. I know them, you don't, hence I'll win every time till you've clocked them for yourself. Second, don't repeat your mistakes over and over. After two or three games, you could see I knew what I was doing, so you should have asked yourself why, worked out what I was doing that you couldn't, and changed your game accordingly.'

He's getting a bit carried away, parsing the game like Rashi on Ritalin. I try to care but fail miserably.

'If it took you too long to work out the combinations, you should have stopped playing – found a reason to convince me to quit rather than keep banging your head against a brick wall. It took you twenty games to do that – I'd have kept going to two hundred if you hadn't eventually called time.'

'And? What's the moral of the story, then? How does your wise words work in the big bad world of spy vs spy?'

He leans forward in a flash and grabs my chin in a vice-like clench.

'I don't mind your lip, for now at least, but don't start running your mouth about the work I do. I'm only gonna tell you once, so be very careful what you say, right?'

I nod, then pretend to yawn when he lets go of my face. He's undeterred, keeps going with his matchstick megillah.

'If you make it far enough to work with us, you'll need to remember lessons like this. Never play anything you aren't guaranteed to win, and if you find yourself out of your depth, get the hell away from the situation till you're properly prepared to go back to it.'

Makes sense, I suppose. I shrug out of goodwill, feel my pocket under the table. The wrap's all present and correct. I stand.

'Excuse me, I'll be a minute.'

Nicky nods, picks up the menu and studies it as I head for the toilets. By the time I reach the door I've relegated nim to the back of my mind, can't wait to rack up and calm my nerves. I lean over the cistern and pull out the packet, empty it out onto the porcelain top, gasp in shock as I take stock of what's happened. The entire fucking gram's been swallowed whole, torn from my grasp and drowned in a sea of Vaseline; I've leaped headfirst without looking and paid the ultimate price. The greatest trick the devil ever pulled is smearing a layer of Vaseline over all flat surfaces. There is no viler act of spite. If that's what this place has come to, then fuck my patronage, I'll never set foot in the restaurant or hotel again. I'm short of breath, fuming and fretting and clucking my head off. The gram tells its own sorry story, buried in a see-through tomb as I sob uncontrollably at the graveside. I vainly check my pockets for a back-up wrap, sink to my knees in distress, jump up, barge out and storm back to the table not caring who sees my fury. Nicky clocks it, of course, seems to be enjoying the show.

'Everything ok, son? You look like you've just seen a ghost – get bitten by your fly, did you?'

I breathe heavily, down the glass of Shiraz that's appeared by my knife. I say nothing, wish I could just walk out, bell Steve, pick up and fuck off. Nicky's grinning with unbridled pleasure at my pain.

'That was my second little pub trick, as you so charmingly put it, though I had to prepare it in advance before I joined you at the table.'

What a wanker. I don't care what life lesson he was trying to teach me this time, I've had enough of this. I don't mind being got the better of once in a blue moon, but getting between a man and his powder is a whole different ball game. Nicky revels in my pain, then sets his jaw and points a meaty finger at me like a wide boy Lord Kitchener.

'Just calm down, and drop the brat act. There's plenty more coke where that came from – don't act like a fiend who's just lost the last rock on earth. Here, take this if you're so desperate.'

He flicks another wrap at my chest with a look of pure contempt. I let it drop to my lap and leave it where it lands.

'What we're here to talk about is of infinitely more

importance than you and your grubby little habit, so give me a bit of respect for the next couple of hours. I know you think you're Teflon-coated and just gonna coast through life without a second thought, but past performance is telling another story, isn't it? You're in a parlous state, and this is your only way out.'

He bangs the table for effect, and the couple on the next table practise their synchronised lip-curling routine. Nicky goes from snarling to hissing by way of compromise.

'I want you on a plane within a fortnight – no ifs, no buts. The next draft starts in a month's time, and I want you to spend at least two weeks getting to grips with the country before you're called up. We'll rush through the paperwork, give it all to you on a plate, you just need to resign yourself to the inevitable, and do it quickly and quietly. Or I'll just throw you to the wolves myself, cos I'm ten times worse than you when I don't get my own way.'

I gulp more wine, swallow it down with my pride, nasty aftertaste from both. Nicky puts his Jekyll hat on again.

'Look, it's a gamble for us both, and I wouldn't be taking the risk if I didn't think you had the right qualities. We're not asking you to sign your life away, just to go through the first stage and see how it suits you. If things don't work out, you can turn tail and flee all the way back to where you started, but we both know deep down you don't want that. And if things do work out, you might find for the first time in your life that you're part of something that actually gives you pride, gives you meaning, and gives you purpose day after day, year after year.'

Pep talk over, he gets started on his drink, leans back in his chair and rests his chin on his left fist. I take my cue.

'Ok. But there has to be a hell of a lot of detail, because it's all been smoke and mirrors up to now, and I need much more to go on than that.'

My wish is his command. He spills more beans than a Heinz packer with Parkinson's. By the end of the main course it's clear my life is in his hands. By the end of the meal, my head's in mine. Exit the dragon.

Paranoid, sitting in a deep sweat, thinking: I've got to mip somebody before the weekend.

Done and dusted, in every sense. Bags packed, links severed, house cleared and conscience too. Leave tonight or live and die this way. I'm keeping Daisy in the dark, don't want her to try and talk me out of it, gonna take her to Laura's and leave her outside the front door for her mum to find. They'll both live ever after, hopefully happily on Daisy's part, not overly concerned about Laura's state of mind. Three hours to go, Nicky's on his way over for a final farewell, he's been acting like a doting father ever since I caved in, nice to see someone is. Scroll through my emails, laugh again at my parents' response to my news: 'Proud of you, hope to see you soon.' Buy eight words, get one comma free. Not sure what part of me leaving London, joining the IDF and putting my life on the line they don't understand, or why they've suddenly stopped dictating terms and conditions for my continued bankrolling. Maybe it's me with the comprehension problem. What they lack in interest they make up for in interest-bearing bonds stacked up in my trust fund. Worse things happen at sea.

Nicky rings the doorbell. I throw a book over the line I was racking, jump off the sofa and let him in. Whoever's on reception should have buzzed up to warn me; we pay them double the going peanut rate but still get fucking monkeys for our trouble.

'Boaz says hi, wishes you all the best – you've probably worked out by now he's a sayan – a helper – yeah?'

I haven't, but I nod that I have. Nicky said the other day there are a close to a million sayanim round the world; if Boaz is on the books then k'nayna hora. Can't imagine he's in the thick of the action, given he spends his days staring at a hall of mirrors, but maybe he's working his way up.

'He's been keeping an eye on you for us since Saul's crash, which is why we decided to approach you when we did.'

Yeah, yeah, change the record, Nicky. I've got the point already, I know he wants me to think the way they roped me in is up there with Entebbe, but I really don't care now the deal's been done. Nicky reaches into his rucksack and pulls out a crumpled hemp sack.

'Just one last thing I want you to do for me before you go – you got any newspaper?'

'What for?'

'Just get me some. A lot, in fact'

I go to the kitchen and find yesterday's *Sunday Times*, bring it back to the lounge and put it on the empty bookshelf. Nicky's stroking Daisy with one hand, flattening out the sack with the other.

'This is your last test, I call it the akedah – see where I'm going?'

I snort derisively; he can only mean one thing.

'What do you think I'm gonna do, slit her throat? Give me a break.'

Even as I'm protesting, I realise I don't mean it. He's growing on me, I have to admit. I've got over the ridiculousness of his presence in my life, got to grips with my imminent reincarnation as best I can. Nothing seems out of the ordinary from here on in. Either he's right and I've been perfectly suited to all this for years, or he's a master at the art of brainwashing – whichever it is, forcibly casting Daisy onto a funeral pyre feels of as little consequence as leaving my broken chest of drawers outside for the binmen.

'No, not unless you want to – I thought you'd prefer something a little less messy. Here, take this and I'll lay out the newspaper in case she throws up from the dose.'

He proffers a syringe. I think for half a second and take it. Daisy's looking from me to Nicky and back again, senses something is amiss but she's too shy to ask questions. I'm feeling more indifferent with every passing moment, my mind's already fast-forwarding to the other end of the rainbow, already chalishing for the next chapter to begin. Wonder if Nicky's disappointed or delighted that I'm not putting up a fight, wonder what's missing in my neural wiring that I care so little about each and every bond I have or ever had. Wonder if there's a William Hill at Ben Gurion airport – I'm not letting that old habit die for as long as I can hold out.

'Come here, girl, come and lie down.'

Nicky's a natural, he's got Daisy calm and collected and curled up on the sports section. He beckons me, points to a spot on her thick, muscled neck and guides my hand to an inch above the skin.

'You're on, son, nice and quick, she'll be out like a light.'

Ready, aim, fire. One shot, one kill. *Baruch Dayan Emet.*

PART II

11

It is a country of dark glasses and blood. Home at last.

Got up from the shiva a month ago, I'm still saying Kaddish but the pain's a distant memory. Ashes to ashes, off-white dust to off-white dust. I wander round the base in a euphoric haze, I whistle while I work on my locking and loading and ducking and diving and crawling through thickets and kicking down doors. I'm a bit too happy for my own good, bit too compliant with the officers' orders, but better to grin and bear it than let their sadistic straws break this camel's back. I put up with it eighteen hours a day, seven days a week, I bark like a seal when prompted, I perform like one, too, on demand. The only chink in my armour is at lights out; when the wind whips the canvas and the dark sucks us all in, there are brief moments of doubt but I don't let them breed. Don't listen to the voices, don't let history get any ideas about repeating itself. I fade into six hours of blissful sleep, get up with the lark, aim my gun at its chest and salute the flag. *Amud noach, amud adom*. Mach 3 my head and shoulder my way to the front of the breakfast queue.

And it's one, two, three, what are we fighting for? Don't ask me, I don't give a damn, next stop is Vietnam, or Israel's version at least. The rumour mill's been churning out all kinds of bollocks this week, my favourite being that we'll be thrown into a tent full of tear gas this afternoon to see how long we can last in there. We set off on our latest hike, forty kilometres in five hours. I volunteer to carry one of the stretchers so that I can march at the front of the pack and not get caught amongst the handicapped clowns in the middle. 'Left, right, left' is as alien a concept to them as remembering not to put the lit end of a fag in their mouths, my cheishikometer's still not at a sufficiently high level to put up with them round the clock. We finish the march under clear blue skies, sun shining down benevolently on us, gather round the Mem-Pay's quarters to hear what's next on the schedule. Something isn't quite right, cos Mefaked Dvir can't wipe the smirk off his face and, since his lapdog Yoni is on leave, it can't be because he got his balls licked after breakfast. Even the Mem-Mem is smiling, something he normally saves for news of another Hamas leader getting his head blown off.

As the Mem-Mem talks, I tune out and watch the activity over at the entrance to 705's turf. New York Lenny trudges past, a shadow of his usual ADD self. When he spots me he makes retching noises and mimes throwing up. He's too far away for me to get away with talking to him, so I just nod quizzically and turn back to my unit. People are jabbering away now that the talk is over, so I ask David what the score is. He shakes his head ruefully.

'We've got five minutes to get down to the tent by the firing ranges. And then we get gassed.'

What the fuck? I don't believe they are really gonna do this. It's a bit close to the bone to herd up a bunch of Jewish boys, chuck them into a sealed room and turn on the gas – a bit too 1940s Polish retro for my liking. Why do we need to learn about tear gas the hard way? It's like teaching kids the green cross code by running each one over with a two-ton truck. But no, in their infinite wisdom the army have decided that there's nothing like the real thing to ram the lesson home. So off we traipse, lambs to the slaughter. I get myself a place well back in the line – this is the opposite to mealtimes, everyone wants to be last to get served. As the torture gets underway, I watch with trepidation the transformation that comes over my mates after barely ten seconds in the tent of doom. Natan is up first. Gas mask on, he waltzes in with his standard cocky-slash-Down's perma-grin splashed all over his face. We wait with bated breath. Seconds later, after a flurry of movement at one end of the tent, he bursts out, sans mask, screaming, vomiting and crying worse than a ketamine comedown. He is laughed at and consoled in equal measure; no one knows quite what to do with him other than keep his hands away from his face to stop him making it worse.

As the queue shuffles along, it occurs to me that maybe it won't be that bad. I've ripped my body and mind to shreds for years, I've battered myself harder in a week than this lot have in a lifetime. Fuck it, I'm a tough bastard, I've got nothing to fear. Oppenfuhrer Dvir hands me a gas mask, I slip it over my head. The last thing I see as I'm pushed inside is Vadim flying past me on his way out, clawing at his face like a PCP junkie. I can see the gas canister burning away in the middle of the tent, its plumes of acrid smoke filling the space from top to bottom. I stumble in, where I'm poked and prodded by the Samech Mem-Pay, who's masked up and loving every minute of the pantomime. He drawls through the rubber of his headgear, I stare straight ahead at the toxic cloud.

'On the count of three, take off the mask. One, two . . .'

I rip it off, enter a world of pain. My senses implode, I'm fighting to stay alive. I charge for the doors, but the Samech and Dvir block my path. They throw me back in, I try to smash my way past them again like a wounded bull. Again I'm repelled. Do these cunts know how much pain I'm in? Apparently they do – on my third dash for freedom they part like the Red Sea, I dive through the flaps and out into the fresh air. Which is no fucking better, the breeze on my face only serving to heighten the agony. I throw up repeatedly, David and Amit grab my arms to stop me patting down the fire on my face. I collapse onto the grassy verge where the others lie convalescing, I swear bloody revenge on my tormentors. Then five minutes later it's all over. Pain gone, vision restored, but with a memory that will stay burned on my brain forever. Can't fucking wait till I graduate to gasser from gassee. I think I've fallen in love. Are you watching, Palestine?

Nicky sends me a text, wants me to call him on the secure line during my next cigarette break. Fuck knows what he wants, he checks up on me even more than Laura used to. No point arguing, I dial as I'm told.

'You should be in touch with me more – don't make me have to chase you. I don't want you forgetting why you're here in the first place.'

Don't know how he thinks I'd forget, I live every waking moment with his spectre breathing over my shoulder, and most of my sleeping ones too.

'I know, Nicky, I'm sorry – I've just been getting properly into the routine here, like you told me to. I'm just trying to act like all the rest of the boys here.'

Which is true, up to a point. I'm definitely not trying to emulate the other members of the foreign legion though. The native-born Israelis are all right, they've got their heads screwed on and are just going through the motions of conscription; the Diaspora volunteers on the other hand are a bunch of lunatics. American psychos, South African sociopaths, Mexican militiamen and French fanatics. They bare their fangs when asked why they joined and spit out hate-tipped bullets preaching death to the Arabs and anyone else who stands in the Chosen People's path. My dad missed a trick becoming a shipbroker.

'That may well be the case, but remember your roots, all right? You should act a lot more grateful to me – I got you your money back from Saul, and I set up Tina's miscarriage of justice, didn't I?'

He loves that phrase, thought he was so clever the first through fiftieth time he used it, but it's getting a bit tired now. Inducing her to miscarry was a mechaya, granted, as was sorting out Saul's debt, but even so. Piling pressure on me now when I'm not so much as putting a foot wrong seems a bit harsh, but I suppose even Mossad agents need a bit of love now and then. I tune out of his droning, say what's required, pat my gun on the back and kiss my grenades on both cheeks.

DECEMBER 2007

Night falls over the backwater West Bank village, though it makes no difference to us slumped against the walls of the nagmash. Ten of us crammed into a space not much bigger than a double bed, paying for Amit's poor driving by getting flung around the interior every time we hit a boulder in the road. We share the space with the remains of our lunch, as well as tomorrow's breakfast, but in the heat we'll be lucky if it hasn't decomposed by the time we get round to eating it. The sweat pouring off our heads and down our faces is black with dirt, everyone's tops are stuck fast to their backs. A wet T-shirt contest but without the girls, David looks like being the winner. He resembles a melting snowman, only his sporadic moans stop me thinking he's passed out in the back. Occasionally I muster the energy to stand up and crane my neck towards the small panes of bulletproof glass at the top of the nagmash so I can get my bearings, but it's a waste of time. The windows are too thick to see anything clearly, and what I can make out appears to be yet more and more winding country dirt tracks. We've been through the town centre once, and now seem to be circling the deserted backstreets over and over. Need to keep my mind occupied, but there's nothing doing in the real world. Time for a trip down memory lane, take the long way round to avoid the pile-up on the '06 junction. Not a place or time I wanna revisit, not even just to rubberneck it with the rest of 'em.

I lose myself in a reverie of my top-rated London lays, rewinding the tapes in my mind, replaying the highlights like an erotic *Match of the Day* special. A faint burst of gunfire in the distance snaps me out of my trance, I relegate Tina & co. to the back of my mind and try to focus on the here and now.

The sun's gone down but it's still hot as an Auschwitz oven, plus the roar of the engine shows no sign of abating. We've been stuck in the cauldron for fifteen hours. I couldn't care less by now whether we catch our prey or not, I'm up for calling it a draw and arranging a replay for two weeks' time. Not so our beloved Mem-Mem; he still stands at the front of the nagmash like the figurehead at the bow of a ship, urging Amit to drive ever onwards towards God knows what. The Mem-Mem mans the MAG mounted on the roof, swivelling it in the direction of anyone unfortunate enough to be sharing the cobbled roads with our mini-tank. Eventually we notice that we're slowing down. It sounds like we're now driving off-road, which is usually a sign that the Mem-Mem is looking for a place to park up and rest.

Perking up momentarily, we debate whether this is a five-minute leg-stretching pit stop or the couple of hours' sleep we've been promised. It turns out to be the latter. We pile out of the back door and survey our surroundings. We're in the back garden of a mansion-sized house on a residential backstreet. The owner's family peer at us from the porch with a mixture of bemusement and disgust. We take positions, everyone covering one another, guns loaded, safety catches off. We edge forward towards the house on the Mem-Mem's orders. The squad from the second nagmash are also here, approaching from the other side of the garden, and we are now twenty strong as we descend on the impromptu hotel we're commandeering for the night.

The Mem-Mem delivers curt instructions in Arabic to the family members sitting on chairs on the veranda. From the way they shoot out of their seats it is plain he hasn't gone overboard on the charm. Taking Natan with him, he disappears inside the house and sets about locking the family in the basement, before letting the rest of us in to search the upper floors of the building. Once we declare it clear, we gather in the lounge to receive our orders. We are to guard in pairs, everyone doing twenty-minute shifts over the next four hours while the others sleep. We strip off our shirts, roll them up as pillows, crash out on the tiled floor of the living room. The place is a proper palace compared with some of the shacks we're used to searching. We don't stand on ceremony though, just pass out half-naked and sprawled out all over the floor of the lounge.

Business is business, my dear hosts, sorry for the inconvenience, sorry for keeping you locked up like human shields. We can't sleep in the nagmashes, you see, we'd be sitting targets for any RPG-toting militants who might fancy their chances, and we can't be having that. Hope you don't mind being herded like cattle into your own cellar so that your enemy's troops can grab a few hours' kip – you can always lodge a complaint with the UN by phone or email or maybe even fax. Apologise to your dad for me, can't be easy for the man of the house to suddenly have to kowtow to a gang of IDF soldiers, but *c'est la vie*, that's the way the pita crumbles. And if you look at me like that again, you'll be giving deep throat to a snub-nosed M16, and I'll make fucking sure you swallow. Good night, sleep tight, don't let the sniffer dogs bite.

MARCH 2008

Out on patrol, our radio blares out a call from the 'eye in the sky' camera crew. They direct us to drive to one of the local schools, where kids are lobbing rocks at Jewish cars. That's music to Dvir's ears. He morphs into A-Team mode, rams his magazine into his gun, checks his grenades are in place, gets pumped up for action. A bit strong, given we're gonna be at least ten years older than our opponents, but when in Dvirland, you do as the Dvirs do. We fly through the Bet Jalla backstreets, nearly upending a donkey and cart when we tear round one blind corner. We drive with the back doors of the jeep open, David and I keeping our guns trained on anyone who stares at us too long. David turns to me as we speed along, endorphins sluicing at full pelt through his bloodstream.

'I'm on it, I'm feeling the power, you know? I'm in the zone – and I'm much less scared of being around Palestinians than I used to be.'

No shit, mate. Not surprising seeing as you're in a bulletproof jeep with three other soldiers and enough firepower to turn the whole town into Swiss cheese. Can't see how this clown's going to last the course once we get stuck into the hardcore missions; he's hardly special forces material according to the misguided words that pour out of his mouth and the misaimed bullets that fly out of his gun. We approach the school, park hurriedly on the grass, then alight and split into pairs. David stays with the driver in the jeep. I'm Dvir's zug so wherever he goes, I trail in his wake, Marlboro-coated lungs protesting at the pace we're running at. We round the final corner, where we're met with the sight of fifteen ten-year-olds holding rocks bigger than their heads, which they toss off the side of the hill into the path of the cars below. Their fifty-year-old teacher stands off to one side, supervising them as he puffs languidly on a cigarette. Our appearance doesn't perturb him; when Dvir barks at him in Arabic asking what the kids are doing, he just shrugs insouciantly.

'It's their break time, yani, what do you want from me?'

Dvir is not amused, points his gun at the teacher's chest.

'Get the little fuckers inside, now. You've got thirty seconds.'

Playtime's over, ours is too. We pile back into the jeep, the other three depressed there's been no action, me depressed we haven't had time for a cigarette break. I turn on my iPod and ignore Dvir's debriefing, can't see what there is to talk about given fuck all has happened. Ten minutes pass, we're on the road again, the radio bursts into life, we're ordered back to the school like overworked OFSTED inspectors. The brief this time is to detain a boy spotted in the school grounds who's wanted for a week-old Molotov attack. Our team stays with the same formation as the first half – Dvir and me up front to make the arrest, David and the driver shoring up the defence and gorging themselves on bags of Bamba. This time we're on higher alert, every corner we round we go guns-first, we've got no idea who is lying in wait or where we are going. My senses are heightened like I've been hitting the powder, flashbacks fill my mind to the brim. My pupils are dilated, my heart's pumping, I have to fight back the urge to chat breeze to break the tension.

It's eerily quiet as we round the perimeter of the school. I can just about make out snatches of chanting from an upstairs classroom, but otherwise the only sound is our M16s banging against our bulletproof vests as we run. The eye in the sky girl directs Dvir via his earpiece, we finally find the playground where a football match is taking place – twenty kids in their mid-teens hurtling around the concrete pitch in hot pursuit of a worn-out leather ball. We edge up to the fence. One or two of the players notices us in the background but barely look twice before going back to the game. Finally, Dvir gets word of which boy we want and, after shouting at the kids in Arabic, marches determinedly into their midst and grabs his quarry.

I'm keeping guard at the entrance to the pitch. Something feels wrong here, nothing to do with ethics and everything to do with edginess, an odds-on hunch that we're walking into a trap. The other boys turn their backs on the scene without a word, continue their game, unruffled that one team is now a player down. Dvir manhandles the suspect towards the jeep, we turn left up an alley and stay close to the wall. Dvir's let go of his gun, he's holding the boy's collar with his right fist, his left hand trying to coax the radio back to life. I keep my finger on the trigger and spin my head like Linda Blair in *The Exorcist*, looking frantically for any sign of danger. I don't find a thing, start to relax, see the jeep up ahead, hear a muffled shout, a gate swings open, flash of metal, two pairs of eyes, rush of air, heavy thud at the back of my head, teeth smash together, neck snaps down, chin hits vest, spit fills mouth, all gone slow motion, all gone pear, noise becomes smell becomes taste becomes touch, can't see a thing though, can't run won't run, vertical goes horizontal, day becomes dusk becomes moonless night. Logic and proportion have fallen sloppy dead, the white knight's talking backwards, fuck the red queen though, fuck the light and the dark and the concentric circles, try and fight it, try and hold on, but I'm not here and not now and not long for this world. Speak to myself in semibreves and quavers, sight-read the music but can't hit the keys. Swallowed, sorrowed, I'm with everyone and yet not.

The stitches are out, the fury's still bottled up inside. Dying to get back on the frontline, I've got scores to settle and demons to banish. Soldiers do it, terrorists do it, even educated fleas do it: revenge is a dish best served to complete strangers. Another week of sick leave though, another week of papering over the cracks in my willpower. It's one thing staying clean when I'm busy round the clock and my every move is monitored by a phalanx of superiors, quite another when I'm lying in bed in my Tel Aviv flat, time on my hands and hedonism on my mind. My head looks like a boiled egg after a short, sharp crack from a spoon, the scar spreads across my skull in a pentangle. Temazepam takes the edge off the pain, whisky takes the edge off the temazepam but drags me back to a crossroad I thought I'd never stand at again. I forgot how much I missed my hangovers, forgot the thick, comforting blanket they used to spread over me to keep reality's bitter cold at bay. I take stock, look and listen, wish I hadn't started because now I can't stop. Hate what's bubbling to the surface, hate what I've uncovered under the overturned stone. One year on the wagon and I was looking good, looking like I'd broken into new terrain on my life's point and figure chart. Problem now is it's obvious I'd gapped up, and every gap gets filled in the end (see Centrepoint's client base for details). Sobriety can suck my dick. I don't wanna be left alone to think – wanna be left alone to drink, to snort, to bet, to spiral out of control and back into insanity's loving arms. Want madness to tuck me under its wing, want lunacy to draw me in close to its bosom and let me nestle there forever. Want a meal first though, haven't eaten for close to thirty-six hours. Walk outside into the blistering April heat, turn left on Ben Yehuda and wander south to Allenby. Starting to majorly miss London life, or at least the velvet-lined version I used to live. The minstrel boy to war has gone, but I fucking wish I hadn't. Wish my M3 was parked round the corner, wish my plasma was waiting patiently for me at home. Wish the toughest decision I had to make was whether to chase the whisky with a line or the other way round. Wish the only Arabs I saw were the ones cleaning my flat and washing my car. Wish it'd all be over by Christmas. Sit down heavily at an outdoor table, fuck knows what the restaurant serves, fuck cares either, my engine's been on empty all day and now it's finally given up the ghost. A waitress sidles over, gives me a demure smile, I respond with a blank stare and a plaintive plea for help. My Hebrew vocabulary's been solid ever since army ulpan, my affected Essex accent ruins it though, the girl struggles to decipher any of my opening sentence. I point at a picture on the menu, looks edible enough, easy enough, can't convey strongly enough how little I'm fussed what appears on my plate. Five minutes later and my stomach is trying to punch its way out of my ribs, pummelling on the bars and screaming for attention. I push myself weakly out of my chair, walk inside to hunt for my lunch. A familiar smell smashes me square in the face with a straight right. For a split second I struggle to place it, then the floodgates open as I realise it's the smell of high-grade charlie, and I'm back in my Hampstead hell, and the vision that was planted in my brain still remains. I'm twelve months older but none the fucking wiser. The guilty party is a vat of hummus bubbling away in the corner, the baking soda simultaneously softening the chickpeas and my resolve, its aroma straight out of the scratch'n'sniff version of my tortured autobiography. I snap out of my trance, march back outside, determined not to be dragged over the edge by a cutting agent in chef's clothing. There are two Soviet Union escapees sitting at the next table now, husband and wife, Pinky and Perky, bodies ravaged by communism, minds ravaged by Stoli's cheap and nasty imitators, souls ravaged by the raw deal they got cut when they disembarked in this neck of the woods. The man looks at me with barely concealed envy, he's clocked the Blackberry from the off, plus the iPod, the stuffed wallet, the Bulgari sunglasses, all spread out in front of me on the table, not to mention the diamond stud in my earlobe, the hundred pound flip-flops, the half-a-grand T-shirt and shorts combination, the whole pretty little Western package. He's clocked the snub-nose too, knows not to try anything clever cos bullets speak Russian just as fluently as Arabic. Even *Pravda* readers get the blues. I'd love to help but I've got cravings to crush, hummus to wolf down like a chazer or chazer down like a wolf, don't mind which, just got to get it in me. The next time I look up it's to see who's saying hello, flash a fake grin at a face and try and remember her name, think it's Sharon or Karen or Taryn or something, think I met her last weekend, last month or last year. Just another beck without a cause, without a care in the world or an original thought in her head, got to be friendly cos it's more than my job's worth not to, can't queer my pitch or blow my cover. Part of the deal is I've got to fit in, blend in, mix in with the rest of the aliyah faithful, got to play the game and make the friends and press the flesh and kiss the cheeks and be sugar and spice and all things nice so that no one suspects a thing. It's a tall order, but I'm a fucking pro at pretending. I'm a master manipulator, king con, just read my CV. I jump up and we hug, I shoot the breeze with her, shoot a smile at her mate, *du bist sehr schön*, but we haven't been introduced. They flit away at last, I turn back to my food, try to read the vine leaves but nothing is clear. I watch the girls sashay their way down to the beach, shayna punims both but what a waste of two tongues, should be seen and not heard and so play to their strong suits. Pay for my meal, overtip the waitress, she'll be grateful at first then resentful on reflection, she'll wish we could swap places but she wouldn't if she knew, wouldn't want to spend more than a second in my head, wouldn't want to walk more than a stride in my shoes. Yesterday, all my troubles seemed so far away, but now they're back and badder than ever, now they jeer and they mock and they curse and they cuss. I've run but can't hide, I've found out the hard way. I get back to the flat, drop the gun, grab the Scotch, down half a bottle by ten, send my liver the bill, moving slowly, drinking fast, fading even faster. My M16's far from happy, far from impressed, won't say a word, won't even look at me. We both know I'm sleeping on the couch tonight.

SEPTEMBER 2008

Tension is rising across the West Bank, the natives are restless and baying for blood. We're spending the day reacquainting ourselves with the noble art of grenade throwing; I'm happy as a sandboy and ten times as tough. Night time sees us switch weapons – I'm in the Makach squad but would rather be toting a Negev. We sit on a hilltop and hone our skills, blow up car after car with armour-piercing incendiary tracers, big name for a bullet, even bigger fireball when the target is hit. Dvir turns to me during a lull in proceedings, wants a quiet word away from the others.

'You're being sent to try out for a new unit we're forming, the Mem-Pay thinks you're right for the role.'

I say nothing, listen to the RPGs spitting hell at the heavens, watch the sodium flares parachute their way to the desert floor.

'This is a prestigious promotion, if you get it, that is. Only six of you from the whole mahlaka are being put forward, passing the gibush will mean great things for your combat career.'

I'm all ears, kvelling that they chose me, plutzing that I won't pass. I still walk on eggshells eighteen months on, still don't believe that they haven't seen through my act, that they haven't put two and two together and worked out what I was before. I might have a healthy body now, but my mind's far from healed, at least that's what it looks like from where I'm sitting.

'When's the trial? And how long is the posting for?'

'Next Thursday, it'll go on straight through to Sunday night. Once you're in, you'll be signed on for an extra thirty months kravi duty, plus you'll be committed to between two and three months reserve duty a year once you're demobbed.'

Sounds perfect, sounds like just what I need. I don't trust myself on the outside, don't want to put myself to the test for a long while yet. Weekend leave here and there is one thing, not enough time for the bacchanalian spirits to hitch a ride back to my mind's town centre, but I know as soon as I'm out of my nine-holed boots for good I'll be staring into the abyss again.

'B'seder, I want in, thanks for passing on the message.'

Dvir looks me up and down with pride. He doesn't know a thing about my past, doesn't have a clue about my deal with the devil, doesn't query my cover in the slightest. Like everyone else in the gdud, he thinks I'm as kosher as chopped liver, as heimishe as a plate of tsimmes.

'Good, I already told the Mem-Pay you'd go. Keep it to yourself until after the gibush, you'll be signed out on home leave so the others won't know what you're up to.'

I nod, poker-faced, follow him back to the firing range. We shoot long into the night; we've got a big match tomorrow so every second counts. We put up our tents at five, fall asleep as the first rays of light arrow their way across the plain.

By midday we're aboard a convoy of Safari trucks, Hebron-bound and bang up for it. The briefing is short and sweet, no time for politics, no time for background, just the bare facts and the key details. It's kicking off in refugee camps in Nablus and Tulkarm, sympathy protests are erupting in six other cities as well. Hebron is our beat, we know the layout like the back of our hands, better in fact because our hands are gloved up whenever we're out on patrol. When we arrive, it's a major anticlimax. The old city section resembles a ghost town, boarded-up houses and barricaded shops line the streets like gravestones, the only people on the street are heavily armed Givati soldiers looking bored as they languidly patrol the deserted, dusty main road. We're all craving action, can't believe we've come all this way only to find we've missed it. We grow restless, badgering our commanders for information, eyes darting in every direction looking for the merest hint of trouble.

'Everyone be ready, prayers are almost finished and they'll be leaving the mosque soon.'

Excitement lights up a dozen faces, magazines slam into a dozen assault rifles. We all know the drill – Friday prayers are when the Muslims get whipped into their most frenzied state, when they hear Paradise calling and feel the hate surging through their veins. If they wanna play rough, ok, there are at least fifty little friends they can say hello to spread throughout the four Safaris parked in the square. Our resident frummer Elimelech says his customary prayer for deliverance – needs must, in God he trusts – while the rest of us are happy to rely on Messrs Colt, Browning and Uziel Gal. There are a few Jewish worshippers wandering up near the Cave of Machpela, but they would do well to make themselves scarce like the rest of their flock, the line of fire will encompass every street as far as the eye can see. The imam's voice is still droning over the loudspeakers, we smoke cigarettes behind the trucks and slug from our water bottles. The sun has got his hat on, the Samal's followed suit, helmet strapped on tight, he's always quickest off the blocks, always first into the fray. Doors open in the Muslim side of the Cave, the penitent pour out, pent-up rage etched on every face. They spot us straight away, don't make a move though, they're not going to walk into our trap that easily. Off to one side stand a gaggle of aid workers, milling around the checkpoint like animals at a watering hole. All the species are there: TIPH observers in their royal blue jackets and hats, Christian Peacemaker Team members in trademark red caps, even the lesser-spotted Ecumenical Accompaniers in beige fatigues are present. Fuck them all, if they wanna lay down with dogs, they can wake up with hollow-tipped fleas as well, it's no skin off my nose. Trigger fingers are itching in every direction, the tension mounts, the ball's in the centre circle, kick off's only seconds away.

Yalla, incoming – two rocks land five feet from our line, can't see where the throwers are, but that's of minor importance right now. Shouts erupt behind walls and up alleys, 'Allahu Akbar' the cry of the shabab faithful. Dvir gives us hand signals but he needn't bother, we all know the drill, all know what's coming next. We charge the crowd of scrawny teens in pairs, beginning our assault with a volley of tear gas canisters, but to no avail. It's like the locals have mutated and become immune to our weapons, like mosquitoes in the Sahara morphing into Lariam-resistant clones. The more we fire, the more they mock us, and the more fucked off the Samal becomes. Blessed with a fuse shorter than a baby Uzi's barrel, his way of exorcising his demons involves fusing Palestinian skulls with brick walls to make a dusty, bloody concoction that calms his nerves like Xanax. So it is now, as he grabs two of the slower-moving youths and forcibly introduces them to the outer fence of the checkpoint compound, before hurling them to one side and tearing off in pursuit of more prey. Calev, ever desperate to emulate his hero, delivers a bone-shattering blow to the temple of one of the already dazed boys, who staggers two steps forward before crumpling in a heap by the side of the road. His friend doesn't fare much better, Kobi leaping towards him and kicking him in the chest while emitting his trademark war cry, then bounding off up the street after the Samal.

As I follow a few paces behind in my role as second spotter, I catch the eye of a ten-year-old girl watching the proceedings silently from her first-floor bedroom window. Thumb in her mouth, belying the maturity evident in the pubescent rounding of her chest, she stares dumbly at the sight of the two battered boys – her brothers? her cousins? who fucking cares? – who've felt the full force of the 704th brigade special forces. I point my gun at her head and motion sharply for her to move away from the window frame, the fewer witnesses the better, for us and for them. Rubber bullet rounds are taking out rioters all around me, live fire crackles intermittently at first, then the tempo is upped and it becomes the dominant sound. Keffiyeh-clad youths run for cover wherever they can find it. They're not looking so tough now that our big guns are blazing.

Glass shatters above my head, I don't stop to find out why. I'm running into the souk, burning tyres and piles of rubbish block my path, visibility is down to less than ten feet, smoke billows in every direction. I've shot at least a dozen bullets, all rubber so far, now I reload with live, not taking any chances. Bottles and stones rain down from above, I fire a couple of rounds upwards as I run. No time to line up my sights, I've got my eye on a far bigger prize at the end of the alley. Dvir's bossing things there, he's got three men up against a wall but no support, I sprint full pelt to assist him, Amit ten paces behind me. We run into a thick black cloud, air acrid with fumes, emerge just in time to see Dvir hit the deck as two sharp cracks peal out. One man holsters a pistol, the trio sprint up the passage. No time to think, no time to waste, I drop to one knee, stare down my sights, take out two with neck shots. Gun jams but Amit's on it, he's struck the same pose as me, hits the third in the shoulder. We're back on our feet, running over to Dvir. His face is pure pulp, jaw poking through the mess of pottage. I throw up against a wall, legs weak and resolve even weaker. Amit fares no better, we slump against the metal grille of a bakery then remember where we are and snap out if it sharp. I cover the street while Amit works Dvir's radio through trembling fingers, calls for the medics, tells the segel the score. We scramble back to our feet, let adrenalin do the talking. We get up and do what we've gotta do, don't let the side down, the final score's heavily in the IDF's favour. We're through to the next round, Hebron Athletic are left to regroup and lick their gaping wounds.

12

The funeral seals it, I've never felt so alive. Tears streaming down my cheeks, full magazine jammed into my waistband, red beret perched on my head, I'm finally at peace. War is hell, but it's fuck all compared to life in a vacuum. The bodies crumpled by the graveside are my comrades, my brothers, my flesh and blood, their pain is my pain and mine is theirs. Twenty-three years on the planet and I've finally found a family, I've got kith and kin at last. Dvir may be gone, but there are scores of us left – a community, a kehila, a shell-shocked society. The cemetery heaves with mourners, emotions run high, none higher than mine, mine are scaling Everest, scrambling their way up to the peak to plant a blue and white flag in the snow. I grip my gun tightly to my side, the barrel pressing hard into my thigh as I gather my thoughts. I'm still crying, still loving the sensation, my tear ducts haven't been put into play for going on two years, and even when they last worked they were only in crocodile mode. I vaguely recall breaking down in my flat, must have been connected to coke or the City or Laura or life, but there's no way I'd have mustered even a tenth of the passion I'm feeling now. I break away from the group, walk down the rows of military graves, scanning names and dates and broken-hearted couplets chiselled into the stone, catch sight of my reflection in the opaque glass of the mortuary window. The silhouette of the gunman staring back at me should be a template for the Diaspora, should wake them all from their slumber, should ram home what it means to defend our people from those who rise up to destroy us.

I'm transported back half a decade to Camden Road, sitting in class with an eighth in my blazer. I sleepwalked through the day, marking time until I could dash back to the Suburb and share the spoils with the others. By mid-morning, the weed was burning a hole in my pocket, and I'd taken to pulling out crumbs of the white-haired skunk and surreptitiously chewing on them in class. I was buzzing by the time the lunch bell rang, and after messily munching down the standard chips and beans on offer in the canteen, I retired to the back playground with a couple of friends to watch the clouds go by. We spent ten minutes shooting the breeze, before an abrupt, perceptible chill swept over everyone standing on the cracked asphalt. Phil spoke in an urgent voice, pointing at the fence separating us from the skateboard park next to the school.

'Look, look – who the fuck are they?'

Our eyes were fixed on the two black bodies in black blazers scrambling up the fence, their Holloway Boys uniforms in stark contrast to the hundreds of blue-clad JFS students in attendance. They were flying up the metal wire ('what's a fence to them when they're used to swinging through the trees?' scoffed Phil, who'd have got on famously with my dad, assuming he didn't tell him he was from the NOCD capital of Redbridge, Essex) and the tension was mounting amongst those of us looking on. This was safari park stuff: a herd of gazelles grazing peacefully, their calm suddenly shattered by the arrival on the scene of two predatory lions. Living up to their role, as one the entire student body turned tail and fled as the first of the boys reached the top of the fence and prepared to jump down into the playground, and who were Phil, Max and I to disagree with herd psychology? Arms pumping furiously, we dashed for the safety of the lunch hall with the rest of them, not stopping till we'd barged through the doors and slumped down on the plastic chairs within.

The room was abuzz with breathless speculation and theorising: who were the intruders? Who were they after? What had happened after we'd all made it inside? But the one question no one asked, and which they fucking should have done, was what the hell was wrong with the lot of us? Why, when there were close to five hundred of us in the playground, had we not stood our ground and dealt with the break-in? I mean, our odds were pretty good: two hundred and fifty to one put us in what most pundits would call a fairly strong position. Except, of course, our generation of Jewish youth had been conditioned to see ourselves as physically inferior to the goyim that surrounded us; smarter than them, maybe – though that was debatable in terms of the JFS faithful – but definitely weaker when it came to brawn, and that was a major Achilles heel for us both as individuals and as a community.

As we gathered our thoughts, the smell of fear and overcooked lunch mingling together in the cramped hall, I could see my granddad's face looking on with stern disapproval. A veteran of Cable Street (I had to take him at his word: every East End Jewish male you met over seventy told you they were in the thick of it in Cable Street, even if they were born paralysed from the waist down or spent the first forty years of their life in the Amazon Delta), he'd be disgusted by the current crop of Semitic surrender-merchants. I was too, but since I'd not exactly covered myself in glory either, I was hardly in a position to do much preaching, though it didn't stop me trying.

'Fuck's sake, if I wasn't mashed I'd have done something, I swear.'

I pointed at my blood-red eyes as proof that it was weed that had held me back, rather than my lily-livered approach to conflict resolution. They weren't convinced, Max getting in the first withering retort.

'Yeah, course you would, but calling daddy's PA to send in a couple of bodyguards doesn't really count, you know.'

We stood up to take a tentative look out the window at the deserted playground, which now sported a crude, spray-painted swastika slap bang in the middle of the pitch's centre circle. A strange choice of tag given the interlopers' own Nazi-unfriendly skin tones, but this seemed rather beside the point as the dust settled over the student body.

I believed the hype as much as the next boy or girl. The dark forces of Holloway Boys, Richard of Chichester, and the other schools that flanked us in every direction were, in our eyes, as frightening a prospect as Cossacks were to our cowering Russian predecessors. The walk from the school gates to Kentish Town station every afternoon was approached with trepidation by all, fevered imaginations running wild as to where and when the next assault would come from. In the event, the attacks by the local council flat kids usually took the form of showering us in a hail of pennies, which did far less damage to us than it did to their skint families' Sunny Delight savings funds. As I got slightly older and significantly more lairy, I took to hurling back pound coins just to prove a point. I'd have progressed to fivers and tenners as well, but paper aeroplanes were too much of an effort just to remind the slum-dwellers what they already knew: namely that they were always gonna be at the bottom of the barrel, and we'd always be laughing heartily at them from on high.

As the final lesson of the day drew to a close, the tannoy at the front of the classroom crackled into life, our sombre head of year announcing that we were to assemble in the back playground for a briefing from the local police before heading home. Intrigued, we gathered en masse in the spot where just a few short hours earlier we'd turned tail and fled, as two uniformed policemen prepared to address the coward-filled crowd. Epaulettes bobbing up and down in time with the puffing out of his chest, the more senior of the pair stood up to speak.

'Following the intrusion earlier today, we have decided to increase the level of protection afforded to the school. In order to stay vigilant, we are planning several foot patrols along your routes home – both to Camden Town and Kentish Town stations – and we would ask that you all remain alert and on guard as well, so as to minimise the risk of any unsavoury incidents taking place.'

As the crowd digested his words, two massively built, shaven-headed figures strode into view, marching purposefully towards the policemen, who gave assenting nods before making space for them on the wooden pallets upon which they stood. Both men bore stony-faced expressions, their eyes fixed straight ahead and their mouths pursed into thin-lipped grimaces. They had their hands thrust tightly into the pockets of their cheap bomber jackets, whether to keep warm or restrain themselves from flashing involuntary *sieg heils* it was hard to tell. However, rather than being exchange students from the Tufnell Park chapter of the National Front, it turned out the new arrivals were on our side in the holy war that was about to be waged the length and breadth of Camden. The policeman continued his monotonous discourse.

'I would like to welcome Elliott and Jason. These two gentleman are part of the recently formed Community Security Trust, or CST, who will be assisting both us and you in our campaign to ensure students' safety. Both Elliott and Jason are highly trained in martial arts, and even more importantly they are both experts in the realm of personal protection, and I believe their work on your behalf will prove invaluable in keeping you out of harm's way.'

As soon as they were outed as closet Jews, I became entranced by L+J (as they quickly came to be known by a student body for whom having to pronounce more than one consonant at a time was seen as an intolerable breach of their human rights). Whereas when they first appeared on the stage they'd seemed like any ten-a-penny pair of goyim, now that they'd been properly classified, they became instant objects of fascination. Set against the backdrop of the hundreds-strong crowd of stereotypical weakling Jewish students, L+J stood out like sore, skin-headed thumbs. I couldn't fathom how they'd emerged from the same soil as the rest of us.

The pair quickly became part of the JFS furniture: they strutted up and down the roads by the school like clockwork Golems, the adoration showered upon them by their grey-skirted teenage admirers fanning their feathers on a round-the-clock basis. They had an instant effect on the hate-crime rate, or so our headmistress claimed in her crowing missive to parents at the end of term. 'Since joining forces with the local constabulary and the CST, there has been a dramatic reduction in incidents of attack against JFS students,' she wrote, 'and we are proud to announce significant new measures in our fight to protect those in our care from violence.'

Those significant new measures amounted to an electronic gate being installed in the back playground, a few cameras mounted on poles above the perimeter fence, and a third member of the bonehead brigade being added to the paramilitary force who scowled their way up and down Islip Street and Camden Road as though leading the Israelites out of Egypt. The spray-paint swastika affair had been immortalised in communal legend as no less a catastrophe than Kristallnacht, and the CST's exhortations to sandbag ourselves in and prepare for battle had been swiftly acted upon.

Five years on, and I'm doing my bit. Stalking, walking in my big black boots. Swapped anomie for enemy and now I let my bullets do the talking.

The gibush is a walk in the park, I don't doubt myself for a minute. Only four of us make it – Lucas and Michayel drop out before Shabbat is even over. Ain ma l'asot, I'm not crying for the Argentine or the Israeli. Strip out the dead wood, sign out of 704, salute the flag and swear allegiance to the Black Panthers. That really is the new unit's name, not sure they've quite thought this through but the insignia looks fucking fierce. Arkanovi Tigrovi, IDF-style – same black balaclava chic, same air of extra-judicial entitlement, same all-out antipathy for Muslim militants. We stand in a chet as we swear our allegiance, forty-four faces all as fired up as mine. They're grrrrrrrreat, and so am I, with or without milk, with or without a clue what we're in for.

Thursday night and we're painting the town red, Panthers on the prowl, let loose on Jerusalem's unsuspecting jungle. Gap-year girls are the easiest prey, the tastiest too, they go weak at the sight of a bullpup TAR-21 – I know how they feel, I'm in lust with my gun like never before. We're only the second platoon to get kitted out with Tavors, they're the newest kids on the ballistic block and they're so hip it hurts. We swagger down the streets like we've got the keys to the city, we pretty much do, we make a pretty strong case. Damn, it feels good to be a gangster. The manager at Zolly's knows the score, clears ten outdoor tables as soon as we arrive, he can see our potential through the shekel signs in his eyes. We're strictly banned from drinking when armed, but tonight is different from all other nights, there are no rules and no regulations and no military policeman in the country who'd dare stop the Panthers toasting their good fortune. Lap one begins, I hold my own, neck a Corona and chaser, shiver with pleasure as the drink hits the spot. I'm in control, my foot hovers over the brake, I'll keep pace with the others but stay well under the speed limit. Laps two and three are fine, no veering off the track, steering comfortably clear of the wall of tyres. We laugh, we joke, we sing, some dance, our numbers are swelled by giggling groupies. I take my pick, line her up in my sights: nineteen, New Yorker, no discernible morals so far as I can tell.

'You want to go up the road for a drink on our own?'

That's her, not me. I like her style, like her chest even more. A pair of oversized kneydlach, barely contained by a layer of gossamer more see-through than chicken soup. No need to check the hechsher here. I nod my assent, we wend our way through the maze of yellow-brick alleys to the heaving terrace at Blue Hole. We're under no illusions, our small talk's minute, one Black Russian each and we're off again, quickstep to the park and duck into the bushes. She knows what she's doing, could suck an M33 through a Makach. I come and we go and we're both looking sated. Not sure what she gained from the experience aside from a facial, but I'm not arguing the toss in every sense of the word. Zolly's is mobbed, it's standing room only, my mates are getting restless and they want to move on. I kiss her goodbye, we swap numbers for show. I don't bother pressing save, couldn't even if I wanted to cos I swear she never told me her name. What a little k'nanyna, what an eishet chayil she'll be. Shame there's no word for a female mensch, they should conjure one up just for her and her ilk.

Mike's Place is next – out of the frying pan, into the gap-year fire. Drinks get downed but not by me, doubt's been gnawing at the back of my mind long before the girl started gnawing lower down. Self-preservation and self-control flank my craving like prison guards, I'm in awe of myself but not in a good way. If I won't let myself drink then I might as well call it a night, I'm not the type to get drunk on good times alone. There are too many memories, too many triggers. I either stay and smash myself into oblivion or bow out gracefully and soberly and cab it back to the hotel. I opt for the latter through gritted teeth, the others feign disappointment but they're too wasted to care. I back away despondently, staring green-eyed daggers at the scene; it's straight out of a Hogarth etching but there's no place for me on the page. I've been requisitioned to sit for Cayley Robinson, more's the fucking pity, the drink has worn off now, the disappointment isn't in any hurry to depart. I lie on the still-made double bed, I wrap an arm round my Tavor, I gaze at the ceiling and sigh for effect. For what shall it profit a man if he gains a soul but loses his whole world?

13

My mind's made up, I'm a Panther for life. The training was brutal but that was then and this is now. We've reached the promised land, we're still standing, we're taking the intifada by the scruff of its neck and showing the West Bank who's boss. Hamas wanna party like it's 1939, but not on our watch. An eye for an eye was the old model, now we're subscribing to the One Jewish Fingernail doctrine. Harm so much as a cuticle and the walls come tumbling down: shops, houses, schools, whatever, nothing is sacred when the law needs to be taken into our own hands and the savages tamed. I haven't walked down Civvy Street for a month, but I no more miss Ben Yehuda than I do Baker Street; out of sight, out of mind, out of the equation. Gunpowder is the new fishscale coke, I crave it more and fear it less, I go through gram after gram, get higher and higher, no side effects, no comedowns, no damage done. My Meprolight bathes the world in an emerald glow, I squint and scope and set my sights. I don't wait for Bentley's orders, I just let him have it whenever and wherever and however I can. Of course him can be her can be them can be young can be old can be any shape or size or any colour of the rainbow. I know the drill, know who to aim for, Xs line my gun like a teenager's love letter. I'd rather be dodging bullets here than on the trading floor, especially since Lehman's walls came tumbling down and the City streets became lined with more corpses than could fit in the entire Gaza Strip.

I love my lot and my lot loves me. So do my comrades, commanders and base crew. The only fly in the ointment is Nicky's Middle Eastern emissary. I haven't seen Nicky since I touched down in the country. He's hardly ever in town; this isn't his turf, galut is his beat. Instead I answer to Chana, frecher extraordinaire and fierce as a dragon. Whoever she answers to has clearly told her to give me the iron fist treatment, I take it in stride but it gets a bit tiresome. I've lived up to my side of the bargain ever since I got here, give or take a couple of short-lived bouts of recidivism. She could acknowledge my efforts and cut me some slack. It doesn't really matter though, especially now that I want out of the deal. I'm meeting her this afternoon in the usual spot, a third-floor flat in Malha, selected for its proximity to a military medical centre which provides cover for me travelling to and from the area in between shifts of guard duty.

I arrive early, sit on a wall at the back of the building and bask in the sun. My uniform is filthy, I can't remember the last time I changed it, or the last time I showered. This week has been the hardest yet, but if it was up to me I'd keep going for months. Two old men shuffle past my perch, the shorter of the two gives me an affectionate salute. I salute back with a smile, hold my chin up proudly and stick my tongue behind my top lip. Jerusalem sparkles in the background. I feel like I'm in a psalm but there's no time for that now, Chana strides up the path and I jump down to greet her. We get into the lift, she doesn't look at me, too preoccupied with her blood-red nails to pay me any attention. I inspect my own, the claret on mine didn't come out of a bottle, wonder if I should point that out to Chana, wonder if she'd be as impressed as me or just flash me withering look number seven from her extensive collection. She opens the door to the flat, makes herself at home in the lounge. I follow suit but with far less conviction. I feel nervous, I feel like a naughty schoolboy even though I've been anything but. Chana fixes me with a steely gaze, parts her over-glossed lips.

'We're hearing good things about you from your commanders, it sounds like you've come a long way.'

She means hearing in the loosest possible terms, there is no way she or any of her colleagues have been talking to the segel, more like they've been eavesdropping and snooping in time-honoured fashion. I take it as read, no need to ask for clarification.

'Yeah, I'm really comfortable in the Panthers, and I'm really grateful you let me move out of 704. Thanks again for that.'

Obsequious to a T, bide my time, wait for the right moment to list my demands.

'We're all very satisfied with how you've got on so far. Your psych tests are all coming up clean, your field reports are more than adequate and it looks like you're on track for the next part of your training.'

Keep shtum. Let her talk, let her think I'm letting it all sink in.

'In six weeks' time you'll have done two years of service, which is ample for what we wanted you to learn. We'll be taking you out of the Panthers in due course, probably at the start of June, and we'll cover all the bases to give you an honourable exit from the unit – maybe a fake transfer to military intelligence or a discharge on health grounds, something like that.'

I knew it was coming, doesn't make it any easier to hear though. I sigh theatrically, shift a bit on the sofa, lean forward towards her. I rest my mouth on my knuckles, widen my eyes in dismay, try and look like a cross between *The Thinker* and a model for a male impotence advert. Not sure it's possible to soften Chana up, but I might as well try. Would rather talk to the organ grinder anyway, but the Mizrachi monkey is my only option right now.

'Chana, I need to speak to you about that. I really don't think I'm ready to leave yet. I know what I agreed in London, but I'm not well enough to come out of the army environment yet – I don't think I'm strong enough to stay off the drink and drugs.'

She holds up a hand, her palm demanding my silence. I comply, heart pounding and head grown suddenly heavy.

'Halas, that's enough, this isn't the time or place for your input. I'm telling you what's next on your schedule, not asking for your opinion. Since you've brought it up, I'll tell you that we're no fools, we've given your situation a lot of thought and we know you're ready for phase two, whatever you might think.'

More fool them. I open my mouth to speak, Chana shakes her head sternly, I snap it shut again.

'Off the record, I don't have a clue what's going on in your paranoid skull, but if I were you I'd change your tune immediately. This is happening whether you like it or not, and if you've managed to get this far without fucking up, there's no reason you shouldn't be strong enough to keep going just by willpower alone. And anyway, like I said we're not seeking your advice, you're in our hands and you'll do our bidding as long as we want you to. Barur?'

I nod glumly, already working out my next plan of attack. Appealing for clemency from Chana is utterly futile, but I'm one hundred per cent not giving up my fight to stay in uniform. Surely Nicky would side with me – he knows the score better than this tart and her faceless superiors. For fuck's sake, it's not like I'm not serving the country when I'm in the Panthers – I've found my niche and surely it's to everyone's benefit I stay there. I've got a fortnight to change their minds, I reckon, any longer and they will have already put the wheels in motion to get me released from my unit. I'll let her win this battle, just for the sake of shalom bayit, but I won't be backing down till the war is won. This isn't about ego and pride, this is my life on the line.

14

Two minutes since the shift started, my gun's getting bored. I'm getting bored of my gun and its non-stop moaning, especially cos we're all in the same boat. I'm tired of staring over the rooftops of the refugee camp, I'm fed up of the flickering banks of CCTV. Nothing happens, it's like a morgue in here. I sing a song of sixpence, I eat some of the rye from my pocket, I scan the graffiti on the guard tower wall. Hidden amongst the crude drawings of engorged genitalia and carrot-sized joints is an incongruously intellectual offering in thick marker pen:

Five books for those psychotic enough to join a foreign war:

1. *For Whom the Bell Tolls* (Hemingway) – This is the book you would have written had you been drunk on absinthe and horrifically shell shocked. Oh, wait . . .

2. *The Things They Carried* (Tim O'Brien) – Just so you know how to describe a Vietnamese kid getting his face peeled off.

3. *Homage to Catalonia* (Orwell) – 'Oh, and yeah, once I got shot in the neck.'

4. *Don Juan* (Lord Byron) – The father of all that is holy about running off and enlisting in a foreign war, bedding the local gals, ingesting the local poisons and dying like the local pawns.

5. Owen, Pound, Rosenberg, Graves and the other dead poets of the twenties – In case you want to know what mustard gas did to the Western Front.

It's powerful stuff. I'm intrigued as to who penned it. I'd hazard a guess it wasn't by the same author who scrawled on the opposite windowsill:

Vaginal discharge – delicious and nutritious.

I soon tire of the scribing that adorns the walls like Belshazzar's palace, I need another distraction. I should really make the most of the peace and quiet that complete seclusion in an isolated tower brings, it was for just such R & R that guard duty was created. It's made all the more precious after yet another day pounding the streets of the Al-Aida camp, preaching the law to the locals through the sights of a loaded gun. An hour of hazy half-thoughts does the trick, washing away the stains of the day's violence and purging my mind totally of unwanted memories. Still bored though. I crack my knuckles, I check my watch. It's four in the morning, the pitch black of night is reluctantly giving way to a pre-dawn grey. I gaze out of the camouflage netting at the sleeping town beneath. A cockerel crows hesitantly from the other side of the towering security wall, in the distance a tractor sputters to life in the Gilo olive groves.

I suck languidly on my eighth cigarette of the shift, barely bother to inhale, just go through the motions for lack of anything better to do. The lazy saxophone on 'Ordinary Fool' swirls round the room through the tinny speakers I've rigged up on the table. My eyelids grow heavy as I imagine the bed that awaits me. A flash of light to my right catches my attention momentarily, but as soon as it disappears from view, so does my interest in its source. Then, a second later, it's back again, accompanied by the gentle purr of an engine belonging to a taxi gliding towards my post.

Alert now, I grab the binoculars and focus on the driver, who appears oblivious to the fact that he's right on the edge of a sterile street. All the roads round the base are sterile, meaning that nought but military vehicles are allowed on them, by strictly enforced orders from on high. Thanks to typical jobnik inefficiency, there is no sign warning drivers they are entering a closed military zone, meaning that accidental incursions are a regular – and perilous – occurrence. That said, the unintentional straying always takes place during daylight hours, usually the hire car of a tourist who doesn't realise that not all of Bethlehem's roads lead to Baby Jesus's manger, or a local who forgets that the old short cut through town is no longer the best way to avoid the rush-hour traffic. But this is different: a taxi making a slow but steady approach to the south gates of the base, and mine is the only lookout post with a clear view of his transgression. Not wanting to put a foot wrong during my crusade to stay in the Panthers, I get on the two-way and radio for advice, but all I receive by way of reply is static. No one's taking their nocturnal duties seriously – I'm probably the only guard who hasn't slept their way through the night shift.

The taxi's making firm progress now, it's only fifty metres from the gates. Swallowing hard, I grab my gun and swing it into position, aiming straight for the front window on the driver's side. My heart pulsates audibly against the ceramic plate in my bullet-proof vest; fuck it, this isn't the time for giving the benefit of the doubt. For all I know, the car's full to the brim with Semtex and about to blast the front half of the base sky-high. The driver bears a serene expression as he cruises towards the tall metal grilles in front of him, mouthing silently to himself as he keeps on driving straight ahead. But still I can't bring myself to shoot without consent from higher up the chain of command, and I put out another plaintive call for assistance.

This time the earpiece crackles to life, a faint voice asks me to explain the situation. Speaking in rushed, staccato tones, I describe the scene below the window and ask for immediate orders as to how to respond. The reply is stern and swift.

'Authorisation granted. Fire at will.'

That's all I get, then the radio falls silent, leaving me on my own again. Biting on my lower lip, I steady myself and cock the hammer. As my finger tightens over the trigger, the cockerel crows again, its shrill cry shattering the silence and segueing perfectly into the piercing crack that peals out as I fire a single bullet towards the taxi. Everything freezes, the echo of the shooting rings out on the street, the taste of gunpowder immediately on my tongue as its acrid stench fills my nostrils. I blink once, taking what seems like an eternity to open my eyes again. I don't know what the fuck's wrong with me, I've got a seriously bad feeling about the situation though I can't work out why. The driver's only the latest in a long line of my casualties. I've never cared about a killing yet, they've all been necessary evils to carry out. Maybe it's exhaustion, maybe I'm ill, maybe I'm just stressed about being pulled out of the Panthers – whatever it is, I'm losing the plot. As the dust settles over the blood-drenched scene, my fevered mind begins hurtling down cul-de-sacs where all I can see is me forever branded with the mark of Cain; I see my future, a solitary hell where I stagger under the weight of the shooting like Sisyphus buckling beneath his boulder.

Before I can get swept up any further in the cyclone encircling my mind, the base bursts into life and the post-mortem begins in earnest. First onto the scene is Hevgeny, who stumbles into the guard tower in his bear-like fashion, clawing at his sleep-swollen eyes as he crashes his way over to my post. I stay silent, not trusting myself to speak in the immediate aftermath of what's happened. He sticks his wide, shaven head out of the window, the narrow slits of his eyes contract even further. Incomprehension shrouding his face like a veil, he gradually puts two and two together and realises that the fatal bullet must have come from where he is now standing.

Jumping back as though he'd been shot himself, he roars at me in guttural Russian. He doesn't look particularly angry; if anything it's excitement that propels him on with his tirade, adrenalin quickly putting paid to his previously soporific state. Grabbing my slumped shoulders with his huge hands and shaking me violently, he looks into my eyes for an explanation, finally resorting to stuttering Hebrew to bridge the linguistic divide between us.

'What did you do? Who is he?'

He gesticulates wildly at the body slumped over the taxi's dashboard. I can't reply, don't reply. I'm still in shock, speech eluding me like the spores of a dandelion evading a child's grasp. Try as I might, I can't part my lips to speak, can't utter a sound from the gaping chasm of my mouth. Bright beams light up the still-sunless sky, half-dressed soldiers run to and fro, jabbering wildly and inanely, no clue what they should be doing, but knowing they should do something all the same. Striding through the melee with a steely purpose and a determined grimace, the Mem-Pay barks for the south sentry to check the road for danger before kicking the gates open and heading towards the still-shuddering car. For all that we're used to firing on our foes in the heat of battle, everyone can see that gunning down a driver from an upstairs window is outside the usual parameters of combat, and there'll need to be a damned good reason for taking such drastic action.

The Samal bursts into the room where Hevgeny and I stand, taking two steps towards me and disarming my gun with a deft flick of the wrist, pocketing my magazine in his vest and taking the situation in hand. His radio revs up, orders come flooding thick and fast from the Samech Mem-Pay, who calmly dictates instructions in his Camel-roughened tones. I can barely focus, fatigue and shock combining to pin me to the wall I'm slumped against, head pounding with an intensity that engulfs all my other senses.

I'm on autopilot now, detachedly watching my green-clad commanders swarm around the stricken driver like ants encircling a pigeon's carcass. No one in the unit wants the slaying to become public knowledge – at least, not if it is going to be packaged and disseminated as yet another indiscriminate IDF killing of an innocent Palestinian. A media blackout is swiftly imposed; even the other soldiers in my unit are kept well back from the scene to prevent any chance of loose tongues wagging before the official story can be concocted by the segel.

The internal forensics team roar up in a convoy of APCs within minutes of being called out. The Magad isn't far behind, his driver taking the short cut from the Har Gilo HQ through the still-sleeping town of Bet Jalla. Hevgeny, as acting commander in our lookout team, has been assigned to keep an eye on me while the investigation takes place, which doesn't require much effort on his part. I spend the first few hours staring into the middle distance with a glassy expression fixing my features in place. I answer the barrage of questions in perfunctory fashion, nodding and grunting when necessary, not volunteering any further information, utterly transfixed by my inner turmoil.

The IDF cogs whirr and creak around me as I remain catatonic in the Mem-Pay's portakabin. Once the bomb-disposal team gives the all clear on the car, the measurements are made, the taxi is loaded onto a trailer and moved to a covered corner of the base where it's draped in a thick tarpaulin. The driver's body is long gone, whisked away by army ambulance to a military hospital for storage until his family are located. And then, in the midst of all the confusion and activity, a civilian car pulls up at the gates, is casually ushered in by the Samal, and disgorges its two-man load at the steps of the makeshift office.

A palpable air of apprehension descends over the portakabin, where the Mem-Pay and his Samech have till now been furiously arguing over how best to contain the media storm that is threatening to break at any minute. As soon as the first man steps through the doorway, the two commanders immediately fall silent, before melting away into the weak mid-morning sunshine and leaving me alone with the two strangers. Hevgeny, who'd assumed his chaperoning presence was still required, finds himself persona non grata too, unceremoniously dismissed with a flick of the first man's head.

I'm suddenly wide awake and alert for the first time since the shooting, a mixture of fear and intrigue coursing through my veins and breathing life back into my exhausted body. Hungrily grabbing the cigarette being proffered by the shorter of the two men, I let him light it for me and draw the smoke greedily into my lungs. They sit themselves in the leather chairs behind the Mem-Pay's desk, watching me with an air of amusement as I try to shrink from their gaze and blend into the furniture.

This lasts for thirty seconds, then the first man who entered decides to break the silence. Dressed almost identically to his partner – black, faded jeans, nondescript running shoes and a badly ironed striped shirt – he leans forward in earnest, elbows on the desk propping him up as he stares straight into my eyes. He introduces himself in heavily accented but flawless English.

'I'm Ofer, from the internal investigations branch at the

Kirya. And this is Lior, who, as far as you're concerned, is also a military investigator.'

He raises his thick eyebrows for my benefit, pausing to see if I'll take the bait and question the suspect description of Lior's role. I don't, more because I'm too busy sucking down the cigarette than from fear of reproach for speaking out.

I'm starting to feel a degree of defensiveness. After all, I'd still been following orders, hadn't I? I do everything by the book, just like all the other good little automatons with whom I enlisted. This whole performance is all a bit strong, I reckon, and I decide to stand up for myself and let them know that I'm not about to carry the can for the whole affair. Satisfied that he has my full attention, Ofer announces their intentions in curt Hebrew.

'We're here to lay down the law for you –'

I cut him off in mid-sentence, surprising all three of us with the force of my speech.

'Listen, I don't know who you are, and it doesn't really matter, cos I'm not some renegade soldier who just shot a man for the sake of it.'

I'm spitting blood, words pouring out of me at breakneck speed having been bottled up for so long. Reaching over the table and grabbing my lapel with ease, Lior slaps me across the cheek with his free hand, shocking me into silence, before turning to Ofer and nodding for him to continue. Ofer is only too happy to comply, the gloves now off and his true menace shining brightly through his dilated pupils.

'Listen closely. Lior and I are your fucking judge and jury – and executioners too, if we so desire. As far as everyone out there is concerned, you could either be a national hero or a national disgrace, depending entirely on what emerges from the spokesman's unit when we give them a statement to make in the next few hours. And similarly, what emerges from here depends entirely on what Lior and I want to put out there – so I wouldn't get on the wrong side of us, sergeant, unless you want us to turn you into a pariah who even your grandmother would curse at in the street.'

Suitably chastised and still smarting from the sting of Lior's slap, I breathe heavily and wait for the next barrage of words to spill forth from Ofer's lips.

'I can tell you this: right now it doesn't look good for you. You see a taxi, you don't call out a warning – at least, no one heard you shout to the driver – and now we've got a fucking dead Palestinian on our hands and no motive for his death.'

I swallow hard, my head spinning with the implications of what his cold analysis is spelling out. Lior takes his cue, effortlessly in character as good cop of the duo.

'Or it could be very different indeed. You could turn out to be the last line of defence for a sleeping base that was seconds away from being turned into a fifty-man fireball. Your quick thinking might have saved dozens of families from mourning their children, cut down in the prime of their youth by a murderous bomber with dynamite in his trunk and dreams of Paradise in his mind.'

Back to Ofer, who's snarling for effect.

'The truth is, there is no truth – yet. Obviously, the segel don't wanna look bad, especially given that most of the senior commanders are looking to stay in their jobs for life and don't want this kind of stain on their records, never mind their consciences. But at the same time, the taxi and the driver were totally clean, as far as forensics can tell – the only thing he had on him were three still-warm loaves of bread that he was probably trying to take back to his family for breakfast before they cooled down. As it looks right now, you've just shot a man in cold blood merely for taking a wrong turn in his rush to get home.'

I protest weakly, struggling to convince myself, let alone him or Lior, despite getting a strong feeling I'm being royally set up here.

'But I was given the order to shoot.'

Lior disagrees – *quelle fucking surprise.*

'No, you weren't. We've checked with everyone who was on duty in the radio room at the Gilo base, and none of them had any conversation with you or anyone else for twenty minutes either side of the shooting. So don't fuck around and start trying to pin responsibility on someone else – you took the decision on your own, and if you don't cooperate with us you'll shoulder the blame by yourself as well.'

I reel from this blow as though hit by an uppercut – what the fuck is going on? One thing I'm certain about is that I'd at least waited till I'd been granted clearance before opening fire; if they deny this, and try to set me up as having acted like a lone wolf, then I'm in it up to my neck. Despite my insistence that I'd been ordered to shoot, Lior and Ofer aren't having any of it, going so far as to suggest that I'm hallucinating now, that my overactive imagination threatens to put question marks over the rest of the testimony I've given. Ofer speaks in a cold monotone.

'If I were you, I'd forget about this voice you say you

heard, since you're digging yourself deeper and deeper into a hole you might find you can't get out of in the end.'

As I voice my objection yet again, he abruptly stands up, leans over me and roars.

'There was no order, understand? And if I hear you say once more that there was one, then you're on your own, and you'll regret it for the rest of your fucking life.'

My temples throb harder than ever, and I feel myself slipping away from reality again, visions of the dead man's blood dripping from the shattered car window enveloping me in a crimson veil. Lior notices my retreat into my shell, delivers another, slightly gentler, slap to my face to accompany his instructions.

'Stay conscious, because this is the most vital hour you'll ever go through in your life.'

It turns out that despite their scare tactics, they'd intended to set the whole thing up as a sniper-kills-terrorist incident from the off – but when I find out why, I almost wished they'd just stitched me up for shooting without orders. His voice dropping to a whisper, and fixing me with an even sterner gaze than anything he'd mustered thus far, Lior draws a photo out of his shirt pocket and holds it three inches from my eyes, keeps one eye on the door as he whispers across the desk.

'Don't say his name. You don't need to. All you need to do is clock what's going on here, and fast. The fact that you decided to waste some poor Pali father of six means you've just given him all the rope he needs to hang you with – and, believe me, that's exactly what he's gonna do.'

I can't breathe, the face staring out at me from the black and white passport photo all the proof I need that I'm tangled up in a web from which I'll never escape. Nicky Schwartz – once my saviour from my London nightmare, and now, it seems, forever my Israeli captor. I'd trade all my tomorrows for one single yesterday, but no one's gonna let me off that easy.

15

'Stop being a cunt, just calm down and think rationally.'

Easier said than done, Nicky. It's all right for him, he hasn't got a closet full of skeletons just waiting for any opportunity to retake centre stage. I sit and stare at the two glasses of Glenfiddich. My heart says go, my head says whatever my heart says, the days when it thought for itself seem long gone. It's only been a week since the shooting, but it feels like a lifetime. Nicky picks up his drink, makes a song and dance about swirling it around in the tumbler, sniffs the golden liquid and then downs it in one. He motions for me to pick up mine. I do as I'm told.

'Good. Now neck it, light a fag and listen to me.'

I tip it back, sigh with pleasure, shoulders shiver automatically. Fuck, I've missed this. Nicky refills the glasses, leans back in his chair and looks me dead in the eye. The air in my flat is still and scorching; if June is this bad the next few months are going to be hell.

'If you spend a summer travelling South America in the blazing sunshine, chances are that by the time autumn comes around you'll be sporting a tan several shades darker than when you began your trip.'

He's talking in riddles. He can carry on till dawn for all I care. My whisky makes come-to-bed eyes at me – I think I've pulled.

'But since the change occurs gradually over a period of time, you might well not notice how brown you've become until it's pointed out by a shocked friend when you get home. And that's how it is with you and your bad habits. I don't care what cock and bull story you've used to convince yourself otherwise, I'm telling you how it is from an observer's perspective. You've been clean for two years, you've exceeded everyone's expectations in one of the toughest platoons in the army, and you're on track for great things with us. You've just got to grow up and realise your past is behind you.'

So he says. So Chana says. So the psychiatrist says. So what? They can speculate all they like; they're still wrong. Nicky downs a third shot, not sure if he's showing off or if this is just how he drinks. If the latter, then physician heal thyself. He yawns, lights a Cohiba, carries on speaking in between puffs.

'Look, it's all academic anyway. You're out of the Panthers, you're in bed with us. There's no point looking backwards, just get on with the task at hand. The fact that you don't care about the killing in Bethlehem only reinforces my belief that you're perfect for this job. There are plenty of soldiers who'd have beaten themselves up forever over that kind of situation, but by all accounts you haven't mentioned it once since your head to head with Lior and Ofer'

Fair point, I haven't thought about it since then either. After it became clear the lengths Nicky and his associates would go to just to get me out of uniform, it seemed pretty pointless dwelling on the matter. The shock I felt at the time I now chalk up to panic – it had fuck all to do with remorse for the shooting itself and everything to do with wanting to stay on an even keel in the Panthers. Nicky was never going to let that happen, so I resigned myself to reality and went through the motions.

'We couldn't leave you in the unit any longer. As soon as Chana warned me you were getting too cosy there, I realised we needed to act fast. My main problem with you being in the Panthers was that you were losing one of your most vital characteristics. – I picked you as a candidate because you were a loner and happy to be one, but you were becoming too much of a team player in that environment. I don't want camaraderie to be part of your lexicon, I want you to be an outsider and a one-man band.'

I consider his words as I get started on my next drink, and wonder if he has a point. Back in London, I no more craved friends than I did hooves; I could see their benefit to those leading a different way of life to mine, but there was no place for them in my world. In some ways, that's as true now as it ever was – outside the army, at least – though there is no getting round the fact that I felt differently on base with the rest of the squadron.

'Nicky, that's all well and good, but can't you see that things have changed from when we first met? I mean, part of me thinks our deal shouldn't stand at all. I was a fucking mess back then, I didn't know what I was agreeing to. If a crackhead signed over his house to you for a rock when he was under the influence and clucking for his next hit, that wouldn't stand up in court – it's the same thing here, I reckon.'

My response serves as nothing more than a red rag. Nicky's raging, but he just about holds it in check.

'No, no, no, son, don't start getting clever with me. That's not the direction this conversation's gonna go in, ok? I lived up to my part of the bargain – I got you out of London in one piece, which is far more than you were capable of doing.'

Fair enough, but I've done my bit to repay the favour, and I'm offering to do more – just in the army rather than Mossad. I can't see what all the fuss is about. He can, so on we go.

'I didn't bring you out here and spend all this time and effort on you just to lose you to some fucking combat unit. Any knuckle-dragger can do the army's dirty work on the front line – you're made for something more sophisticated, and you know it. Bottom line is, you're out of the Panthers now, we've made you a fucking hero, you can get laid from here to Herzliya a hundred times on the back of that story, and it's all set up perfectly for part two of the programme'

On his head be it; he can't say I didn't warn him. My tongue lolls out of my mouth – I'm no match for the whisky, time has turned me into a lightweight. Nicky shows no sign of slowing. He reloads again – shot five or six, I'm losing count.

'Before I go, let's just establish what happens next. Training starts on Sunday, so get yourself together over the weekend and be ready to be stuffed full of a serious amount of information come next week. The course lasts eight weeks, and at the same time I want you to follow all of the instructions Chana's given you about becoming part of the

Anglo scene in Tel Aviv. Hit the beaches, join the tennis club, watch the football, drink at all the right bars, make yourself known and make yourself fit in. That's fucking essential, so don't let me down. Forget what you think of them, just play your part. You're an actor, you're in character, you're following a script. No more, no less, so always have that concept in the back of your mind.'

It sounds like the good life in theory, it'll be a Hitchcock nightmare in practise, becks replacing birds but doing just as much damage.

Four weeks down, a lifetime to go. The training is the least of it. If anything, it's the easiest part, the hard graft comes outside office hours. Tel Aviv is teeming with north Londoners, all of whom prove the Suburb is less a physical entity than a state of mind. Welcome to Suburb-on-Sea. Forget the melting-pot ideals of the country's founding fathers, this corner of a foreign field will be forever England, forever insular, forever impenetrable to unwanted intruders. I've got no problem getting in, I've got a golden ticket, I'm a blue-blood beck when I want to be, and right now I want nothing more in the world. See Nicky for details.

I sit in a first-floor flat on Mapu learning the ropes like I'm in a series of children's books. Topsy and Tim hack into suspects' phones, Topsy and Tim remotely access people's computers, Topsy and Tim encrypt sensitive emails and send them to their handlers. Field trips are even more fun, tracking targets without raising suspicion, all the while taking photos, gathering data, mapping movement, learning habits. If I was high calibre as a Panther, I'm setting new levels of quality in my latest incarnation. Everything about the job appeals,

I live and breathe and dream my work, power seeps from my fingers, my eyes, my shoulders, knees and toes. It's all about the power, just like before, nothing has changed but the faces and places. All roads lead to power, the means vary but the end is always the same. Give me a gun, a Bloomberg, a phone tap, whatever – as long as it puts me in the driving seat, I'll grab it with both hands. Working for the same organisation that decapitated Hamas's top bomb-maker via a bomb in his mobile gives me goosebumps. I'm so excited, and I just can't hide it, though I have to do my damnedest to try as soon as I clock out each afternoon.

Back on the street I'm just another London layabout, kicking my heels in the Jewish Costa del Sol. The mark of true decadence is getting blisters from your air-cushioned flip flops – my feet look like bubble wrap so I know I've arrived. I move and I shake and I stretch out on the beach, sipping Corona or soda. I make my presence felt slowly but surely, surround myself with the right people and do the right thing. Simon becomes my right hand man, St John's Wood born and bred, trust fund fed and watered. I'm a year older than him and a lifetime wiser, but I don't let on because I'm not allowed. He's seeing out the summer till he enlists in November – no Panthers for him, he's regular Nahal infantry like the bulk of the olim. He's as nondescript as the rest of the clones, but his looks kill as often as mine, at times even more, so we work well together combing the beach for treasure. He believes my hype, swallows my lies hook, line and sinker, thinks I trade futures from my flat and live off my winnings. He knows about my past from the grapevine back home – they all do in fact, I've been told not to hide it, but they also all know I saved my base from a bombing, and present trumps past in this part of town. Everyone idolises an IDF hero – just how it should be, just how Nicky knew it would be.

Another day, another dollar, another string to my bow. This morning was spent cracking codes with Chana, she's a hundred times nicer now that we're in an exclusive relationship, now that I'm Mossad through and through, in sickness and in health. I've got tennis in an hour. I walk along the beach watching the matkot faithful at the water's edge, slapping their rubber balls back and forth with mind-numbing repetition. Their game is my worst fear – it's like knocking up for all eternity, where winning is the antithesis of the game, there's no money shot, no possible way to exert one's superiority over the other player, no death, no glory. I have to win, plain and simple – four words I've told myself a million times over the years, four words that should be etched across my face in Indian ink, four words that should flash above my head in neon lights warning anyone who strays into my path.

I'm an on-court Goya: bold, luscious strokes, the forced lessons of my childhood finally paying dividends in the yuppie heartland of north Tel Aviv. Today's partner Nicole is more like Botticelli: precise and detailed, conjuring up anatomically impossible arcs from time to time that cost her more in stretched muscles than they do me in lost points. Her boyfriend Josh watches us from the clubhouse. He doesn't know I've been watching him for weeks – nothing personal, Chana just wanted to check my credentials by using him as a template. What I've discovered is hardly earth-shattering, unlikely to set the Middle East alight or derail negotiations between the region's major players. On the other hand, Nicole might be interested to know about his penchant for live chats with Indonesian slappers on inmybed.com, likewise his offline visits to stop-me-and-fuck-one shacks round the back of the old bus station. New muscles are coming through in my back, might be angel wings, probably just the tennis though – this is my ninth set of the week and it's still only Wednesday. We towel off our faces, pack away our racquets, drain our water bottles. Josh wanders over, kisses Nicole on the cheek, shakes my hand firmly like his dad taught him to.

'We're going to meet up with the others at Mash now, it's Spurs–Chelsea so everyone's going to be there – do you want to come with?'

Not really, squire, I fucking hate both teams, hate Mash, hate you, hate your bird too but slightly less, at least she gives me a good game.

'Yeah, why not? I'll just stop at the bookies on the way, might as well have a dog in the fight.'

This country was mis-sold to me in the brochure; I thought gambling was illegal out here, but it turns out where there's a will, there's a government monopoly. The state runs its own book, all competition is banned, the odds are about eight per cent lower than they should be so that the agents can take their cut. I'm not fussed because I only dabble here and there, I'm keeping the betting in as close check as the drinking. Drugs are still but a distant dream, though some day my prince will come, I have no doubts on that front. We leave the club, cross the park, wander up Dizengoff, push our way into Mash. The bar is modelled on an English pub, the punters playing along merrily with the charade. But without the presence of goyim it's a strange experience;

back home, we used to know our place, joining in the chants if they had already begun, but never being so brave as to start them ourselves. Here, though, it's like the lions have been taken out of the Sahara, the gazelles run riot, freed from the mental shackles of worry, aping those whose positions they'd always aspired to occupy. Josh and his cronies are in the thick of it, urging on Tottenham like a *Fiddler on the Roof* supporters' club. Nicole sits at another table with the rest of the football widows, or maybe it's the boys who are the manicure widowers, the girls utterly engrossed in each other's latest treatments, babbling away in indecipherable tongues. I sit between the two groups with one eye on each, speaking when spoken to but not really needing to bother. My body is exhausted from the tennis, my mind is exhausted from the ennui. I've got my work cut out, but it could be worse. At least there's light at the end of the tunnel. Chana says there are plans afoot – I can't wait for her to fill me in. Spurs lose, I win, Josh scowls, I grin, the flock traipses out into the broiling night, each and every one of them living *la vida becka*.

AUGUST 2009

Chana and Nicky. Two for the price of one, I'm in for a treat. He seems to spend more time in Israel than abroad of late, maybe he always did, maybe I'm just not meant to know and not meant to ask questions. He throws me a file, a lascivious smirk plastered across his face.

'Here, you'll like this. A dream debut, I reckon, I'd have snapped it up myself back when I first started.'

I pick up the slim ring-binder, open it to the first page, scan the face staring back at me. Dark haired and pretty, the latter down to a 50:50 split between nature and a rhinoplasty surgeon's nurture. Doe-eyed – can't clock the lineage, looks like a Sephardi trapped in an Ashkenazi's body, light-skinned but more than a hint of Moroccan about the features. I keep flicking through the folder, which is made up mainly of school reports, medical notes, employers' records and sundry hand-written memos on Mossad headed paper. I look up at Nicky, he nods at Chana.

'Her name's Tanya Ben Shushan, she's just turned twenty-one, she arrived in Israel two weeks ago –'

Nicky cuts Chana off in mid-flow, leering as he speaks.

'Straight off the boat, straight off the psychiatrist's couch and all, just the ticket for a control freak like you.'

I give him a look of confusion, he gives me one back. Clearly I'm meant to have joined the dots up already, but I'm not there yet. Chana steps in to bring me up to speed.

'We're doing a bit of matchmaking here, we want you to get together with Tanya and stay together, it's a crucial part of setting up your deep cover.'

I take another look at the photo. I've got no complaints. They could have given me any old hound, I suppose, could even have made me gay if it suited their scheme. I glance at the brief biography, turn to Nicky and speak.

'Why her? She can't be anything special, I can see it in her eyes. There's fuck all going on behind those pupils, she looks like a waxwork.'

Nicky laughs, holds up a second file, taps it with his free hand.

'True, true, she's not the brightest star in the sky, but it's not her we're interested in, it's Ben Shushan the elder we care about. She's daddy's little girl, and the little girl's daddy is a man we've had our eye on for years. His nickname's Shaiko, that's what everyone calls him. He was born here, he's a '67 vet, then left the country in the seventies to make his fortune. He did a bloody good job on that front, he's worth anywhere between two and five hundred million. Lives in Park Lane, cashed up to the eyeballs, proper Mizrachi macher with all the trappings of success.'

I'm all ears, plus a bit of arched eyebrows. Can't see why they'd want me as a male Mata Hari chasing a Jewish target. Nicky reads my mind, fills in the gaps.

'He runs a tight ship, he's got businesses all over the Middle East, most of them set up under holding company umbrellas cos Jews aren't welcomed with open arms in the countries where he operates. The whole thing's run by his nearest and dearest. It's largely family members at the helm, but there's also a fair amount of friends and acquaintances from his childhood. Shipping and construction used to be the main money earners, actually your dad's probably dealt with him somewhere along the line, but don't breathe a word when you speak to him.'

No need to panic, Nicky, our next call's scheduled for ten past hell freezing over. We only communicate through bank transfers these days, and even then there are three or four middlemen making sure our paths never come too close to crossing.

'Shaiko was kosher enough to begin with, probably a few tax dodges and bribes here and there, but certainly nothing to put him anywhere near our radar. Things have changed though, he's linked to all kinds of dodgy cargo, and he's apparently doing business with some of our sworn enemies.'

I wait for specifics; I should know better. Nicky's whetted my appetite with a few crumbs, but I'm far too low down the food chain to be served a three-course meal.

'Anyway, enough about Shaiko, let's get back to your little damsel in distress, which is a pretty spot-on description of her state of mind. She's the youngest of Shaiko's eight kids, and she's definitely the most fucked up. The five sons are all IDB – in daddy's business, Chana, it's a good one to know – and the other two girls were safely married off to Temani boys years ago. Tanya, on the other hand, dropped out of school, then shacked up with some shvartse she met in Antigua when she was eighteen. Three years later, plus at least six figures of handouts from her wallet to his grasping fist, and Shaiko's finally put the boch on the affair. He's shipped her over here and out of harm's way, she's broken-hearted and reeling and ripe for a takeover.'

Chana looks up from her notes, wants to throw her two shekels in.

'What we're talking about here is a seriously big opportunity, for both you and us. If you follow everything you've been taught, you'll have no problem winning her over or maintaining the relationship for as long as we need you to. But you have to realise from the word go that we only get one chance here – her dad's going to be ultra-suspicious of anyone she goes out with, he won't want to see her go through any more heartache. You're our best bet at getting someone inside the family, so don't fuck it up. On the plus side, you've served in the army, which Shaiko will like, and you're Jewish, and you come from good stock.

At the same time, your born-again status only gets you so far, he'll be wary of your past, and there are no guarantees that even if you're with his daughter long term that he'll let an unknown Ashkenazi into the firm.'

Fuck me, they've given this some serious thought – they've mapped out my future like coked-up cartographers.

'Ok, I hear you, it all sounds fine. But what's the timeframe? It sounds like you're locking me in for a lifetime here –'

Chana starts to interrupt. Nicky overrules her and makes his own interjection.

'You're in for as long as we need you in – end of. I've been waiting for years for a chance to get inside Ben Shushan's camp, and finally it's arrived thanks to a gluttonous gibbon up a Caribbean palm tree. Tanya's the perfect way in – she'll think you're her white knight, I'll know you're my Trojan horse. I'm putting a lot of faith in you, maybe too much, in fact, given how green you are, but I need to move now and you're the best match for the job description.'

Nicky stays for another ten minutes, then leaves the two of us to it. Under Chana's watchful eye, I plan out my attack, formulate my strategy, rev up my engine. Heaven help the fool that walks through my door, cos I've decided right now, I'm ready for love.

Getting to Tanya was the easy part. There were only two degrees of separation, thanks to the tight-webbed world we both inhabit. Pulling her was a piece of cake too, she was crying out for a rebound, and I cruised into pole streets ahead of the pack. Stomaching her inanity is another story though; every time we meet or speak she plumbs new depths of ludicrousness. I bite my tongue and stifle my laughter and act like it's normal and keep up the front.

'This place reminds me of a date I went on once in the West End, but I'm having a much better time with you than with him.'

I smile, refill her glass, widen my eyes to encourage her to go on.

'I got out of the date though, because I had a plan with my friend Georgie that she'd call me after an hour to give me an excuse to leave. She always does that for me, she's my escape goat.'

Jesus wept; I have to make do with an internal howl of laughter.

'That friend of Joe's is as dry as doordust.'

I don't want to, but I have to ask.

'What's doordust?'

She gives me a withering look.

'You know, the dust you get on doors.'

I want a night off, a week off, a month off. I want a hundred years of solitude. I'll settle for a quiet café though.

'This restaurant's packed, maybe we should go somewhere else.'

She looks around, shocked by the melee.

'Yeah, you're right – it's so busy, the people are coming and going like pancakes.'

I don't even know where to begin. The ABC would probably be a good place to start.

16

Nobody does it better. Not even close. This ain't bandit country anymore, this is Tsfonbon terrain. Adapt to survive: forget your past, embrace your present, flash a grin at your future. Brand new Raybans locked and loaded, brand new racquet slung low in its holster, brand new balls six-strong in the chamber. Pristine Ellesse zip-up shining brighter than the sun, tennis shorts, tennis socks, tennis shoes, tennis sneer. Tennis stride, tennis stare, tennis state of mind. Duck out the door, down the path, through the gate. Hit the ground running, turn left, right, left. Fix up, look sharp, feel even sharper, strut down Ben Yehuda like a Mulberry model. See and be seen, either will do, but there's a strict selection process on both counts. Don't wanna see the shvartse sweating buckets behind the bistro, not him or his fear or his stress or his pain. Don't wanna know how few peanuts they pay their mop-wielding monkeys, don't wanna think how I look through penury-tinted glasses. Destitution is so last season, underclass chic doesn't cut it round here. Cash is back, bling's the new black, the haves haven't got time for the hordes of have-nots, not when the court's booked for half seven and there are backhand smashes to think about. Stop at the cashpoint, eyes front, don't look down. Don't look at the drunk slow-roasting in the afternoon heat, don't worry about where his next meal will come from, where his last one went, what he finds at the bottom of his blood-stained bottle. Don't read his pathetic sign, don't get bathetic, empathetic, sympathetic or sad. No guilt, no time, no inclination either. Desperately seeking shekels, but this worm ain't for turning. This worm's off to the end of the rainbow, this worm's following the yellow brick road. This worm's a snake on Jacob's ladder, this worm is bound for glory, this worm. I know why the caged worm sings, why the caged worm sees with eyes wide shut. Filter out the waifs and strays, sift out the detritus. No use crying over spilt lives, no point trying to raise the dead. Let the Ministry of Techiat Hamaytim deal with it, let the Department of Rofeh Cholim pick up the slack. Cross on a red at Ben Yehuda/Gordon, fuck the fuming taxi driver and the horse he rode in on. Fuck the two Filipinos on the bench in the alley, fuck their wheelchair-bound charges and their slow-death stares. Spot three becks on the corner of Ben Yehuda/Ben Gurion, waists smaller than their consciences, bee-stung lips, bee-sting tits, B-grade minds and B-list bodies. They know they're not Premier League, but they're angling for promotion, a top-six finish will suffice for this season. They see me and my racquet and my blacked-out eyes, they tense up, eyes scan me like the laser at a checkout till, I return the compliment without flinching, without turning my head. An imperceptible glance from behind the tinted Raybans, an imperceptible frown at the lack of appeal.

A sherut slows down, disgorges its load, the rabble spills out in confused disarray. They blend into the background, all except one. Ben Yehuda/Nordau, darling, what did you expect? A welcoming party, a string quartet? The girls in the beauty salon don't give a damn, they're only here for De Beers, Des Garcons and Lacroix. The boys in the bike shop won't help you either, they're drunk on cocktails of chrome, cologne, and uncut testosterone. I'd love to break stride and lend you a hand, but in reality I wouldn't and couldn't and shouldn't. I've got a one-track mind, I'm astride a one-trick pony. I'm galloping all the way to Rokach and I'm not looking back. Riding to the end of Dizengoff, crossing the bridge over the River Yarkon, passing the boat club, basking in the glow of my city. Drinking the amber nectar dripping from the skyscrapers, scooping up the ambrosia glistening on every over-watered blade of grass. Hell is round the corner, but Mecca's straight ahead and I'm on my third Haj of the week. The other pilgrims are already here, dressed in puritan white, swaying back and forth as they serve, slice and smash their sins to Kingdom Come. Avadim hayinu, but tonight we are free, tonight we are in the promised land, on the promised court, at the promised time. This is our inheritance, this is what Abraham through Herzl through Ram and Erlich swore to us. I fall to my knees, I reach out my hand in supplication. I spray my thighs with the anointing oil, I stretch, bend, massage, twist. She does the same, my faithful chevruta partner. Three steps forward, three steps back, ease into it gently, knock up till we're ready, and then it begins. Two hearts, two minds, two hours, two sets. Six-four to her in the first. Time to turn on the style, put my foot to the floor. Six-one to me in set two, I'm on it like Sonic. I'm radiant, glistening, beaming with pride. Bursting with pleasure, oozing out lust for the here and the now and the serve and the volley. So is she, so are they, and so it should be. Everyone's a winner, at least everyone who matters. The man in the clubhouse matters less than he thinks, the woman in the club shop even less than that. The cab driver home is another rung down, the girl on the bakery till is lucky to even scrape the barrel. Oh well, what to do, out of sight, out of mind, out of luck. Out of the shop, into her block, into the lift, into her palace. Twenty-two floors up, light years away. His and hers showers, his and hers croissants, his and hers solipsism on the beach-facing balcony. Up above the streets and houses, penthouse flying high. If you lived on Easy Street, here are the people you could meet, here are the people who would share the sights, the sounds, the air. The condescension, the arrogance, the grade-A greed. Onto the second terrace, stare down at the city like Zeus from Olympus. Egos inflated, muscles relaxed, mind over matter and gin over tonic and lemon and ice. People on the ground look like ants – sounds like a cliché but it's much more than that. It's a way of life, dear, it's an ideology, a theology, a branch of modern science. It's a way to exist, it's a way to engage, it's a way to come to terms with the highs and the lows. As long as you've got wings, there's no point not flying, no point not soaring and arcing and wheeling. No point pretending that anything's fair. No point running with the hares and hunting with the hounds. Have gun, will travel. Have racquet, will play. Hava negilah, ve'nismecha.

Everyone just wants to tell their story, Tanya doesn't let minor inconveniences like social niceties or self-awareness hold her back. Her past relationships read like the *Jungle Book* cast list, and in under four weeks she's managed to tell me every deathly dull detail of each affair at least three times over. She sees me as her pro bono psychiatrist, and I play the part to perfection. She lies on her white leather sofa, kicking the cushions with her bare feet, sun streaming in from the floor-to-ceiling windows; I lean forward on a matching chair, fingers pressed together, hands slanted to form a pyramid, my nose resting lightly on the peak.

'Some days are good, some are bad – I'll be ok soon, but it's just such a struggle at the moment.'

'Course it is, darling. Pass me a tourniquet, my heart's bleeding to death.

'I know, Tan, I know. You've just got to try and look to the future, not get so caught up in the past, it's not going to do you any good dwelling on it.'

I turn around and flick my cigarette through the open balcony doors. Fly, little one, fly, tell the world of my plight locked up in this ivory tower. Stop complaining, says the cigarette, who told you a calf to be?

'I think I'm getting depressed again, I can feel it coming on. You know, once someone's had a period of depression, they're sixteen per cent more likely to get another spell of it.'

Yeah, and a hundred per cent guaranteed to bang on about it till Moshiach strolls through the door. I gaze beatifically at her, focus on her eyebrows – not her eyes, that's the first rule of Chana Club. Might as well get some practise in.

'Are you gonna see someone about it? Cos maybe you should, I'd hate for you to feel you don't have anyone here who can give you professional advice. There must be loads of English-speaking analysts in Tel Aviv.'

She lifts her right hand to her forehead, covers one eye with her palm. I'm watching the ships roll in, no question I'll still be here to watch them roll away again. This is shaping up to be an all-day appointment.

'I don't know, part of me wants to call my therapist in London, no one else will understand me like he does. This isn't just about what happened with Patrick, it's much bigger than that. I'm scared, you know, scared of where my life is going, scared I don't know what to do with myself, frightened that I'm a failure.'

I slip a hand into my pocket, press the record button on my phone. Chana wants me to build up a collection of intimate exchanges, revelations, insights, anything that can help to profile Tanya, Shaiko and the rest of the family, or be used as leverage in the future if need be. This might be one of those moments, better to be safe than sorry.

'You should give yourself a break, you've only just got to Israel, there's plenty of time to find your feet and discover what you're cut out for.'

She stares at the ceiling, not a hint that she's listening to me, not a hint that she's even breathing. Half a minute passes, planes swoop low over the beach coming in to land at Sde Dov.

'Yeah, maybe you're right.'

She starts to sit up, rising out of her leather coffin like Dracula.

'In fact, you're definitely right. I should put things in perspective, I'm here now, aren't I? I've got over the first hurdle, and I've got to keep going. I feel like I'm on a path.'

I wish she was under one. Not sure what's come over her, I assume it's chemically induced. Must be the Cipramil kicking in; about time it did, she necked them well before breakfast.

'Exactly, that's the way to look at it. What's done is done, and you've got your whole life ahead of you.'

Congratulations, you have used your one millionth banal cliché of the week. You qualify for entry into our prize draw to win a future shackled by golden handcuffs, punctuated solely by meetings with your handlers who will drive you onwards and downwards for months and years to come. I'd tell her to change the record, but she's definitely only got one disc in her collection. She looks around the room, glances at the world outside her window.

'I wish I could be at peace all the time, not just when I'm doing yoga. And even yoga's stressing me out, I can't work out whether Kundalini or Bikram's better for me in the state I'm in.'

Whichever one requires you to wear a straitjacket, I reckon. Not to mention a gag – she bangs on about her spirituality like she's the reincarnation of Buddha himself. More like Zen and the Art of Cuticle Maintenance. She sighs again for effect.

'I do feel much more spiritual here, this positive energy and religion all around me definitely has healing powers. All I know is I was destined to end up in Israel, even if I don't truly understand my mission.'

Don't feel bad, treacle – no one understands your mission. With the best will in the world, the chances of you having even the slightest purpose on this planet are slim to fuck all. You can take the beck out of Hampstead, but don't let's get too carried away with ourselves.

'Shall we head down to the pool? I can't stay in the house any longer, I'll go out of my mind.'

I don't need asking twice. I stop recording. This wasn't the richest of seams to mine, but there'll be plenty more opportunities.

'Sure, but I'm just gonna duck to the shop first, I'll meet you down there, if that's ok.'

She nods distractedly, skips to her room to slip on a bikini. I grab the spare key from its hiding place in the kitchen – it's time I had easier access to the flat. The doormen know me by now, they won't bat an eyelid at me walking in and out of the block on my own. I ride the lift down to the basement, jog through the garage and grab my trunks from the boot of the Alfa. I go back up to her floor, the apartment is locked, she'll be poolside already and nothing will move her once she's in sun-worship stance. I unlock the door, let myself in and head straight for her desk. I whip out the camera, snap each and every paper I find as I rifle through the contents of the drawers. No time to check them now, I'll go through them later at home. Her diary screams for attention – be patient, I'll get to you, I'll give you all the time you deserve. Her hopes and dreams, such as they are, cover every page in a florid, childlike hand, it's gold dust in terms of helping me win her over, it's got the potential to be even more precious to Chana. I've been reading her texts and emails from day one, but this is even better, these are her innermost thoughts, her raw, uncut views on her childhood, her family, and most importantly her dad. I'll present it all to Chana like a teacher's pet brandishing an apple, I'll get at least a gold star for my efforts. I put everything back just as I found it, I'm an expert rummager,

I practise daily in my flat, photographing the before and after versions and checking for any signs of sloppiness. I stuff the camera at the bottom of my rucksack, make my way down to the eighth floor and out onto the terrace. There are only three other people by the pool, alterkakkers all, whiling away their autumn years in Tel Aviv's summer heat. Tanya's got more in common with them than she'd think. I switch my phone off, my mind off, don't need to worry about my conscience, it's been on standby for years, the little red light the only sign that it was ever on at all.

Clucking's goyish, chalishing's Jewish, it might seem like hair splitting, but it's more than just semantics. I'm chalishing hard this week, though I try to pretend I'm not. I try to pretend I'm ok, that I get enough of a buzz from the work to see me through, but it gets tougher with every passing day. I've had enough of being an extra in a Bond film, I want a part in a different movie, Chocolate and the Charlie Factory springs to mind. All the low-level drinking is driving me crazy, it's like endless foreplay without the sex, and watching Tanya munch pills round the clock only rubs salt in the wound. I want to wed my septum and coke together in holy matrimony again. This time I'll do it properly, this time I'll make it work. I've learned from my mistakes.

A five-foot-four hippy opens the peeling wooden door, eyes me suspiciously through a mist of sweet-smelling fumes. The building is decrepit, the house of the rising damp, though my host doesn't seem the slightest bit embarrassed. He carries on staring at me, dots joining up ever so slowly, the light bulb finally flashing on and prompting a lisped opening line.

'Tho you're Thimon's mate, are you?'

I tilt my head, draw languidly on my cigarette. I'd forgotten how tiresome it is going through the motions with wannabe-Scarfaces.

'Yeah, he said you could sort me out – you're Ronen, right?'

He nods once, looks at me gravely. I'm far from impressed. He looks battered, his hand trembles as he pushes open the door and beckons me inside. I follow him in, walk into a wall of second-hand smoke emitted by a motley crew of stoners dotted around the room. As I go to sit down, a PlayStation controller catches me square in the jaw. One of the more compos mentis characters on the couch rasps an apology.

'Sorry, man, I was chucking it to Lidan, you walked in at just the wrong time. You ok? Come, let me see your face.'

Ignoring the opportunity to get a free check up from Doctor Chong, I rub my cheek and turn to Ronen. He takes his cue.

'What you looking for, then? Coke, yeah? Or did you want thomething else?'

I feel like a kid at a pick'n'mix stall, I want a handful from every jar.

'What are you holding?'

He doesn't need to think, now that he's talking shop he sounds much more on point than before.

'Fucking everything, man – K, P, H, E –'

I cut him short before he can finish reciting his dyslexic alphabet.

'Nah, forget it, I just want some charlie, actually'

No point beating around the bush, stick to what I do best.

'How much?'

I pretend to think for a couple of seconds.

'Er, forty grams, if you've got it.'

All eyes turn from the flickering lights of the TV screen to eye up the lairy Londoner who's just asked for ten thousand shekels' worth of product. The same space cadet who a minute earlier had been throwing joysticks at my head now assumes the role of consumer watchdog.

'You fucking joking, man? You can't just ask for that much – we don't even know you.'

Ronen is not amused, wrestles back the reins.

'Thut up, Edan. You therious about the amount, mate?'

I pull out a wad of hundreds in reply, casually handing them over as I sit down on the edge of the sofa.

'Pretty much. I don't have a lot of time either, you know, so if it's a problem just tell me.'

Ronen leans down towards one of the red-eyed members of his executive board and has a hushed conversation. I only want to score so much in one go to prevent having to jump through any more dealers' hoops for a long while to come – this kind of scene is enough to make a smackhead go straight. Once they've finished whispering sweet nothings, Ronen leads me back out of the lounge and up the stairs. We reach a bedroom, which he unlocks with a key from his pocket. Inside, an enormous Rottweiler sits motionless on the mattress by the barred window. As we enter, the dog starts up in alarm, Ronen grabs the beast by the neck, soothes it with lisped words of reassurance, pulls open the cupboard doors. Signalling that I should look away, he punches in the combination to the small safe on the top shelf, swings it open and reaches inside. From the heady aroma of horseradish wafting my way, I can tell he's got the goods. My hunch is confirmed as I peer at the snowball-sized rock he proffers casually in my direction. He's won the first round of our little posing match. I'd thought I seemed pretty big asking for forty Gs, but he's just shown me that I can have half a key without making him blink. He deftly shaves off a chunk with a switchblade, tosses it to me as though chucking a peanut to a squirrel.

'Thee what you think of that.'

Who am I to argue? Like a wine buff getting acquainted with a new Beaujolais, I hold the lump between my thumb and forefinger, sniffing at it inquisitively before scraping some off with my finger and whacking it onto my gums. A heady bouquet, a charming little aftertaste – and it freezes my fucking teeth off. Perfect. I compliment the chef on his fine fare.

'This is sweet, Ronen. You and I could get along, I reckon.'

He grins for a microsecond, then remembers that scowls make him feel tougher than smiles, hustles me out of the bedroom and back down the stairs. My gums are alive with the sound of music, the coke gets absorbed into my bloodstream and drops in on my brain to say hello. They hug, stand back and stare at each other – wow, you haven't changed a bit, neither have you, how long has it been? Take your shoes off, let me put the kettle on, two sugars, thanks, no milk, come sit down at the kitchen table for a good old catch up. I drive the stash back to the flat, do one more line for luck, then shove the rest into a sock, throw the sock into a suitcase, put the suitcase back on top of the wardrobe. That's the rainy day fund. I have to do it right, I have to stay in control. No more second chances, no more final warnings.

I breathe deeply, light a cigarette, fire up the laptop and log into Tanya's Hotmail.

Ten of them sit in a circle on the beach. Waiters hover round the table like flies, they know they're onto a winner. The group is here almost every afternoon, wining and dining and pining for more, desperate to consume, unsure why but doing it all the same. I know the reason, I read the runes a long time ago, it's all about frantically trying to fill the void, but it can't be done, won't be done, not with drink or drugs or mixed doubles or swimming or shopping or Caesar salad. I'm all right, Jack – at least I've got purpose, at least I've got a higher calling. This lot are fucked though. Tanya's the worst of a bad bunch, but the other nine are hardly doing much better. I watch them from the tayelet, dragging my heels, trying to savour every last second of freedom. I sigh, walk down the slope onto the sand, get in character, walk up behind Tanya and plant a kiss on her forehead. She smiles, reaches backwards to rub my neck.

'Hi, babe, I was just telling everyone about the drama this morning.'

I pull up a chair, sit down next to her, dig my feet into the sand, wish I could bury my head there too.

'What drama? Is everything ok?'

Her eyes light up at the chance to retell the story.

'Well, I was just getting up around eleven, and I looked out the window and saw a fire in the Sea Pearl building.'

Her sidekick Lara looks shocked, raises her hands to her cheeks in horror, a strange reaction given she already heard the story less than a minute ago. Tanya stops talking, lets the opening scene sink in for far longer than necessary.

'Nu, so what happened next?'

She leans forward, sips from her wine glass, savours the moment.

'Well, smoke and flames were pouring out of the windows on two floors. I knew I had to get help fast, so I buzzed down to reception and told them to call the fire brigade.'

She's a fucking legend, her exploits should be immortalised in book, film or song for future generations to learn from and emulate. Her acolytes are just as special – not one of them seems to find anything unusual about the story, each and every one would do exactly the same. Lara is full of praise for our conquering hero.

'It's so lucky you were around, it's like it was fate that made you get up late today.'

Not fate, darling, it's about having fuck all else to do, having nowhere to be, no job to perform, no bills to pay, no purpose to fulfil. And no laser treatment till next week because the salon's shut for refurbishment. Tanya has a faraway look in her eyes, blinks at Lara and speaks hesitantly.

'Maybe that's it, maybe it's a sign of something . . . yeah, or . . . hold on, I've lost my train of thought.'

Let's be honest, 'twas barely a carriage, and a burned-out one at that. More food arrives, more fingers lift more knives and forks, more mouths chew more morsels, more time passes, more words are spoken, more heads are nodded, more nails are filed, more sun cream sprayed. I've had more than enough but I've got more than six hours left, more's the fucking pity. Thirty grams in my flat, but I can't touch a single grain – Chana's got me doing drug tests every couple of days. Funny how they started a week after I scored, funny how they must know I'm holding over an ounce but don't say a thing and just leave me to squirm, funny how I'm such a pushover these days that I roll over and play dead and come to heel when they whistle. Almost. I've spotted the gap, I'm exploiting the loophole, I'm still at the counter but I'm scoring over not under. I'm anti anti-depressants, but pro everything else on the shelf. OxyContin and co-codamol are my weapons of choice, they're my starters for ten, twenty or thirty a day, whatever I need, whatever it takes, whatever lets me get out of my head and on with the job in blissful tandem. Waves lap my feet, I lift my feet and rest them in Tanya's lap, she waves to another of her stunt doubles weaving her way along the sand. The sun sets, the gulls cry, my mind sails away.

17

I cradle the phone between my neck and shoulder, I stare out of the window at the row of palms.

'I can't eat chocolate, in fact my kinesiologist says I mustn't eat sugar at all.'

I listen, I don't reply. She sighs.

'And the other thing is my hair, it's falling out. I was getting a blow dry the other day and the hairdresser told me I lose far more than the average person – what do you think that's all about?'

I panic. The question falls square into the gap between straight and rhetorical, I don't want to put a foot wrong. I've been doing so well so far. I make a nondescript noise, which buys time to see what she does next. She waits. I venture a response, one that should leave me on pretty safe ground.

'I'm not sure, maybe you're stressed?'

She's more than happy with that answer, trills back at me.

'Yes – that's exactly what I was thinking.'

I repeat myself, my voice firmer this time.

'It must be the stress.'

Outside, there's a drunk woman berating a drunk man in front of a sober-looking red setter. Or maybe she's berating the dog in front of the man, it's hard to tell from this angle. All three are flailing their limbs and jerking their heads, I can't decipher the body language. Time passes, and she's still talking.

'I'm going to take some painkillers now.'

Don't stop till you finish the bottle, do us both a favour.

'It's so annoying, I've still got this cold a week after it began. I don't feel ill, exactly, more like a strawberry that's going off.'

Once upon a time I'd have stifled a laugh at her mangling of the English language, but I don't find it funny anymore. Not funny amusing, not funny listen-to-you-you-fucking-spastic-twenty-one-and-talking-like-you're-six. Close to a hundred grand spent on her education, all the private tutors and coaches she could eat, and this is the net result. I'm just bored of it all, bored of playing along, bored of playing dumb, bored of playing for time as I plan the next act of our drawn-out drama. I hang up at some point, hopefully around the same time she stops talking, but I can't be sure. I lie on the bed for somewhere between two and four hours, smoking, drinking, blinking, thinking – nothing too taxing. I nurse one of those lazy hangovers, complete with low-level headache, half-hearted dry-mouth, vision that oscillates between being slightly over single and not quite double. The day goes from blue to black. I get up, shower, think about shaving, realise I've already showered and that the chance to attack my stubble has been and gone. Can't remember when I said I'd meet her, nor where I said we'd go, but I'll call her once I'm dressed and coax it out of her without looking like I forgot. Gucci loafers, darkest Diesel jeans, can't decide on a top though. I can see a mohair Moschino sweater that I haven't worn in years, can't remember why I'm boycotting it. I can see that stupid pair of drunks again, I swear they haven't moved from the spot they were rooted to hours ago. The dog's jumped ship though. Now I look closely, I see they sway in time with one another, waists gyrating ghosts of hula hoops past. Fucking idiots. Ignore them, ignore everything, definitely ignore that Moschino top, there's something sinister about it, though what exactly I've no idea. Can't believe I've got no more co-codamol, not because it's beyond the realms of possibility that I necked them all last night, more because I should have bought emergency supplies when I walked past the chemist yesterday afternoon. There's time to go and get some before dinner, but making nice to the stuck-up Arab behind the counter is not an enticing prospect right now, not with the mood I'm in. Come on then, grab a Dior shirt. Any of them. Not that one, actually, don't like the way it hangs over jeans. Blue one instead. Out the door, into a cab. Dinner, wine, whine, moan, doctor-says-this, physio-says-that, I say nothing, just look attentive, hold her hand, feign sympathy, feign interest, feign consciousness. I pay the bill without checking, she tells me to check it. I say no, she says yes, I pretend to do it just to keep her quiet, oh no he didn't, cry the audience, oh yes he did, I shout back. Not sure what I'm meant to check it for. Head lice? Illegal immigrants? Traces of weapons-grade plutonium? If

they wanna rob me, let them. Don't care. Wanna go home.
I hate you all, wish I was dead. Wish I could throw a real
tantrum, but I've got work to do. Back at hers, on the couch,
jeans off, in bed. My head between her legs, her head twisted
to about ten o'clock. She's gazing up, a blissful half-smile
on her lips. Wish I knew how she felt. Wish she knew how
I felt. She whispers hoarsely.

'Why are you so good to me?'

Ah yes, I thought you'd ask that. It's like this, you see. I
go down on you for pretty much the same reason that Pavlov
fed his dogs. No, not because he loved them, but because
he was using them for ulterior motives and needed to keep
them on side. Why do Vodafone give you free texts when
you sign a contract with them? cos they love you? No, they
hate you. They just want your money, and throwing you a
bone now and again guarantees you'll come back for more.
It's a loss leader, like Tesco selling spaghetti hoops for less
than they cost them to buy, just to entice you into the shop.
Licking you out is my version of discount spaghetti hoops.
Simple really. I don't like it, but I do it cos it's worth it in
the grander scheme of things. And don't think I chose this
method by chance, by the way. I know he didn't go down
on you, cos shvarts in general profess to recoil in horror at
the thought of it. In fact, had you listened to my Giggs mixtape
rather than rabbited round the clock to Lara about Lancome's
latest lip glosses, you'd have heard his classic boast 'Don't
go low, I ain't cannibalistic.' A curious choice of words, I
agree, not to mention a curious choice of topic to broach
with his fans, but I digress. Actually, while I'm digressing,
you probably missed that other gem of a lyric where he
purrs 'squeezing your breasts so hard, baby, I might let out

the cancer'. No, I don't think it's in bad taste, I quite like that imagery, as it goes. But where were we? Oh yes, why I'm positioned down here, why I'm so good to you, as you put it. I think I've explained it by now, yes? Brand loyalty, plain and simple. I want you to associate me with pleasure, with giving, with passion, with whatever other clichéd concept you want to ascribe to me just because I'm playing into some *Sex in the City* fantasy of modern love between modern man and modern woman. In the end, I decide not to put it in quite those terms, cos I don't want to spoil the moment. I just opt for a somewhat less wordy and somewhat less truthful response.

'Because, darling, you're so worth it, and I love to make you happy.'

Words to that effect, or something equally sugar-coated. I'm not really listening to myself, I haven't listened to myself all night. It's not like I couldn't do it all in my sleep. A girl like her doesn't require much exertion on the cerebral front. Just suck, kiss, fuck, caress, repeat as required. Then fade to black. Dream, wake, shower, eat. Smoke. Apologise for smoking. Smoke again when she's not looking. Apologise for smoking again when it turns out she was looking. Stare at the sea from the balcony of the penthouse, wish one of us was drowning in it. Ask her if she's ever been on a jet ski. Wonder what she'd look like under a jet ski. Steel myself for another day, another week, another month. Kiss, leave, smoke, smoke, smoke. OxyContin. Nice. Brush the taste of her off my teeth. Co-codamol chaser, bed.

I peer at myself in Tanya's mirrored lift, pseudoephedrine killing me softly. My eyes are retreating back into their shells, my skin's sallow and my shoulders slump. I whip out my emergency box of omega-3, laugh at the packet like I do every time. The maker doth protest too much: 'Mercury-free' ain't such a mechaya, not worth boasting about in such bold type. I down three, I'm not expecting a nes gadol but you never know. The doors open, I step out into the hall, stumble along to her flat and lean on the bell. Her muffled voice makes its way to my cochlea, but my brain can't or won't convert the sounds to words. I try the door, it opens and I enter, she's not in the lounge so she must be in her room. I make my unsteady way to the white leather sofa. She shouts something indistinct, I mumble something indistincter, the sea looks blurred through the balcony window. I go from sitting to slumping to lying flat on my back, she's still out of sight but not out of earshot. She's cooing like a contented pigeon, must be moisturising or hydrating or plucking or preening. I narrow my eyes, widen them again, can feel myself running out of oxygen, try to yawn with intent to supply. Nothing doing, still slipping away, floating like a butterfly, kreyeching like a drowsy bee. She emerges, hair wet, eyes dancing, legs skipping over to the couch. She leans in close to my face, our lips probably graze but it's hard to tell. My senses have absconded, my mind's pulling on its boots and getting ready to run after them. Somewhere thousands of miles away a kettle's switch is flicked. Give me hope, espresso, till the morning comes. A caffeine defibrillation isn't what the doctor would have ordered, but fuck medical science, mine's a double and don't spare the horses. Don't call this a comeback, but it kind of is, I suppose. I'm sitting up, talking, hearing, tasting, touching, breathing again, still can't see the seashells properly on the seashore. She's smoking a joint, a smile spreads like cancer across her face. She offers it to me, I wave it away, we both know I don't touch the stuff, both know it's horses for courses and I'm on the pseudoephedrine circuit this week. Only just discovered it, can't believe I was so slow off the blocks. Wasted all those years, wasted all those tears, could have been slaying my dragons with a methamphetamine sword for the best part of a decade had I known. Still, I'm making up for lost time now, might have another half before dinner if no one objects. She won't, she's away with the fairies, eyes bleeding like a Virgin Mary statue as she smokes the j down to the bitter end. I've turned to liquid, I trickle down the hall in her wake to the lift and the mirrors and the half light, the doorman nods as we pass his desk, I try to nod back but my strings are snapped. I'm bowlegged and bobbing, a newborn calf getting to grips with terra firma. She's not doing much better but then she never is, really. Stoned or stone cold, how she finds her way home without a trail of breadcrumbs is a Hanukah miracle. She flags down a cab, we get in somehow, I say something, he drives us somewhere over or under or near the rainbow. We're sitting at a table, presumably in a restaurant, there are other people near us, eating, drinking, living, dying. A menu comes over to say hello, chaperoned by a waitress who speaks neither rhyme nor reason. I look furtive, but my look's deceptive. I'm not really furtive, I'm happy and I know it and cos I clap my hands they all know it too. Should probably stop clapping, should probably stop swaying, should probably press rewind and not have done that last half. The waitress returns from her travels, nice to see you, to see you nice, only kidding, darling, I can hardly see my hand in front of my face so expecting me to focus on the menu is a bit of a tall order. I want one in Braille, I want a seeing-eye dog, I want doesn't get so we're back to square one. I play with my keys, I wait to see what happens next, I've missed my cue, I've forgotten my lines. She's forgotten hers too, the waitress exits stage left, we're caught in a trap, we can't walk out, because we've taken too much, baby. Merlot appears as if by magic, I drink it as if by mistake, was reaching for the San Pellegrino but my gullet's just as happy for water to turn into wine. Pick a dish, any dish, swirl the balsamic vinegar around in concentric circles, look at her, look past her, look up, down, left, right like a lulav, would love an etrog over easy, would love a good bit of s'chach to shake. She's laughing hysterically, I step up to the plate and strap in for the ride. Tetrahydrocannabinol versus pseudoephedrine sulphate – place your betsm ladies and gentlemen, there can only be one winner. She's streets ahead, tears and mascara pouring down her face, laughter still pealing out from her lipstick-lined belfry. I want to keep up, but I'm fighting a losing battle, I'm not long for this world, not long for this table at any rate. I decamp to the gents, splash my face with water, stare into the mirror and into my soul and the cupboard is bare and I stare a bit longer but there really is nothing there really, just dust and a few ancient cobwebs and what am I doing getting philosophical here when I could be back there and I could drown my sorrows in gnocchi and quattro formaggi sauce and little pieces of food that might be bread or might be red or might be dead or might be a figment of my close-to-retirement imagination. I'm back at the table in theory, in practise I'm somewhere over Jordan swinging low, I'll hear them tape-recorded angels in lifelike stereo. She's still laughing, still trembling, still eating whatever it is that came attached to her plate. It could be a steak, it could be a fish in steak's clothing, it could be so many weird and wonderful things but I wouldn't know because I don't care because food is just fuel and fuck the frills that go with it. I don't mean to sound angry, don't mean to sound bitter, I'm quite happy, as it goes, quite enjoying the stupor, stuporcalifrajilistic but my sorbet tastes atrocious, wanna send it back but don't know where it came from, she's touching my leg under the table so I let her but I don't touch her back cos I can't move my arm or my hand or my fingers, well I could if I tried really hard but I don't have the koach, don't have the cheishik, don't have the time or the inclination though I do have the best will in the world. It's such a great will they'll write sonnets about it, there'll be frescoes and tapestries bearing its image. Where have all the breadsticks gone, long time passing. I say that out loud because it's so big and so clever and so am I. She doesn't think so but she doesn't think so that's hardly a MORI poll, let's ask the waitress. Actually let's not do that at all because the waitress has turned into a woodland creature, she's shrunk to four foot she looks like a Sylvanian figure she's squeaking something at us about coffees then scurries away which scares me and makes the laughing policewoman laugh even harder and everything stays very very still for a very very short moment and then bursts into life again and it's loud and it's hot and it's fun and it's here and it's now and it's never and if I'm not mistaken we're back on her couch in the dark and the pills keep on popping themselves into my mouth and I've got two choices left either one will do so I get up and walk outside and light a cigarette and throw a ten-shekel coin off the balcony and have one of those moments where you're not sure if it's real and then I decide that it isn't but so what if it's not because I'm here anyway and I'm not going away anytime soon and the pills have taken over my mind it's a coup d'état and the military are backing the rebels and I'd better resign before blood flows in the streets. I can still hear Tanya laughing as I fall through the glass.

Money don't matter tonight, maybe it won't tomorrow either, but I'll be lucky to make it to the end of the week with what's left in my wallet. I walk to the bank on Dizengoff, ask for my balance, get a look of raw hate and scorn in return.

'Of course I can't tell you that – your account's in the Ben Yehuda branch, not here.'

What difference does that make? She's acting like she's Ingushetian and I've just asked how the buses are running in Moscow, for fuck's sake. This branch seems to have seceded from the mothership and become an autonomous, lawless region of its own, but I'm not scared, not budging till my pockets are bulging.

'So?'

'So zeh-oo. I can't tell you your balance from this screen'

'Well can I at least take my money out?'

'How much do you want?'

Fuck knows, I still don't have my balance, do I?

'Er, let's try fifty thousand.'

You don't have fifty thousand'

'If you can see that, why can't you just tell me the balance?'

'Because I can't see the balance from here . . .'

Yeah, yeah, didn't mean to set you off again, let's just keep playing lucky dip then.

'Ok, forty-five thousand, then.'

'Nor that.'

'Forty thousand.'

'No.'

The saga continues right down to zero. Something's seriously amiss here, I need answers, but I'm not getting any blood out of this sallow-faced stone. I withdraw semi-graciously, barge back out of the building while I try to work out where my money's gone. I spit at the bank's frosted window, no one sees or cares. This is the most hi-tech country on the planet, its army can shoot a sheikh in his wheelchair in Gaza from a mile up in the air and plant explosive hundreds and thousands on a West Bank militant's 99 Flake, but it's out of the question for two branches of the same bank to possibly share any information. No idea how they became the money laundering capital of the world, they'd be lucky to be the dry cleaning capital of a fucking high street. I stamp my way down to the beach, call Coutts to find out the score. All I get for my time are abject apologies, bowing, scraping, umming and ahhing, no real information, nothing concrete to go on. Nicky's definitely behind this, my account's been frozen. Time my gums were too, I can't deal with this now, my shoulder's still killing after my dive through the French windows. This is no time for sense and sensibility, no time for worrying about consequences, there's no way Tanya will trust me after last night's lunacy, no way she'll see me as a long-term prospect anymore. That's just what I wanted, just what I planned – if I'm of no use to her then I'm of no use to Nicky, not in the here and now and hopefully not ever again. I stride north, I'm going to my ir miklat on the water, pass the Dan, Sheraton, Carlton, Hilton, pass the drones and the clones and their aches and their groans, see that uber-beck Zoe up ahead coming my way, she's wearing her not-quite-ex Guy's clothes as ever, two skewers short of a shwarma. It's one thing her donning them for the walk of shame home, quite another keeping them on all day like a mind-fucked Miss Havisham. I bare my teeth as our paths cross, don't break stride, don't say a word, don't try, don't care, don't give a damn. Not anymore. My work here is done – move along people, there's nothing to see, I'll just keep on truckin' to the park and the port and the paradise lost. Let someone else tie Tanya up in knots, let some other fool fuck her, it was fun for a bit but the shelf life was short. I'm back where I started and it's *plus c'est la meme chose*. This is God's fault, no question, there's no one else here to blame. He'll try and pin it all on me, try and wriggle out of His responsibility, but I'm not buying that for a minute. He spelled it out, scratched *homo fuge* on my retina, so that's what I did, that's how I rolled, that's why I ended up halfway round the world. I did my bit, and just look at me now. I hit the port running, stumbling, tripping, ocean spray stinging my eyes, bottle of soda chafing my leg through my shorts. I duck through a hole in the fence, jog past the crane, dodge the flakes of rust drifting down from its decaying frame, scramble onto the sea wall and weave my way west. I'm the only one here, nobody's fishing today, not with the waves this high and the clouds this low. I stare straight ahead, eyes honed on the stone hut at the end of the jetty, there's nowhere else I'd rather be, nothing else I'd rather see. Water crashes up over the crumbling concrete, I reach the doorway, step inside, get used to the gloom. A chessboard sits in the corner, a scribbled note on top, held down by a rook. 'Your move, snail' in thick black marker, white's already played, e2–e4, is this the real life, is this just fantasy, I spin around, stare back to shore, spin around again, stare at the board, stare at the wall, stare at the sea, stare at the sun, stare at my Blackberry as it shrieks in my hand, press the green button, clamp the phone to my ear, Nicky is speaking and shouting and screaming, I can see what you're doing, it's not gonna wash, we gave you twenty-four months, there's no going back, if you want to make God laugh, tell Him your plans, if you want to make me laugh, tell me you're quitting, I own you outright and you're not going anywhere. He pauses, I'm silent, wish I could talk but I can't, he lets fly again, blue murder's the colour scheme, I press red, step forward, fling the phone into the waves, run back along the wall, don't care if I make it, too late in the day, too long in the tooth, too young to die but the odds are getting slashed by the second, hit dry land, hit the car park, hit the main road, hit for six, dragged into a van, hammer cocked, gun to my throat, duct tape on my eyes, try to remember what the dormouse said, easier said than done, easier then than now, a rising tide lifts all ships except mine, I'm taking on water, manning the lifeboats, sending out maydays but no one replies, I dreamed I saw Joe Hill last night, now I only see stars, comets, deepest darkest black. *Der derech hayosher iz alleh mol kosher.*

PART III

18

With St George in my heart keep me English. Someone presses a slice of onion into my left hand, I clutch my pen with my right.

With St George in my heart I pray. Faces harden, fists clench. Bitter scowls, narrowed eyes, jutting chins, puffed-out chests.

With St George in my heart keep me English. A surge of anger, a common goal. Lines start forming, feet start marching.

No surrender to the IRA. Flags fly, banners wave, fingers point, knuckles crack.

No surrender, no surrender, no surrender to the IRA . . . Drums beat, voices scream, children run, adults roar.

Jack and Jill go up the hill like lambs to the fucking slaughter, as do Abdullah and Ahmed and the rest of the wannabe-martyrs brigade. I hate Jack and Jill the most, but it's a close call. I'm not here to hate, anyway, at least not my fellow marchers. Not my fellow Palestinians – 'We are all Palestinian now', can't you hear the loudhailer? – not my fellow journalists either, and they're out in droves on a day like this. Last week's demonstration left three villagers dead and over fifty wounded, so it's gonna be on like Donkey Kong today if the hype's to be believed. The Magav border policemen believe the hype, they're no fools even if they look it, knuckles scraping on the dusty path behind the coils of razor wire and electric fence. As we wind our way up the hillside I can read the soldiers' faces: up, down, turn around, kick a Palestinian, that's what they're trained for, that's what they're here for, that's what they're up for, as usual, as ever. Fucking wish I was on their side – literally as well as figuratively. Eye their M16s with envy, lust after their grenade launchers, chalish for their clips of rubber bullets and live rounds. Bet they don't feel the same way about my onion. Lucky bastards. Can't let it show, not even a flicker. I'm a face and a name and fame comes at a price. People know who I am and they all wanna word, foreigners mostly but a few home-growns too.

'Ahlan, I am Hamed, I can help you for your article. You want for me to introduce you to the Resistance Committee leader?'

He's panting as he speaks, eyes darting over the horizon, adrenalin pumping its way round his skinny frame. Mid-twenties, badly shaved head, keffiyeh knotted round his neck, pinched faced screwed up in mock horror for the cameras. We're on the catwalk now, it's all about the pout, all about the anguished features of the poor little townsfolk, the travesty, the injustice, the helpless, hapless Davids getting gunned by Goliath.

'Maybe in a minute, thanks, I'm just taking in the atmosphere for now. Here, here's my card, my mobile's at the bottom, call me later when things calm down and we can sit and chat.'

The embossed *Guardian* logo is my backstage pass, it's my ticket to ride, my keys to every Palestinian city across the West Bank. Ten months on the job and I'm as A-list as it gets.

'Shukran, I do that, for sure. Yalla, habibti, stay safe, use the onion when the gas come, and tell the world what these dogs doing to us.'

Yeah, mate, no worries. You can count on me, chief. I flash him a peace sign, he jogs up ahead, we're a hundred metres from the fence, the tension mounts. Masks cover faces, slingshots appear in teenagers' hands. Still we march forward, still Magav hold fire. Smiling broadly like jackals, making no sudden moves, the first rows of protesters walk up to the soldiers and sing their songs with gusto. The soldiers beam beatifically back, watching with expressions of benevolence and amusement. Some Israeli activist-cum-traitor takes up a prominent position at the front, smugly preaching his message to the troops a foot away from him. The press pack stand on the ridge above, filming and photographing, enjoying the show. I keep my place among the commoners; I'm a new breed of journalist, I'm meant to be hands-on and knee-deep and one of the people. It's what the *Guardian* wants, and far more importantly it's what Nicky demands.

The calm's getting boring. Everyone wants a storm, pantomimes are meant to be far more crowd-pleasing than this. A burly Palestinian scrambles up on the gate by the fence and walks across it like a tightrope, the onlookers cheer. As he attempts to repeat the trick the other way, a Magavnik gives him a shove, sending him tumbling down to the ground. Immediately, another Arab cracks a heavy blow to the soldier's arm with a wooden club. In the same instant, a hail of rocks flies towards the rest of the troops behind the gate. Act two begins – he's behind you! Or behind that olive tree, anyway, and that one, and that! Shoot to kill, boys – I'm with you in spirit, ignore where I'm standing. They don't let me down. We turn tail and flee, the sound of tear gas and stun grenades ringing in our ears. Plumes of smoke criss-cross the sky, youths gather on the path below, hurling projectiles from their slingshots, drawing a hail of bullets in return. Blood starts flowing, medics don't know where to begin. Red Crescent ambulances bounce along the rocky grass, stretcher-bearers double as pall-bearers, it's take-no-prisoners day at the zoo. I can see through a girl's skull, bits of grey matter peeking out, wails encircle her limp body, tear gas encircles the wailers. Cries of 'murderers' go up, then get silenced by another wave of live fire. Fuck this, I'm not staying here, I go into Bambi-mode and prance my way to freedom. Look like a mug as I tear off in my press-issue flak jacket but that's the whole point when in Rome, got to imitate and emulate and concentrate on fitting in. I'm winning this lot's trust, but it's not as easy as I thought – it's taken months to convince them I've truly switched sides. Being ex-IDF raises more than just eyebrows, there've been plenty \tof fists and occasional veiled threats of more, but Chana taught me how to counter it, and I'm earning trust by the day. Clutch the onion to my nostrils, hurtle blindly through the fog. More screams behind me, more pleas to Allah up ahead. A commander's voice booms over a speaker, orders everyone back, gives us to the count of ten, then they're coming to get us. Hide and Seek meets Grandmother's Footsteps meets a real-life, real-time, bite-sized intifada. We keep running, so do the others, the playground suddenly empty.

We take shelter in a village backstreet. A gaggle of teenage boys appears, eager to show off their scars. One rolls up his torn trouser leg to reveal a badly gashed calf and a jagged wound just above the ankle, blood filling his cheap trainer as he dashes round in a zigzag. A crowd of sycophantic dreadlocks immediately engulfs him, the activist foreign legion latching onto their latest pet Pali, kneeling round him in distress like he was Christ on the cross. Digital cameras capture his pain, their compassion, the town's struggle, the Zionists' evil. I elbow my way through the throng, ask questions, feign concern, take notes. Heavy stress on the notes – I'm doing two jobs for the price of one.

The army's final flourish is a choreographed shower of gas grenades, as perfectly staged as an Olympic fireworks display. All that's missing is a neon sign flashing 'Better luck next time, Bil'in.' They've done me proud. Now it's my turn.

Shira grips the steering wheel with both hands, cigarette clenched between her front teeth, smoking furiously, driving lividly. She veers across lanes as we race towards Tel Aviv, cutting in, cutting up, cutting out again for more. I pretend to scan my notepad, chewing thoughtfully on my pen as I flick through the pages. The car's scorching, hot wind blasting in through the open windows. The air conditioning's off, in a nod to either her penury or her eco-politics. Sweat gathers in beads, rolls down my cheeks and drips onto my T-shirt. Tears trace a similar route down her face.

'It never ends, it never, ever ends. It never will, and we'll just keep losing more and more comrades to their bullets.'

I sigh, shift uncomfortably in my seat, skin sticking painfully to the ageing black leather.

'And look around us, look at all these people, they couldn't give a damn, they just buzz up and down the highway totally blind to what's happening. I hate them all, I hate this whole fucked-up place.'

She makes a broad sweeping gesture like a windscreen wiper, damning her country and countrymen as far as the eye can see. I sigh again, clear my throat, get ready to speak, get ready to soothe, get ready to sympathise.

'I know, I know, it's their ignorance that allows shit like today to happen. People would be up in arms if they knew what really went on just a few miles from their home.'

They wouldn't, of course, I'm just teeing her up so she can let fly again. She doesn't disappoint, her voice now a screech of helpless rage.

'That's just it, though – even if they did find out, they'd just carry on as before, because what do they care about a few smashed Palestinian skulls? What do they care as long as their coffee shops in Basel aren't blowing up, what do they care as long as they can still smear themselves in oil and fry on the beach all day?'

I cock my head to one side, make like I'm mulling over her words. I yawn on the inside, on the outside I burst into life.

'Well, that's it then, isn't it? The Palestinians should bring the struggle back to the Israeli streets, shouldn't they?

Nothing else is gonna get any results, and the status quo's hardly doing them any favours.'

She glances at me, then back to the road, spitting her cigarette out the window in a polished motion. I check myself – don't get too carried away, she knows your background and she's definitely not convinced by the act yet. Hers is the worst type, the domestic dissidents, the ones who've rejected their heritage and work twice as hard proving their commitment to their newfound cause. Insanely suspicious, they think everyone's undercover: their partners, family, friends, acquaintances, old, young, rich, poor, black, white, red, blue. They think their phones are tapped, their email's hacked, their offices are bugged and their houses watched. Self-important little Malcolm Xs to a man (and a woman). Still, just because you're paranoid, don't mean they're not after you, or sitting next to you on the drive home, or slipping a tiny recording device into a crevice down the side of the seat.

'Look, they're entitled to do whatever they want to throw off the occupation, so if they start attacks again in the cities then we have no right to tell them not to. But I think they respect civilian life too much for that – it's the Israelis who don't value life, more's the pity. If someone gave me a gun, I'd shoot a soldier after what we saw today.'

I don't respond to her fighting talk, to her rank hypocrisy, to her arguments boasting more holes than a slab of Emmental. According to the script I'm meant to keep shtum. I chew a fingernail, then another, think about a third but opt for a cigarette instead. I'd love to fuck her for research purposes, would love to know whether she drops the act when she's juiced up and otherwise engaged. She's worth a go looks-wise too, but only if she was dipped in disinfectant first. Matted hair, dirt under her nails, never been within a mile of mascara. The Magav water cannon is probably the only shower she's had this month. Pointless train of thought anyway, the only dick she'd suck would have a PLO tattoo on its shaft. I jot down a note as she rabbits on.

'You know, you've got a lot of power to tell the Palestinians' story to a whole new audience, especially because you used to be in the IOF.'

IOF, how terribly right-on, sister. O for occupation, not D for defence. Bet if she had twins she'd call them Sabra and Shatila. I wait for her to continue, subtly trying to ash on the dashboard.

'Even though I think it's indefensible to serve in the army, you can start to make amends if you keep writing like you have been. Especially because people on the right can't dismiss an ex-soldier in quite the same way they do someone like me.'

They don't dismiss you because you're a radical, they dismiss you because you're wrong. They dismiss you because you're a useful idiot, because you provide cover to terrorists and succour to savages. You'd be up against the wall and shot with the rest of us if your precious Palestinians ever did manage to realise their dream. I keep listening, keep ashing.

'There are some people I can introduce you to if you want to do an article about our group, but I'll be honest, they might be a bit wary of speaking to you, because of your past. I am too, though having met you today I'm less apprehensive than before.'

Praise from Caesar, or Leila Khaled at least. A military

jeep speeds past, Shira flicks it the finger. Stupid little one-state pony.

'Thanks, I'd love that, if you can. And I know what you mean about them being suspicious, but I can only be honest with them, and hope they take me at face value.'

My phone rings. It's got to be Chana. I'm due at hers in an hour for the debrief, plus there's an article to write and she's a harsh taskmaster. I hit the clear button, turn back to Shira and arc another stream of lies her way.

'Sorry, that was my editor at the *Guardian*, I'll call her back. I'm doing an op-ed on the march for tomorrow's paper. I'm gonna hammer the army for what I saw – whatever missiles the shabab were throwing, there's no excuse for that kind of carnage. I think there'll be a feature on it in the news pages too, because the correspondent was there today as well and she's usually great with those kind of stories.'

Shira grimaces; not a good look.

'Well, I hope she does a better job than her predecessor. I don't mean to be rude, but the *Guardian* are almost as bad as the right-wing media, worse in some ways because at least you know what you're getting with the likes of the *Jerusalem Post* or Fox – you expect them to suck up to Israel. The *Guardian* should be backing the Palestinians one hundred per cent, given their so-called love of equality and tolerance.'

Change the fucking record, the vinyl's wearing through. Thank God we're already coming off the Ayalon onto Kibbutz Galuyot Road. We sit at the lights, a beggar approaches. Shira undoes her seatbelt, starts rummaging in the handbag on the back seat. She proffers a handful of change, mumbles inaudible platitudes. She shakes her world-weary head, he shakes his too, their lice high-five each other in mid-air. The lights change, we drive on towards Jaffa.

'He's another victim of the occupation, you know?'

She says this thoughtfully, I ignore it artfully. My work here is done. I've introduced myself, made nice, said the right things, but now I wanna go home.

'I'll jump out here, if that's ok, I need to pick something up from the bakery.'

She slaloms into the kerb, pigeons scatter. I can't wait to join them.

'Nice to meet you, and here's my card, it'd be great to meet up with you again if you have time.'

She glances at the card, places it in her bag. She scrutinises me as I climb out and lean back through the passenger window.

'Nice to meet you, too, and good luck with your work. It takes a certain type of person to admit they were wrong and to work to correct their mistakes. I'm pleased you're on the right path.'

I flash her a grateful grin, spin on my heel, walk ten paces and dial Chana. Delighted to set foot on Israeli soil again. I feel ethnically cleansed.

We don't meet in Mapu anymore, Tel Aviv's but a distant dream. I grin and I bear it and I follow Mario's lead. He doesn't get nostalgic for the airship when he's moved on to Bowser's Castle, he just gets on with the job and lives in the present. Hummus is the new tennis; I play doubles every day. Abu Hasan's the venue, I'm already part of the furniture. Me and the rest of the do-gooder corps, halos burning brightly as we float through the front door. I'll be there tomorrow at one, shovelling masabcha in my mouth then spitting blood back out, raging and railing about the shock and the horror of today in Bil'in. But first I've got to get it all down on paper in a thousand words or less.

Chana's still showing me the ropes, but I'm almost ready to strike out on my own. I must be by now, cos it's hardly rocket science and I'm on my fortieth piece. Open with a sound bite, get to the meat by line two, paint a picture, take a stance, get self-righteously angry till the penultimate paragraph, then pull back, calm down, end on a cliché. Wham, bam, thank you ma'am, straight down the pub. I've been drawing the crowds ever since my debut last year, an overnight sensation who couldn't put a foot wrong. A bit of string-pulling by Nicky set up the gig in the first place, but from that point on it was a walk in the park. I was every *Guardian* reader's wet dream: ex-IDF combat, ex-north-west London Jew, born again and seen the light and ready to stick the boot into Israel. Every article elicited hundreds of responses – letters sent to the paper, comments scrawled on the website, reprints and syndication across the globe. I was given a weekly column in the print section, another slot online, plus an occasional feature for the Saturday magazine. Just what Dr Nicky had ordered, demanded, arranged. He set it up, Chana delivered the goods, and I just had to act the part on both sides of the Green Line. The only collateral damage so far is my dad – he hasn't been in touch for nearly six months, his last email accusing me of selling out both the family and the Jewish people at large. *Ain mah l'asot.* I wouldn't tell him the truth even if I could.

The politics was hard at first, but it was just another form of training. Just like learning to trade, just like learning to shoot, just like learning to act and pretend and perform. I fake caring about the conflict like I faked everything else. Faked loving Laura and Tina and Tanya and more. Faked friendship and ethics and morals and trust. Faked all but my time as a paid-up Panther, and I've even got my doubts about that these days. Doubt trumps every emotion, doubt rules the roost. Doubt's body double is fear, and between them they've got me just where they want me. Drug-free, drink-free, doing exactly as I'm told and learning not to fight back. I've had my final warning, I'm on my ninth life. Fuck this one up and the fat lady sings. For now the only sound is Chana's tutting as she scans my first draft.

'Too harsh, you've got to start sounding more sympathetic to the villagers. Stop attacking them for provoking the soldiers, that's not a progressive position. You're meant to be on a leftwards journey, not staying stuck in the centre. Ten months of writing means you should have left your post-army posturing far behind.'

She's never satisfied, she might as well write them from scratch by herself. We go back and forth for a while, but for far less time than we used to, the whole thing's over in under an hour. She leaves my final two paragraphs intact, as strong a signal as any that I've almost come of age:

Winning hearts and minds is not one of Israel's top priorities when it comes to the Palestinians, but it ought to be. For every child who witnesses the violence meted out against their people firsthand, there is a freedom fighter in the making – who will graduate from the school of shabab rock-slingers to fully-fledged militant so long as he feels there is no other way to protect his people's freedom.

The tragedy of Bil'in, as well as so many other villages and towns throughout the West Bank and Gaza, is that the people the protestors really need to reach with their flags and banners are miles away in Israel's cities and for whom the Palestinians' torment is out of sight, and out of mind. The settlers and the soldiers who witness the demonstrations couldn't care less about the trauma they cause; the only hope is that those moderates left in Israel one day take up the Palestinians' cause.

What a load of bollocks. My editor's gonna love it. Type in her address, attach document, copy in the subs, hit send, done. Let the games begin.

Everyone wants a piece of me now. The rep grows bigger and the pleas grow louder. Emails flood in begging me to write an article about this or that NGO, this or that grassroots project, this or that coexistence group, and I'm duty-bound to follow them up and present pitches to my *Guardian* superiors. Dialogue Circles, Dialogue Oblongs, Dialogue Trapeziums, Anarchists Against The Wall, Mothers Against Occupation, Mothers Wishing Their Anarchist Kids Would Shut Up About Walls And Get An Occupation, Jewish Voices For Palestine, Palestinian Voices For Freedom, The Freedom Theatre, The Freedom Circus, The Freedom Spearmint Rhino, Physicians For Human Rights, Magicians For Human Rights, Electricians For Human Rights, Care International, Care Intercontinental, Care Intergalactic, Peace Now, Peace

Soon, Mushy Peace, Mind Your Peace and Qs, Operation Dove, Operation Love, Operation Love A Dove, Operation Shove A Dove In A Glove, One State, Two State, Red State, Blue State, Peter Piper Picked A Peck Of Pickled Palestinians. And that's just the tip of the iceberg.

I keep banging out the pieces, carefully sounding more and more radical with every passing week. The strategy's paying dividends – arms once folded sternly across chests now open to welcome me with a hug, I'm becoming the darling of the hard-left hardcore. Persona non grata in Israel proper, of course, but that's just collateral damage. There are only two Israelis I have to please, and they're both patting me on the back again like their favourite pet, so I wag my tail happily and fall asleep in my basket.

19

I wake to the sound of an incoming text. I squint at the phone, curse the chutzpah of whoever's breaking the nine o'clock rule. Nicky's the guilty party, probably worth letting him off on a technicality. He's sent me a link to a site and one word: 'Higanu'. 'We've arrived'. I click on the web page, and a Palestinian flag is the first thing I see. The acronym PWC is the second, the Palestine Welfare Coalition, who Chana routinely denounces as agents provocateurs, apologists for terror and all-round anti-Semites. Sounds about right, given the members I've come across so far at protests and rallies – Eurotrash students and drop-outs screaming blue murder at soldiers, lobbing bricks and bottles and ratcheting up tension wherever they go. They've denounced me from day one, their leaders warning anyone who will listen not to trust me, to take what I write with a pinch of salt, to refuse to assist me in any of my research. Yet now their homepage is devoted to my latest article, under the crowing headline: 'Former IOF Soldier: Occupation Breeds Terror'. They attribute my volte-face to my 'finally realising the futility of the Zionist project', and announce their acceptance that I am 'genuinely on the side of right and truth'. The condescension continues for ten paragraphs, in which my born-again status is paraded like a trophy of war, with the urgent directive that 'only through our vital work revealing the horror of apartheid Israel will we convert thousands of others like him. More power to his pen.' The olive branch has been extended. Nicky's spot on: we've arrived.

Your cave is at risk if you do not keep up payments on your mortgage or other loan secured on it. Someone should translate that to Arabic. Someone should tell this waster to stop sitting around smoking shisha and moaning about his lot. Get a job, get a gun, get whatever you need to get up and stand on your own two feet. The world keeps turning, time waits for no man or his rake-thin goats. Time doesn't, but these starry-eyed Swedish sycophants do, they're all over him like a rash. He and his family tick all the boxes, don't they? Brown-skinned – tick. Swathed in robes – tick. Honest, farming folk just trying to make ends meet – tick. Driven to penury by the oppression of Zionazi soldiers and settlers – tick, tick, tick. And the *coup de grâce*, they live in a cave. In a cave. In. A. Cave. Just imagine the kudos we'll get back in Malmo, imagine the tales we'll be able to tell. We slept in a cave with a man and his three wives and ten kids and twelve goats and ate with our hands and became one with nature and worked in their fields and ensured their safety and documented their suffering and told the world of their plight. Book me a one-way ticket to heaven – I'll have a window seat, please, and a vegan meal too.

I lean back on the cushion and stare at my host. His mouth spilleth over, words bubbling out as he lists his litany of woe. A middleman translates – some gawking, wide-eyed clone straight off the aid worker production line. His name's Karl but he wishes it was Khalil, stricken with Stockholm Syndrome in every sense of the phrase. I take notes, as ever, my eyes glazing as I try to focus on the issue at hand. Same old story: Arab tends his flock, settlers attack Arab, goat gets shot, Arab gets angry, army gets called, Arab gets arrested, settlers get away with it, Karl gets on line one to alert the world press. Hardly hold-the-front-page stuff, more like Billy Goats Gruff, and I'm not in *Jackanory* mode anymore. I'm coming up to eighteen months in the job, I'm bored of fucking around in the middle of the desert. I want action, want results, want to be bathed in glory not goats' milk. Chana needs to up the ante. I need a proper pillow, it's almost time for bed.

Darkness engulfs the encampment, but the wild dogs' barks reverberating across the hills make sleep close to impossible. After just a few hours the dogs wake the cockerel, who wakes the donkeys, who wake the muezzin, who wakes me at an ungodly hour, and then we're up and out into the dim morning gloom. A battered space wagon struggles across the rocks, a window is rolled down and my name shouted out.

'You are suhafi, yes? Journalist? You must come, hurry.'

My heart leaps – maybe a chicken's been raped or a mouse has been kidnapped. Can't fucking wait. I amble reluctantly over, Good St Karl dashing in front of me, his wings flapping frantically as he jumps in the car. He doesn't even know what's happened, no idea why he's so agitated in advance. I climb into the back, remember my role and step up my interest.

'*Ahlan, salam alaikum*, what's the problem?'

Throwing the car into reverse, the man turns round and gives me a piercing stare.

'They are coming. Across the hill. The army coming, we must to protect our village and you must to report what they do.'

Karl's on his phone, frenziedly rallying the troops in Scandinavian slang. He hangs up, turns to me.

'This has been brewing for more than a week, the army want to raid the village and arrest men they accuse of assaulting a settler. The charges are false, it's a set-up, and we've got activists coming to act as human shields.'

Yeah, that should work. Just ask Rachel Corrie.

'Ok, how many activists will be there?'

'At least fifty. There are many NGOs working in the fields near here, PWC are sending a jeep as well from Hebron.'

Sweet. Time for a bit of networking. The car crawls along the track, the sun's starting to light up the plain. In the distance we see two IDF Hummers headed towards us. We'll meet in the middle.

The village is buzzing with drones, barricades being hastily erected by women and children, the men have already made themselves scarce. Fierce-eyed activists run zoom around the hive, ordering each other around and turning on cameras and camcorders ready to document the troops' imminent incursion. I assiduously take notes, then feel a tap on my shoulder and turn around. I shake the proffered hand.

'I'm Steve, media liaison for PWC. I wanted to introduce myself properly before things kick off.'

Enchanté. I nod, try to look confident and contrite at the same time. He's got a strong London lilt, another wide boy in the wilderness.

'Hi, good to meet you. I saw your article last month – I appreciate what you wrote about me. I hope bygones are bygones, yeah?'

He nods enthusiastically, all smiles, all sweetness and light. Prick.

'Yeah, of course, we need more people like you. Did someone explain what's going on here?'

'I heard a bit, something about a raid, arresting villagers, right?'

He spits a jet of saliva just in front of his scuffed Reebok Classics.

'At the least, yeah. If we're really unlucky, they'll knock down a couple of the huts as a warning. It's all part of their terror tactics against us.'

Against us, not them. We are all Palestinians. We are the Daleks. We will ex-ter-mi-nate.

'Fucked up. It's madness man, total madness.'

He's pawing at the ground with his right foot, he's dying to dive back into the fray.

'What's new, you know? That's what these bastards do, can't expect leopards to change their spots – sorry, I don't mean that about you . . . You know what I mean, right?'

Not really, but who gives a fuck anyway. I just want your head on a plate, an apple in your mouth and a fork in your left eye. He's about to make his excuses and leave, then remembers something and leans in conspiratorially.

'One thing though, and I hope you'll treat this in total confidence, yeah?'

I nod gravely.

'Good. You might see a few things today that we really don't want reported on, ok, cos this is a bit of a one-off event, and it's not what PWC ought to be associated with.'

I'm all ears, wish I was recording this. Chana's gonna kill me for not switching on my recorder when I had the chance.

'We're gonna give the soldiers a bit of a run for their money, because it'll give the men a chance to escape across the fields, as well as send a message to the army that the village won't just roll over and play dead.'

Do that and you'll be dead for real, darling – has he got no clue what he's up against? What the hell could he and his crew do to stand in the army's way, short of boring them to death with their sermons?

'Sure, I get you, I'll turn a blind eye where necessary. I'm here to do a piece on settler attacks, so I'll leave out whatever doesn't fit the story I'm telling.'

Smiling gratefully, he gives me a clenched fist salute, and jogs to the nearest hut where sandbags are being hauled into place in the window frames. The Hummers are almost at the perimeter of the village. I dash the other way up the hill and sit on a rock with a decent vantage point. The dogs are going wild. They can sense the tension, so can the cockerel, but the sheep are pretty quiet. They've seen it all before, can't be bothered to get involved. A speaker crackles to life and orders are barked out in Hebrew by a commander.

'This is now a closed military zone. Anyone not a resident

of the village must leave the area immediately. Any resident must emerge from his home and stand in the street with both his hands on his head.'

No one pays a blind bit of notice. The activists keep scurrying around, camcorders trained on the troops like bazookas. Soldiers pour out of the vehicles, fingers on triggers and covering one another in pairs. A two-second spell of unnatural silence, then it all kicks off, starting with a fairly innocuous hurling of a can of yellow paint over the first Hummer. Tear gas grenades are fired in every direction, no bullets yet though, but as soon as the rocks and bricks fly the soldiers' way, bursts of gunfire pepper the air and announce round two of the fight. I see Steve and two of his gang crouch behind a wall, metal pipes in hand, waiting for the moment to pounce. They never get it, thanks to four soldiers creeping up on them from behind and smashing into the trio with brutal krav maga swings of their rifles. They don't stop till all three are out cold, then give them a few kicks for good measure and move on. It's the same story all over the village – as the plumes of smoke clear, I can see at least twenty prostrate bodies lying in the dirt, and a similar number being cuffed with plastic restraints and herded to the side of the Hummers. Ten to fifteen Arab men are dashing at full pelt away from the village to my left, some with shotguns slung over their backs, all praying to escape the clutches of their would-be captors. I'm praying for an Apache – someone should pick them off from above, fuck knows where they're headed or what they'll do when they get there.

I'm not sure what I'm meant to do at this point. More army jeeps are heading over the plain towards the village.

They'll be carting off everyone they've arrested, and I have no intention of joining the agitator activists in a cell in downtown Hebron. My brief is clear – if I ever do get picked up: go with the flow, act outraged and incensed and claim press immunity. Under no circumstances blow my cover in even the tiniest of ways. Take what's coming to me as just part of the job. Doesn't mean I have to be a sitting target though, so I scramble up and away from the village, planning to make my way back to the caves where I slept. The screams behind me suggest I'm making the right move. Some other cunt can take my place in the Paddy wagon.

I don't let Steve down; my next column exonerates the activists, heaps blame on the soldiers and settlers in equal measure, earns me the opprobrium of the Israeli right and another surge of support amongst my newfound friends. I don't let Chana down either, providing ultra-precise descriptions of Steve and his would-be warrior mates' activities, and she's baying for blood when we meet up a week after she's finished digesting the details.

'It's time to make a move on these manyakim – what you've told us seals it.'

'That's great, but isn't it a bit obvious that I'm the one fingering them if you just go and arrest them now?'

She fixes me with a steely glare – *plus ça change*.

'Clearly we've already thought of that. You just worry about what you've got to do, because you're the one with a habit of fucking up your tasks. We're not going to simply dive in and arrest them, we're going a more circuitous and clandestine route, as you should have come to expect by now.'

I bow my head meekly. She doesn't fall for my act, doesn't care either.

'What we've planned won't even implicate Israel, let alone our office or your precious self. And there's no rush either, we'll just wait till the next time your new best friend summons you to his side.'

She picks up her phone, starts dialling and strides onto the balcony. Class dismissed.

It's the archetypal Israeli demonstration – sun blazing away in a cloudless sky, a busy intersection in the heart of Jerusalem choked with traffic, two opposing camps of protesters separated by police lines and a few metres of tarmac. In the blue corner, the peace activists of Women in Black are gathering to celebrate their twenty-third year of protests against the occupation. In the red corner, a counter-demonstration of rabid religious nationalists pour scorn and derision on their opponents across the road.

And, diving into the fray with well-rehearsed investigative curiosity is the *Guardian*'s most fearless op-ed fighter, pumped up and ready for antagonistic action. My brief is to savage the right-wingers to ensure my love-in with the left continues, meaning I need to provoke my interviewees hard, then let them have it with both barrels when I write up my piece. My first port of call is a mouthy English-born religious woman brandishing an outsized poster of Palestinian gunmen in the direction of oncoming cars, whose scowling visage marks her out as just the person to explain her group's rage.

I stroll over and ask whether she has a problem with one

of her fellow protesters clutching a sign with 'Israel for the Jews' scrawled across it.

'Don't you think that sends a bit of a racist message?'

I suggest that if she'd seen people holding 'England for the English' banners in her youth, she'd have been understandably upset. Not sure I'd have cared myself, after all I'd have proudly flown a 'Suburb for the Jewish' standard, but I've got to keep up the *Guardian* act for now. She replies through gritted teeth.

'Of course it's not racist. Look, you have to understand that they want to kill Jews . . .'

She points angrily at the fairly placid-looking Women in Black over the road, then continues with her rant, straying further and further from the question I'd asked her to answer.

'The Arabs support a caliphate . . .'

I can see what's coming, and take out the bingo card I carry for occasions such as these.

' . . . they want to dissolve Israel . . .'

I check the right box on my form.

'. . . they've got twenty-two countries of their own . . .'

Check.

' . . .there's no such thing as Palestinians anyway . . .'

Check.

'. . .they teach their children hate . . .'

Check.

' . . . you should know what I mean – you're from Londonistan too, aren't you?'

Stifling the urge to shout 'house!' and claim my prize, I patiently and patronisingly explain that the world according to Melanie Phillips isn't necessarily in tune with reality, however much my frothing-at-the-mouth friend would like to believe it is. Then again, it might be – what do I know or, more importantly, care? She rounds on me defiantly.

'Don't think I don't read the papers. I read eight newspapers every day – in fact, I was just reading in the *Daily Mail* . . .'

Bonus check.

'. . . this week about the Muslims wanting to have a public call to prayer in Sussex.'

She pauses dramatically to see my reaction. Sorry to disappoint you, darling, I'm in work mode today.

'So? How's that any different from church bells calling the faithful to prayer?'

She grimaces at me in disgust.

'It *is* different. For one thing, church bells are softer . . .'

Defeated by that impeccable logic, I withdraw from the arena and try my hand elsewhere. Soon I'm surrounded by baying middle-aged men throwing lame sound bite after lame sound bite at me in a relentless verbal assault. 'Every time there's a ceasefire, we cease and they fire,' one man exclaims triumphantly, as though he's just given Confucius a run for his money in the adage stakes.

Another wise man, waving a placard reading 'Death to the traitors – black is the colour of death', chimes in.

'Anyone against Jews in the land of Israel is morally bankrupt.'

His opening salvo signals him as another rapier-like wit with whom it would be enlightening to cross swords, so I get stuck in.

'But don't you think claiming Israel is just for the Jews smacks of racism?'

He explodes like a cluster bomb.

'I will *not* hear anyone accuse Israel of being racist. Not when the Arabs have been racist for hundreds of years.'

But we're not talking about 'the Arabs', I reply, resolutely remaining in *Guardian* columnist character despite not giving a fuck which side holds the monopoly on truth.

'I was asking whether you thought Israel shouldn't sink to racist levels in its dealing with its non-Jewish citizens.'

He swiftly changes his position as his blood pressure rises.

'I don't care if it *is* racist. Israel's not meant to be some kind of multi-cultural democracy – this isn't England.'

Well into his stride by now, he carries on digging his hole.

'Non-Jews shouldn't have the vote, otherwise we can't safeguard Israel's future.'

I keep shtum, entranced by his complete lack of self-awareness, dazzled by his idiocy. He puffs his chest out even further and gets rhetorical on my ass.

'I bet you think the Arabs want peace. Well, let me educate you, as someone with experience – they don't. When they say they do, they're lying.'

I concede that I am obviously devoid of the same kind of 'experience' as him, observing that he clearly has a far greater depth of understanding of 'the Arabs' collective psyche than me. A yapping little woman who has joined our impromptu debating circle pipes up in a nasal whine.

'Listen, Mohammed broke his hudna in Medina after two years – that's the kind of attitude we're up against.'

She flails her arms like an amphetamine-fuelled windmill, attracting the attention of a burly policeman, who muscles in and demands I tell him 'which side' I'm on.

'I'm not any side, I'm just interviewing these people about their politics.'

He considers this information, then issues instructions like a teacher keeping order in a classroom.

'Well, do it without shouting'

Only too happy to oblige. My job here is done anyway. The readers will love it – first-hand proof that the right wing really are as meshugana as it says on the tin.

20

Lying through my teeth is second nature; I blur the truth in my mind as well as my articles. I have to, says Chana, because unless I believe what I say I run the risk of slipping up. I'm playing for high stakes now, wining and dining some of the most extreme elements in the radical camp, and in the places I've started hanging out there's no margin for error. Especially now that I've been invited for my first sleepover in Shechem.

Except I can't say Shechem, because that's the occupiers' name for the city. If I want to keep my street cred, I have to call it Nablus. PWC have a heavy presence there, and Steve's zealous attempts to brainwash me have given rise to a daytrip to see the work they do in the teeming refugee camp. Chana is chomping at the bit as we finalise the plans on the eve of my visit.

'You use the Huwara checkpoint, ok? And you get in the line second from the left – Golani brigade are guarding the mahsom tomorrow, and the platoon commander knows to wave you through without fuss.'

I nod. The checkpoint is the least of my worries.

'Sure, second from left. Got it.'

'And make sure the bricks are taped tight to your stomach, seriously. There won't be any body search at the checkpoint, but if anything comes loose and falls out, they'll have to act accordingly because there'll be cameras on the gates.'

She pulls out a couple of sheets of paper and lays them next to the cellophane-wrapped slabs on the coffee table. She fixes me with an evil smile, growling with menace.

'You leave these papers in a separate location in the house. They're got the names of local teenagers who your foreign friends have been dealing to, notes of who owes what and when they're due to pay. It doesn't matter that it's all fake, the police won't give a damn. We just need to give them enough rope to hang all the manyakim with, and this will be more than sufficient once they find the bricks.'

Fair play to her, we're onto a winner here. According to the briefing, the chief superintendent who covers the Nablus region recently lost a nephew to a heroin overdose. His men are searching high and low for someone to blame for his death, and Steve and co. will soon find themselves taking centre stage in the investigation after the police are tipped off about what they have stashed under their floorboards, 'or wherever else you can leave all this without getting spotted. I don't care how you do it – just make sure you pull it off, because we want this done and dusted by Wednesday morning.'

I grin; hope the little fuckers can bear it. Chana bares her fangs.

'This is justice, Shabak style.'

I know it's only rock and roll, but I like it.

I follow the yellow brick road up to the Huwara checkpoint, the two brown bricks strapped tight below my ribcage. I wear a rucksack slung casually over my shoulder, and a soft expression on my face designed to assuage the soldiers' suspicion. I approach the gates via the pre-ordained path, am ushered through with barely a second glance, then wait by the roadside for my pick up.

My guide for the day is Hamed, six foot two of pure, raw hate. All he's missing is a T-shirt with 'I'd rather be suicide bombing' stencilled across the chest. The refugee camp is a fucking mess. Alleyways barely two feet wide between crumbling concrete houses, raw sewage flowing unchecked down the broken pavement, pockmarked walls bearing the scars of years of battle. Totally NOCD. I miss Hampstead.

'The army doesn't give a damn about civilians getting caught in the crossfire.'

Not the time or the place to tell him I don't either. Better just to pull a Disgusted of Tunbridge Wells face and let him carry on foaming at the mouth.

'You can never truly know what it's like till you've lived here yourself. Every family's either had someone killed, wounded or arrested by the IDF; dozens of houses have been smashed apart during raids. But, inshallah, our time for revenge will soon come.'

Allah's phone's been on voicemail for years, my friend, but keep kidding yourself if it helps you get through the day. Steve stands next to me, seething as ever, mumbling Arabic curses like a local as Hamed leads us onwards.

Children swagger round in bomber jackets in imitation of the gun-toting fighters adorning the posters plastered on every available surface. The militants have become instant idols for the Nablus youth, who stare wide-eyed at their chiselled features in the posters just as their peers overseas gaze dreamily at boy bands and footballers. No point trying to win hearts and minds here, better just send in the carpet bombers.

At the PWC house, we sit around for hours, eating, drinking, smoking, fawning over anyone in a keffiyeh, and there are far too many of those for comfort. On a trip to the gents, I secrete the packages in their bathroom ceiling, stuff the papers in a hallway drawer, come back to the table two kilos lighter and a hundredweight happier. I spend the rest of the meeting in good spirits, heaping praise on their work, pledging allegiance to the Palestinian cause, sucking up hard to my hosts and even harder on their nagilah. Here's to you, my friends, better hope you don't drop the soap.

To put distance between my visit and the wrath of the Palestinian Authority police being visited on the threesome, Chana waits almost a week before setting the wheels of justice in motion. When it happens, the press gives heavy coverage to the harrowing story of the foreign aid workers languishing in a West Bank jail, having allegedly confessed to using their positions in the Palestinian community to sell drugs to minors and get rich off their addiction. Chana's in heaven, Nicky is too by the look of it. We sit at the back of Honey Beach, papers spread out on the table as we toast my success. He raises a glass of Chardonnay, beams at me as he drinks.

*   *   *

Life is sweet. Cogs whirring, wheels spinning, fit as a fiddle and firing on all cylinders. All the fun of the fair, all the thrill of the chase, plus all the activist pussy I can eat – the girls are easy prey now given my standing on the hard-left stage. The book's coming out in a few weeks, a collection of my best columns bundled up into the intellectual anti-Semite's perfect Christmas gift. I'm spreading my wings, doing pundit slots on BBC News and guest gigs in the *Washington Post*, my influence spreading and my stock soaring.

But there's always a nagging doubt. This can't last forever, and once my expiry date is reached, where will they send me next? I'm too high-profile to seamlessly slip into a new incarnation, I can't be reborn and rebranded again. Fifteen minutes of fame, but then what? Putting me out to stud seems the only logical solution, but I know – and more importantly Nicky and Chana know too – just how that will end up. They don't trust me to stay off the gear even when I'm up to my neck in work, so as soon as I hit retirement age they must reckon I'll be straight back on it. Chana plays dumb whenever I ask her about the future, she's cagey and cryptic and can't be drawn on a thing.

'What are you worried about that for? You've only being writing for two years, there's a lot left in your tank.'

I don't believe her, she's speaking too softly, acting too placatory.

'Yeah, but surely there's only so much I can do for you in this role, and anyway the *Guardian* aren't gonna keep me on the books indefinitely, are they?'

She wishes I'd shut up, I wish she'd open up. Odds-on she wins.

'You don't know that. They're delighted with what

you've done up to now, so why should they want to get rid of you?'

Because they're just as ruthless as you and Nicky, and fresh blood is what the readers feed off.

'There's a shelf-life in this business, and they'll never make me the correspondent here, they said that right from the off. You can't go from taking sides in an op-ed column to expecting people to see you as impartial in a reporter role.'

She gives me a withering look. I wither.

'Well then we'll cross that bridge when we come to it, ok? We're meant to be discussing Midnight Mass, not having a careers advice session.'

Two weeks till the festive season's showpiece event. The great and the good of the media circus will be out in force, and I'll be on duty doing serious eavesdropping. There's no better time to pick up the off-the-record gossip than when they're half-cut on mulled wine or egg-nog or whatever the fuck goyim guzzle at this time of year. First up is the service at the Church of the Nativity, then the after-party at a mansion in downtown Bethlehem where the real fun and games will commence. I'll be off duty that night, in *Guardian* terms at least – I'll be hard at work for Nicky and Chana, miked up and recording every drunken word uttered.

Adam's gonna be my wingman, the *Economist*'s new correspondent who's sorting us out with tickets to the Mass. They're harder to get hold of than Zacharia Zubeida, but he knows a man who knows a man who knows a monk, so we should be sorted. He and I have been out on a few stories together lately; Chana encourages me to build up the rapport between us because she wants to keep an eye on him for reasons as yet unknown.

'There's really nothing to worry about. You'll use your press pass to get through the checkpoints and our soldiers and their police will all be acting relaxed. The eyes of the world will be on Bethlehem, so no one's out to make their side look bad in front of the cameras. Even the most lunatic Islamists wouldn't dare stage an attack on Christmas in Bethlehem, so people crossing won't be checked too carefully. You can wear a body mike or carry a recorder in your pocket, we'll decide on the day.'

Sounds fucking boring to me, just more data gathering and pointless legwork. Still, ours not to reason why, ours but to do and drink. It is Christmas, after all.

We swagger up to the checkpoint like Ant and Bee. I'm Ant, no question, he's blatantly Bee. Kind Dog can't come, shame cos he was gonna be the designated driver. The bottle of red we downed at the American Colony is starting to wear off, no guarantees where the next drink's coming from, there's only one off-licence in Bethlehem and fuck knows where that is. Cross the border, jump in a cab, use mime to express our desire to get drunk. Driver smiles, speeds off down the road, Christmas lights flashing from every tree, PA police standing on every corner. Lonely place for a Jew, but single malt is a man's best friend and the offie's packed to the rafters. Buy a litre of Glenfiddich and a back-up Balvenie, pay through the nose, swig from the bottle, climb up the hill, slump on a bench. Wind whipping around us, tighten our scarves and do up our coats, dreaming of a white Christmas but I'm not allowed that anymore, crowds flooding into the town centre, bells starting to peal. Adam's matching me slug for slug, *k'nayna hora achi*. Hhe's starting to grow on me but that's not saying a great deal. Half a bottle down, drinking way too much way too fast way too early way too casually. Loose lips sink ships but I know what I'm doing, I know what I'm thinking, I know what I'm saying, let's get going, I want a front-row seat for when Jesus comes on stage. Push through the throng, smiling, slurring, slapping strangers on the back, face to face with security, slap their backs too, not a good move, say sorry times ten, show our tickets and press cards and say sorry again, pull ourselves together, fall back apart, slip through a side door and up three flights of stairs. Emerge on a stone roof, massive bell tower ahead, sounds like a plan, let's climb it, ring it, wing it before we're caught, Adam's game, I'm gamer, we laugh like hyenas, scramble up the ladder, no clapper in the bell and that's no bad thing at all cos two guards have appeared, sans festive spirit, avec sawn-off AKs, they wanna know what we're doing, I'd like to as well. Adam calms them down, fobs them off with a lie, they don't understand but decide that we're harmless, wander away and leave us alone. We slug more whisky, chat more breeze, lose more marbles, hunt more danger, start singing carols at the top of our lungs, don't know the words so make them up, I saw three ships come sailing in, all made of tin, and donkey skin, good king Wenceslas looked out, and he saw a chicken, away in a manger, no hair on his head, the little Lord Jesus got up and he said, we hate Tottenham and we hate Tottenham, too cold out here, through the door, down the stairs, standing room only but neither of us can, lean on a wall, laugh at a nun, laugh at another, turn round and run, hide in a courtyard, drain the last of the dregs, bottle two begins, too much light, too much sound, voices shouting, boots stamping, tension rising, convoy arriving, Mahmoud Abbas and his phalanx of minders, sober up in an instant, put a foot wrong you're dead, hold our breath till they pass, exhale and reload, more swigs till we're battered, goes black and I'm gone.

Santa didn't come this year.

It could have been worse, though. Adam rescued me, slung me in a cab and got me safely to Jerusalem through the Bet Jalla back route, I slept it off at his place for over a day then went home to face the music. Don't remember any of those forty-eight hours, but my face definitely does. Black eyes take longer to fade than my drunken memories. Might have walked into a door, I suppose, but I'm a pound to a shekel bet Nicky's to blame. Thank fuck I still had the mike on me when I made it back.

I can't remember the last time I was this scared. In fact, I can't remember the last time I was scared at all. Back in my army days, I was too busy fighting my inner demons to pay much attention to the Armageddon all around me; even when Dvir got shot in Hebron I still didn't fully grasp that it could just as easily have been me. There's something about being strapped up with a semi-automatic that keeps the terror from taking hold, but these days the only protection I've got is a pair of plastic biros. Fuck pens, give me back my mighty sword.

Adam seems far calmer, but then he's not Jewish, Israeli or an IDF vet. He's not going undercover on this particular story, whereas I'm cloaked in more deceptive robes than ever before. When Nicky set this one up, even he seemed concerned about how it would all pan out. An interview with one of the most notorious Palestinian militants ever to stalk the earth, a man who only gives interviews every five years or more, and who'd sooner cut the head off a Jew in his presence than shake his hand. Nicky had a contact who could arrange the meet, told me to offer the scoop to Adam and ask to tag along as his stringer. Adam likes the idea, is happy to go along with my subterfuge, thinks I'm just thrill-seeking rather than anything more sinister.

I told Adam I'd rather give the story to him than the *Guardian* correspondent, because at least with Adam I'd get to come with, whereas the haughty bitch above me in the *Guardian* food chain would just nick the story and leave me out in the cold. Adam's too grateful to stop and think about my motives, too trusting to wonder why I'm so keen to be present. Even if he asked, I wouldn't be able to tell him the true reason; all Nicky's told me is that this is act one of a two-act play. I've got no equipment with me, I'm not meant to do anything other than genuinely act as stringer when we're there, so I know this is some sort of test. Whether of me or the terrorist General Darwish is harder to work out, but something is definitely brewing and I'm gripped by panic as we cross the border at Qalandia. Adam gets suddenly anxious too.

'Hold on, what if they ID us when we get there? Your cover will be blown as soon as they check your papers.'

Nicky was adamant they wouldn't bother with our papers, said Palestinian officials are far more lax than their Israeli counterparts, because we're the ones expecting – and receiving – terror attacks, not them. He'd better be right.

'Don't worry, it'll be fine, the PA fixer who set it up said they won't check us – he's vouched for you, they've looked you up and they're happy to let the *Economist* carry the story. They won't worry about who I am, as long as you just say I'm Simon, your stringer.'

'Ok, if you say so, but what if they recognise you anyway?'

I laugh, make light of the situation.

'I wish . . . I'm not that big a name. Even if any of them has seen something I've written, they'll definitely never have seen a photo of me.'

Adam gets distracted by a six-year-old selling matches who tugs at his sleeve and begs him to buy one of her bundles. He fumbles for change in his pocket, a sign of how green he still is. After a couple of months, every foreigner – journalist, aid worker, whoever – gets sick of the beggars and learns to look right through them. I flag down a cab, hand the driver a scrap of paper with an address scrawled in Arabic. We roll through Ramallah, the stench of burning rubbish choking us, our eyes tearing as the fumes pour through the windows. My teeth are chattering, but I don't know why. Everything is going to plan so far, and none of Nicky's schemes have backfired yet. Christmas aside, of course, but that was my fault, and my Boxing Day beating was the only fallout from that incident.

We arrive at a nondescript house on the edge of a patch of scrubland where two men in badly fitting suits lean against a gleaming SUV. The cab driver glances at them, then back at us, hurriedly gives us our change and speeds off down the hill. The smaller of the men strides towards us, breaking into a strained smile as he approaches.

'*Salam alaikum*. You are Adam, correct?'

Adam nods, smiles warmly.

'Hello. Yes, it's a pleasure to meet you'

The man ignores Adam's outstretched hand, turns to me.

'And you are for to help him?'

I give him a thumbs-up sign, reduced to mime by my fear but I'd better snap out of it fast. He looks at me pityingly, probably thinks I'm a mute. He beckons us to follow him back to the car, his partner is already in the driver's seat revving the engine.

As we reach our final destination, five scowling bodyguards lounge on plastic chairs next to the mansion's high front wall, smoking and drinking coffee as the sun begins its slow descent. We are ushered into a car park through a set of wrought-iron gates, our driver steering the Hummer past four mammoth Mercedes with Israeli plates and another SUV. We pile out, and follow the suits to the front door. Nicky was right, as ever – none of the guards even pat us down, let alone ask for ID. They're so confident no one white and English would ever try and dupe them that they can't be bothered to perform even the most perfunctory of checks. Suits me down to the ground.

The house's interior is vast, packed with outsized, extravagant pieces of furniture: ornate sofas framed with carved wood are positioned around the main room, garish upholstery matched by the elaborate sculptures all around. As we wait for Darwish, I wonder whether I'm the first Israeli ever to set foot in his home, and what he or his foot soldiers would think should they discover my true identity. I doubt Ghostbusters would make it here in time, and I'm praying I don't have to make the call and find out.

The general arrives twenty minutes late, everyone in the room stands on ceremony. As the interview begins, I survey the scene from my vantage point on a sofa behind Adam. Again, I'm stunned by how fucking slack the security is here: rather than pointing a microphone and camera at the general, either of us could be aiming a gun at his forehead. Ha l'vai, it's no more than the bastard deserves.

Darwish fixes Adam with narrowed, hard eyes and speaks with a gravel-laced drawl like Don Corleone. He pays no attention to me, barely notices Adam's questions either; he's just here to grind his axe till it's razor sharp. He hardly pauses for breath as he fires out rabid sound bites about why Israelis should be quaking in their boots over an imminent Palestinian uprising. He should know, I suppose, he's been ordering attacks on our people for decades, leaving widows and orphans and cripples in his wake. As we wrap up the interview, Darwish is at pains to point out his own continued commitment to the cause.

'I am ready to sacrifice myself for my nation. I am ready to give my life.'

'Course he is. Don't mind the life-sized marble eagle statue in the dining room, or the Mercedes string quartet playing their sweet music outside, this man's one of the people, no question. Happy to send the slum dwellers' sons off to die for the cause, he'll toast their courage with a glass of Moët in the outdoor jacuzzi. *Viva la resistance.* We'll see ourselves out.

'That all went fine, just fine.'

Nicky paces up and down the lounge, Chana sits hunched over her laptop. I struggle with the cellophane on my third pack of the day. He stops in front of my chair, puts a hand on my shoulder.

'Are you ready for round two?'

Yes/no/maybe. What difference does it make?

'You and Adam will do the same again, though this time it's not a practice run. Darwish was just to get the ball rolling, and that's exactly what's happened. It's a domino effect – the more underground militants know that he's speaking to the press, and they want their moment in the sun too. Things are picking up pace on the Palestinian streets, and every group's jockeying for position to show they're the ones worth backing when the shit kicks off again.'

I light my cigarette, try and keep up, but he's not giving me much to go on. Chana taps the keyboard non-stop, Nicky carries on freestyling over the beat.

'We're working on a major-league target. He never puts his head above ground but it looks like he might take the bait now. Abdul Mesleh, head of an al-Quds splinter cell called al-Asifi. It means 'The Storm'. Here, look at these headshots.'

I glance at the grainy photos on the table. Yeah, yeah, very nice, seen one seen 'em all. RPG over his shoulder, death in his eyes, blood on his hands but his PR's airbrushed it out.

'We're close to getting him to agree to a meet – our man in the PA is just ironing out the details now. This is why we kept you and the *Guardian* out of the Darwish story – if they get any hint a Jew's involved, they'll dive back into their shells. Your man Adam's the perfect cover.'

Seconded. Adam's as malleable as a Mars Bar. Still don't like the sound of this job though, it's ten times higher risk than the Darwish job, because at least Darwish is a semi-public figure. This guy looks like he couldn't give a fuck what he does or who finds out. Nicky clocks my concern.

'Look, we know what we're doing, we're not going to leave you out there on your own. We just need to put a trace on them, we need to map out their routes and know where their base is. Chana, pass me the chip.'

Chana stops typing, pulls a box from the shelf behind her and hands it to Nicky.

'Look, this can be inserted under your skin to track your movement. It's got enough power to last seventy-two hours, which is way more than we need – you'll be in and out in less than six.'

He's got to be fucking joking. That plastic grain of rice is screaming out a warning, urging me to cut and run while I've got the chance. If Nicky sees the need for this level of protection, he might as well be signing my death certificate. He probably is, actually – what do he and Chana care what happens anymore? Or maybe I'm just letting fear do the talking. Fuck knows. But things haven't felt right for a while, and they're both acting far too tense for me to be able to relax either.

'Nicky, what's the risk though? I mean, if anything goes wrong, there'll be no one within fifty miles who can pick me up.'

He doesn't slap me down like usual, just squats to my eye level and looks me straight in the face.

'Listen, there's always a risk, isn't there? But that's part and parcel of what you do, what we all do. Look what happened with Darwish – you were all worked up and then it went like clockwork, right?'

I nod, but I know this isn't the same.

'Just go through the motions the same as before. Adam does the talking, you're just the bag carrier – only difference is this time you'll be leading us straight to one of our top ten targets. This will be such a fucking score if – or rather when – it comes off.'

I breathe heavily, run my hands through my hair. It's happening, whether I like it or not.

'Look, I've got to go. Chana will give you the details, and then later I want you to get onto Adam and offer him the story. There's no way he'll turn it down, this is a proper scoop for him and his rag. All being well, we'll set it up for Monday. Just trust us, ok, like we trust you.'

My stock is suspended pending a further announcement. My heart's not doing much better.

21

JANUARY 2011

I can't deny I'm excited. I'm the gambler whose favourite thirty seconds are while the roulette wheel's still spinning. I've been fired up ever since last night, when Chana shot the chip into the top of my thigh with the implant gun. I'm a bit worried that the cut still shows, but – as she pointed out with a forced air of joviality – if it gets to the point that they're seeing me without trousers on, then the game will have been up for a while, and the discovery of a chip won't make much difference. I banish the thought to the back of my mind, let the adrenalin surge and get into role.

Adam's wired too, albeit for different reasons. He's stalking round his flat like a madman, making last-minute calls to his editor, running through the list of questions for Mesleh, checking the flash on his camera and firing off emails. He kisses a framed photo of his wife like it's a mezuzah – bit too sentimental for my liking, bit too disquieting as well. He doesn't shut up all the way to the Hebron roadblock, babbling away like we're on a school trip, but it's better than letting silence reign and fear set in again.

My thigh has been throbbing all morning, and my stomach starts churning as soon as we drive into Area A. The day has an unnatural feel, the sun is shining too brightly and there are too few people on the street. I keep catching sight of my reflection in shop windows, I look pallid and tired and, most of all, edgy. That's not a good look to give off to our hosts; I might as well wear a yellow star on my chest. I chew gum non-stop, including when I'm smoking. My teeth are going off on one again, I didn't even grind them like this on pills. A white minibus waits for us at our arranged meeting point, a feeble old man sitting in front of it on the kerb. He's seen better days, so has his chariot. He hauls himself up, gives us the once over.

'I take you first part of the journey. Get in fast, you are late.'

We comply, getting comfortable in the middle row, checking our phones for emails and texts. The driver watches us in the rear-view mirror, catches my eye and snarls.

'You stop with phone now. Give them to me, no phone permitted today.'

Adam looks at me and shrugs, we pass our mobiles forward and he stows them under the dashboard. We leave downtown Hebron and head out into the suburbs. After twenty minutes, the driver flings the minibus into a side street and shoos us out with a mixture of gestures and grunts. He drives off, still with our phones, and we're left on our own with not a soul in sight. Not much we can do, so we sit on a wall and wait. I picture Nicky and Chana charting my moves on a screen in Neveh Tzedek, wondering why we've stopped, thinking I might have been shot and dumped by the side of the road, questioning whether to send in a rescue squad or wait to see what happens. There's no way of communicating with them. I'm just a black dot on a map and a faint pulse on a detector. Adam's even less traceable, but they won't care about that any more than a fisherman worries about the worm at the end of his rod.

A battered, beige Peugeot estate hurtles towards us down the street and backs into a drive. The front passenger motions for us to approach. Four of the five seats are occupied by stern young men with knotted brows, the last space is taken up with a large metal box. The men in the back get out, move round to the boot, open it and start clearing space. The driver opens his door, climbs out and stands inches from our faces, speaking to us brusquely in near-flawless English.

'You do understand that we have to take security precautions, yes?'

We both nod. I'm watching the two men by the boot. Both have pistols in their waistbands, one has a second visibly bulging under his trousers at his calf.

'Good, good. Now, you will be uncomfortable on the ride but it will not be for long, and you will be perfectly safe.'

He holds up two lengths of black cloth.

'We will need to blindfold you, and you will ride in the back of the car. I apologise again, but as I say, you will be perfectly safe during the journey.'

During the journey. After that is anyone's guess.

We bounce around in the boot for what seems like hours, but is probably no more than fifteen minutes. From time to time the men murmur to each other in Arabic. Other than that the only sounds are the wheels churning up dust as we drive off-road. I can't even open my eyes under the cloth, my eyelids are getting friction burns and my head is pounding. Adam and I lie head to toe next to one another, we could speak but neither of us does. He's probably loving the danger, mentally fashioning every last detail of the experience into the perfect dinner party anecdote. I'm feeling sick, both physically and mentally, but there are also moments of calm now that my fate is out of my hands. The last few months have been a hard slog; keeping up the act has left me exhausted, and part of me wants it all to be over sooner rather than later. But on my terms, that is, and that's never gonna happen. The chip in my leg tells me all I need to know about my constitutional rights right now.

The car shudders to a halt, doors open and slam. I can hear birds chirping in trees, the smell of manure wafts into the car. When we're pulled out of the boot and our blindfolds removed, I take in the scene. We're in the middle of a vast network of fields, most of them lying fallow and brown, a few bearing signs of a recent harvest. Two grain silos flank a corrugated iron barn to our left. One of the men jogs off in the direction of the buildings, another turns to Adam and me, smiles broadly and gives us a mock bow.

'Welcome to Palestine. I hope you enjoy your stay.'

At this, two men pull on ski masks, slip their pistols out of their holsters, run headlong towards Adam and me and put us both on the floor with vicious headbutts. I see stars, the bridge of my nose collapses in on itself, I feel blood jet out of my nostrils like a dying dragon. Adam's moaning to my right, the synchronised butting team drag us by our arms across the rough earth, cursing us in Arabic, spitting on our limp bodies. My head bounces off rocks and stones, I fade in and out of consciousness. Can't say I didn't see this one coming.

I come round, mouth crusted with blood. Other than that I'm not in too bad a state. My ribs are sore but nothing feels broken. I'm lying on the dirt floor. I can move my legs and my left arm. My right wrist is shackled tight by an iron manacle attached to a wall, I don't even bother trying to claw it off. On the other side of the barn I see Adam tied to a pole, eyes shut, head lolling forward, chin sunk into his chest. The only silver lining is that my trousers are still on, the chip still in place somewhere under my skin. I open my eyes, stretch my legs. A boot smashes me in the temple, white pain sears my skull. I'm out in a flash.

I'm dying for water, maybe I'm just dying full stop. Maybe it's darkest before death, not dawn. It's pitch black in the barn, freezing cold too. No idea where Adam is, no idea if there's anyone around. Not gonna call out, not gonna draw attention to myself, I learned that the hard way last time. The only sounds come from crickets and my laboured breathing. I run my tongue over my front teeth – two are loose on the bottom, one's missing from the top. Don't remember that happening, but it obviously did. My body is in a far worse state than before, my right hand is numb all the way down to where the manacle bites into my wrist, and I can hardly move my legs even though they're still free. Insects crawl over my bare feet, I can feel them gathered round my toes, feeding off the congealed blood where the nails once were. I shiver uncontrollably, my mind races. I still don't have a clue what's happened, I've got no facts to assess other than my gaping wounds. Do they know who I am? Do they know this was a trap? Are they just looking to kidnap two journalists for their own ends? I pray the last scenario's true, but even then we're as good as dead. Where's Nicky, where's Chana? Where are the cavalry who are meant to ride over the hill and rescue me at the first sign of trouble? I stifle a bitter laugh. Nicky once told me to put things in perspective, said to remember I'm not the centre of the universe, that it's not all about me. No fucking kidding. He's as bad as Darwish sending the youth out to die, as bad as all the commanders on either side, as bad as the fire-breathing politicians, the rabble-rousing rabbis, the paradise-promising imams, every last agitator stirring up trouble for the masses. I don't matter to Nicky, none of his paternal praise means a thing, his promises are worthless. Chana's no better. Her sweet nothings are just that, at the end of the day I'm no more than cannon fodder. If I don't make it back I'll be just another statistic, and not even one whose true purpose was known. I'll be the traitor who was hoist with his own petard, the sell-out soldier who learned too late what you catch from sleeping with the enemy. Footsteps get louder, I tense up, they recede. I stay coiled like a hedgehog. A muffled scream from outside – it can only be Adam. I don't want to think about it, there's nothing I can do for him now.

I wake up, sunlight pouring over me through the open doorway to my right. I prise one eye apart – no one in sight – look myself over. My clothes are soaked in blood. I don't move a muscle, and then I see my feet. Ants cover every inch of skin, I'm black up to the ankles, small clouds of flies hover over the festering mess, they dive-bomb in to scoop up supplies. I thrash my legs and my free arm, scream at the top of my lungs, don't care who hears me, don't care what happens, want the nightmare to be over, want the curtain to fall. Fuck Nicky, he's never coming, the chip's probably not even real, fuck all of this, fuck the pain, fuck the fear, fuck my imploding mind and my tortured soul. Another door swings open, Laura runs in, brandishing a cleaver, Tina behind her, dead baby at her breast. They stand at my feet, watch me flail on the floor, Laura opens her mouth, forked tongue darting towards me, I reel back, feel leather under my neck, twist round, see boots, look up, see Saul, his face lined with scars, hands bunched into fists and swathed in bandages. He lifts up a leg, brings his foot crashing down on my arm, I try to cry out but my lips are glued shut. Tanya peers in through the window, crying with laughter, she cocks a silver pistol and fires a round at the sky. My mouth fills with water, I swallow hard, dust pours down my throat, I shut my eyes and see my parents, open them again and see JoJo, he swaggers around the room wearing a chain of MAG bullets like a necklace. I'm begging for someone to finish the job, but I can't make a sound and I can't move my limbs and I can't see a thing and I'm back on my own with my ants and my blood.

I'm lying on a bed, the mattress is soaking. Someone is slapping my face. It doesn't hurt, I'm past pain now. I take a punch to the chin. It fucking kills.

'Wake up, Jew.'

I doubt he's made me breakfast. I open my eyes, stare down the barrel of a Tavor. Such a beautiful gun, wish it was in my hand though.

'Your little friend wouldn't talk when we needed him to, and now he can't.'

The man behind the mask nods over his shoulder. I look past him and see Adam strapped to a chair, mouth gaping, blood bubbling over his lips and a crimson stump where his tongue should be. His eyes are rolled back in their sockets, he emits low moans interspersed with unearthly growls. I shut my eyes. My captor forces one back open with a thumb and forefinger.

'He won't last much longer. We don't need him anyway. You're the valuable one, you're worth a thousand times more alive than dead. Get up, we need to have a talk with you.'

He yanks me out of bed by my hair, my knee smashes into the metal bedpost as I'm dragged from the room. I avert my eyes from Adam, concentrate on keeping my elbows below my body to soften the impact each time my back and sides hit the floor. I'm pulled down a hall – we're not in the barn anymore, we could be anywhere in the West Bank, could be even further afield than that. For all I know we're in Jordan or Lebanon. What does it matter anyway? I'm propped on a stool, I'm still being held by my hair. Another man in a balaclava sits at a table, smoking, sipping coffee, leafing through a notepad. He turns to me and folds his arms.

'We know who you are, we know why you are here.'

He pulls a cigarette from a pack of Marlboro Reds, lights it, offers it to me. I grab at it greedily, inhaling heavily, gulping down the smoke.

'We know who you work for, we know who sent you.'

I bet he doesn't. If he did, he wouldn't be fucking around keeping me alive. He'd know the risk of me being rescued was too high to chance it, even if they could extract a higher ransom for me while I'm still a living hostage. They're no fools; they know their enemy too well to underestimate them.

'Over the next hour, you will sit with me and tell me everything. I want a full confession, I want every last detail, and we will film it for our records.'

I've finished the cigarette. I want another one but I'm still determined not to utter a single word in their presence. He's bluffing, it's written all over his ski mask. I doubt he even knows I was lying about being Adam's stringer; they probably only worked out I'm Jewish when they saw that I'm circumcised. But if they saw that, then they'll also have seen . . . Fuck . . . I look down – these aren't my clothes, I'm wearing nondescript rags. They've stripped me at some point and that means only one thing. I look back up, he's watching me carefully, clocks that the penny just dropped in my black and blue skull.

'I see you have put, how you say, two and two together. Good. Now you will believe me when I say that we will get every single word out of you. We will not waste time, so you had better begin.'

The man behind me reaches round and slices my forehead with a blade, blood instantly dripping down into my eyes. Not sure what prompted that, but something snaps inside me. Fuck it. Give 'em what they want. It's all the same to me now. It's always been all the same to me. They're just doing their job, Nicky's just doing his, I've just been doing mine. All I ever wanted was to win, but I admit defeat. I know when to fold 'em. Should have quit when I was streets ahead, when my portfolio was overweight in coke futures and hard cash, and I'd hedged every position by staying uncaring, unconnected and utterly untouchable. Should have gone out on a high, in every sense of the word. I peaked aged five: the Jew-only gang was the pinnacle of my success. I was living the dream before I was even out of infant school, doing the Suburb proud, blissful in my ignorance, picking up my father's baton and tearing off down the track. The only way was down after that as soon as doubt set in. Who's to say Nicky's right and this lot are wrong? Who's to say which side I should be on, which team I should pad up for? Everyone's only out for themselves – they talk a good talk but that's really the bottom line. Feather your own nest, line your own pocket. I should know, I've been doing it from birth. As did everyone before me, as will everyone after. These men are only doing what Nicky did to me in London. I'll go through the motions like I did back then. I'm not selling out cos I never bought in.

The camera rolls. I say my piece, don't need any prompting, I remember my lines. They can't understand why I've buckled, and I don't bother to explain. Let them think what they like, my work here is done. We wrap up the shoot, I'm led back to the bedroom, more gently this time though I still take a few slaps. My captor throws me down on a mattress, chains my arm to the wall. He leaves. I lie on my back and stare at the ceiling, the window – anywhere but at Adam's body. My eyes drift downwards. A bent nail pokes through the cement by my legs. I reposition myself on the bed, arm twisted painfully, but it will be worth it in a minute.

Jerusalem will never be builded here, let's stop pretending, let's get it over with. I grit my teeth, slash my free arm repeatedly over the rusted spike, jagged cuts immediately pouring blood, covering my chest and my legs and my red-raw feet. I don't make a sound, don't want to be rescued, just want to melt away, drift away, fade away, sleep. Came, saw, conquered nothing, job done, Kaddish.

ABOUT THE AUTHOR

Seth Freedman was born in 1980, and grew up in Hampstead Garden Suburb, London. Upon leaving school, he went to work in a City stockbrokers, where he traded equities for six years. Aware that his heavy drug and drink habit was in danger of doing him permanent damage, he left the Square Mile in 2004, opting to dry out in a combat unit of the Israeli army. He demobbed in 2006, and has worked as a writer ever since. He lives in Tel Aviv, and has written over 300 articles for the *Guardian*, mainly on the Israeli-Palestinian conflict, but also on subjects ranging from art to business to drugs and gambling. *Binge Trading*, his non-fiction book based on Freedman's trading career and interviews with some of the City's biggest players was published by Penguin in 2009. There are still lots of people who think he's a Mossad agent.

DEAD CAT BOUNCE

A term used by traders to describe when a spectacular decline in share prices is immediately followed by a moderate rise before resuming its downward movement.

A dead cat will bounce if dropped from a high building but it is still a dead cat.